"Murder by the Cup"
Le Doux Mysteries #1
By Abigail Thornton

MURDER BY THE CUP

First edition. June 8, 2021.

Written by Abigail Thornton.

DEDICATION

Every first book is dedicated to my husband.
Without you, I would never have put pen to paper.
(Or finger to keyboard)
Here's to Eternity.

ACKNOWLEDGEMENTS

No author works alone. Thank you, Cathy.
Your cover work is beautiful!
And to Laura, for your timely and thorough editing!

NEWSLETTER

Stay up to date on all my new releases by joining my newsletter!
You can find it and other exciting news at
abigailthorntonbooks.com

CHAPTER 1

Wynona Le Doux set her pestle aside and leaned down to get a good whiff of the crushed herbs. "Mmm..." she hummed, her dark lashes falling against porcelain cheeks as she enjoyed the fragrance. "Just like Granny taught."

At the thought of her grandmother, the usual sharp pang of longing struck Wynona's chest. Granny Saffron had been gone for close to three months now, and yet there were times when it still seemed like only yesterday.

It was made worse by the fact that Wynona had not been able to give her grandmother a proper goodbye. Unbeknownst to Wynona, her grandmother's passing was the distraction that had allowed Wynona to escape the clutches of her cruel but powerful family. The loss still hurt deeply, but Wynona found gratitude amidst the pain. Without Granny's help, Wynona would still be her family's dirty little secret, stuck in that large castle with no hope for a future.

Instead, she was just about to open her own tea shop in honor of Granny Le Doux, using all the skills Granny had taught her in her greenhouse when the rest of the family was too busy running the paranormal world.

Setting aside her morbid thoughts, Wynona brushed the contents of the mortar into a jar already labeled and ready to put on the shelf for her grand opening next week. Because of Granny's tutelage, Wynona was able to offer a unique experience to her customers. Personalized, custom made teas. There were some teas that Wynona made in large batches, meant to cure certain ills and help in specific ways like the mixture she was shelving. The mix of gingko, rosemary, lavender and a hint of peppermint should work wonders with anyone, from fairies to werewolves, in helping grow thicker, more luxurious hair.

For a higher fee, however, Wynona was also offering herself out for private consultations. Teas made specifically for an individual that resonated with their body chemistry and more importantly...their magic.

Granny Saffron had been one of the paranormal world's most powerful witches and her specialty had been in earth gifts. Growing plants and knowing how to use them was a coveted hobby and since Wynona had no powers of her own to claim, Granny had taken the lost child under her wing and taught her everything she knew that didn't require magic.

The warmth and kindness of the powerful woman had been the only thing that had helped Wynona keep going when life became hard. Having been cursed since birth so her powers were bound and useless, Wynona had become an instant disappointment to her family. Instead of embracing and consoling Wynona for something that was out of her control, Marcella, Wynona's mother, had passed her off to a nanny and never looked back. Without powers, Wynona was worthless.

Her family, and most witches in general, viewed magic as power. Lucky for Wynona, or unlucky, depending on how one looked at it, Wynona's family was the most powerful of all. An unbroken line of powerful political succession...until Wynona.

"No more," Wynona whispered to herself. She pushed out a short breath, put her hands on her hips and surveyed her storage room. The space was clean and neat, with every jar and plant labeled and put precisely in its place. Much smaller than the palace Wynona had grown up in, the room was small and cozy with a wonderful warmth emanating from the cheerful fire in the corner.

It was perfect.

With a firm nod, Wynona walked out of the room and into her small home. On the night she'd escaped from her family, Granny had given Wynona the information for a bank account with enough money to allow Wynona to take care of herself for a couple of years, but not enough that her family would come after her when Granny's inheritance was passed out to the masses.

Instead of relaxing for a time, Wynona had taken her newfound freedom and instantly jumped into running a business. With her money she'd been able to rent a building in town, renovate it to her liking, and still buy a small cabin farther out of town with a small attached greenhouse. It had belonged to a dryad at one point in time and was perfect for Wynona's nature loving ways.

She could grow her own inventory right outside her house with the magic of the forest close enough to infuse the plants with a little something extra, yet close enough to town to keep Wynona safe and have easy access to her shop.

She snorted. *Safe. As if there's anything anyone could do to me at this point that would be worse than taking away my powers.*

Her good humor faded. There were plenty of things that would be worse than that, but sometimes they were hard to imagine. Dangerous hexes and wild paranormals were things that Wynona had only ever read about or heard in the news, despite the fact that she had turned thirty on the night she'd escaped. Her family had not only kept her out of the limelight, they had never even acknowledged that she existed, which meant her experience with the outside world had been isolated to media outlets and servants' gossip.

The media had been unaware of Wynona's existence until she'd started to advertise her tea shop's grand opening. In fact, Wynona was almost positive that the fact she'd had so many advance bookings was largely due in part to her last name. Le Douxs rarely condescended to mingle with the peasants, so having access to one, even if she had no powers of her own, was enough to have people booking her tea shop months in advance.

"Good for business," Wynona said with a sharp grin. "It might actually be the only good thing my family has ever done for me."

A soft tinkling sound caught her attention and Wynona looked around for her cell phone. The technological advances money could buy were the closest Wynona got to magic and she had enjoyed having access to many of the luxuries her family had denied her.

Finding the device on her kitchen counter, Wynona opened the screen and groaned.

Scones will be available tomorrow. No earlier.

Chef Atherton Droxon was the best baker in town. It had taken a lot of finagling and name dropping for Wynona to get a contract with him to supply the baked goods for her shop. It was going to cost her a bundle, but anyone who ate one of Chef Droxon's goods *always* came back for more. There was some speculation that he was using some kind of gnome magic to keep people addicted, but Wynona knew that had to be false. Gnomes didn't have much magic. Not enough to tamper with baked goods, that was for sure.

Every species contained a certain type and limit of magic, all except witches and warlocks, that was. Which is exactly why witches and warlocks were the ones who ruled. Witches were born with a limited number of powers, but with the right combinations and genetics, they could create offspring with much greater abilities than any other species. And that didn't take into account the increasing of their natural born abilities through study and work. Just like any creature, what they could accomplish as children was nothing compared to what they could accomplish as an adult.

Wynona punched the call button. She wasn't about to let this deal go sour. Chef Droxon had promised to have a taste test with her tonight and Wynona had planned her entire schedule around it. He couldn't cancel or it would throw off everything she was doing in order to be ready for her opening next week.

"No sooner!" Chef Droxon answered the call with a loud yell. His accent sometimes made him difficult to understand, but Wynona had no trouble at the moment.

"Hello, Chef Droxon," she said conversationally. Perhaps that was another thing to be grateful to her family for. Wynona was extremely cool under pressure. It didn't matter how rude, cruel or dramatic another person was, she had learned how to keep a level head. She'd been forced to, or her family would have destroyed her long ago. "How are you doing today?"

"It is no good," Chef Droxon snapped. "I cannot bake like this. The scones will not be ready."

"Now, Chef Droxon, I know that you're a man of your word," Wynona said pleasantly. "You told me everything will be ready for our little get together this evening, and I'm so looking forward to it." She paused, but he didn't speak right away, so she continued laying the sugar on extra thick. "You're so wonderful at what you do that I'm sure if you put your mind to it, you can have everything ready just like you promised." Wynona held her breath. She didn't like working with spoiled personalities. She'd had enough of that at home, thank you very much. But she needed his food. If she truly wanted her tea shop to stand out, Wynona knew she had to offer things no one else could offer. She couldn't magic up her own offerings, so she needed to rely on the magic of others. Right now, that meant dealing with the drama that was Atherton Droxon.

"The scones do not want to bake," he grumbled, but Wynona could hear the softening in his voice. She might lack magic, but she had learned to compensate by learning to read people.

"How wonderful then that the scones aren't in charge," Wynona said with a smile. "You are the master of your kitchen," she cooed.

"And I just know that all the patrons I have coming to the opening will simply adore your food!"

Droxon huffed.

"You'll be an absolute sensation!" Wynona continued. "Why, I'm sure that the news reporter who has promised to come will want to speak to you more than me!"

"Well..."

She had him. Now to seal the deal. "Imagine all the *free* publicity you'll get! In fact, you're being paid to be there and yet you're the one who everyone will want to meet." Gnomes were notoriously cheap, and when he didn't automatically argue with her again, Wynona gave herself a mental clap on the back and relaxed, knowing it was all going to be okay.

"I suppose I can come tonight," he muttered.

"I'm so excited," she said brightly. "I'm just going to freshen up and then I'll meet you at the shop."

"Will be an hour," he said sharply. "No more. No less."

"An hour is perfect," Wynona said, a triumphant smirk on her face. She tried to wipe it off, but it was difficult. Any victory felt so good after thirty years of failure. She glanced at her watch. An hour gave her enough time to make sure the shop was in perfect order. Having a neat facility would help her vendors know that she meant business. "I'll see you then."

The line went dead without another word, but his abrupt leaving didn't worry her. Gnomes weren't always easy to deal with, but their word was their bond. He couldn't go back on it.

She hurried to the bathroom, making sure her hair was in place. Wynona had thrown it up in a messy bun earlier in the day, and half of it had fallen out as she'd been working. Tsking her tongue, Wynona let down her waist-length black hair. No matter what her family said about the curse, Wynona still looked every inch the witch.

Her family had been bred for power and glamor for generations and even Wynona had been the recipient of decent genetics. Her hair was thick and silky, an attribute she was very proud of. Her skin, however, was another matter. She was so pale it looked as if she'd never seen the sun, and even since being free, Wynona could not get her body to recognize that the sun actually existed. It appeared that she would be milky white until the day she died.

Rewrapping her bun, Wynona let a few pieces of hair down to soften the sharp lines of her face, then pursed her lips and put on her favorite lip gloss. Her lips, plump and naturally red, had been a gift from Wynona's mother. Celia, Wynona's older sister, was constantly remarking on how distracting they were. They were rather large, but Wynona knew her mother was a renowned beauty. Surely her mouth wasn't going to be enough to keep Wynona from finding love...if she ever got to that stage of life.

She'd spent so much of it alone that it was hard to imagine sharing something more than a casual greeting with another person, but secretly, in her heart of hearts, Wynona hoped a soulmate would eventually cross her path. She might never have spoken the words out loud, but they were there nonetheless. And who could blame a girl? It was a natural inclination after all. Now that she was out from under her mother's thumb, Wynona could marry for love rather than position and that, above all, had been a victory for her. Soulmates were not common, though not unheard of, among the paranormals, and for the first time ever, Wynona had the freedom necessary to look for hers...provided he actually existed.

"But first..." Wynona looked herself over and nodded. "Business." There would be time for romance later, after she had turned Saffron's Tea House into the best tea shop in all of Hex Haven.

She grabbed her purse, computer bag, a couple jars of newly created tea tinctures and headed out. If she was as powerful as her mother, Wynona knew she'd be able to snap her fingers and arrive at the tea shop without messing up a single hair. Unfortunately, that little trick required a skill Wynona didn't own. Magic.

She sighed. It always seemed to come back to that. Would her life ever feel normal? Or would she always long for something she didn't have?

"Get a move on," she told herself. Walking to the small attached garage, Wynona punched in her code and the door slowly lifted. Inside was an array of boxes and bubble wrap that she had yet to throw away. The first few weeks of homeownership had been filled with purchases to add onto the few possessions she had managed to smuggle out of her family home.

Clothes, furniture, kitchen supplies... She'd started with literally nothing, but Parazon had been all too happy to help supply her with anything she needed at the touch of a button. Their fairy delivery service was almost instantaneous and Wynona had been grateful for it.

Amidst the aftermath of unpacking, Wynona pulled a mint green Vespa out onto the gravel driveway. Her computer bag and purse were wrapped around her shoulders, but the jars were carefully placed in the storage basket on the front of the scooter.

Throwing her leg over the seat, Wynona settled herself comfortably, then pushed back the kickstand and started off. It was only a ten minute ride and, unless she was in inclement weather, it was a beautifully scenic adventure.

Sighing in contentment, Wynona let her eyes wander as she rode. She was building a good life for herself. One to be proud of and one Granny would approve of. She just needed to get through the grand opening next week, and then life should be nothing but roses.

CHAPTER 2

The sounds of a soft bell rang through the air, alerting Wynona Le Doux to a guest entering her tea shop. She had expected Chef Droxon to come through the kitchen entrance, but maybe he didn't know his way around to the back of the building.

Tucking a piece of hair behind her ear and patting the bun on her head, Wynona put a pleasant smile on her bright red lips and walked out from the kitchen. The smile grew immediately brittle when she spotted who was walking around her dining room. The flashy, metallic, mini dress and six-inch heels stood in stark contrast to the vintage furniture and floral upholstery that peppered the open space.

The shabby chic look had been carefully cultivated in order to invite patrons to curl up with their teacups and stay awhile. Wynona had been very proud of it when she and her new fairy friend Primrose had finished.

Primrose was the premiere flower artist in Hex Haven and when Wynona had been shopping for a supplier, the two women had hit it off immediately. Together they had planned the look and feel of the tea house in order to showcase Wynona's teacup collection and Prim's flower arrangements. The resulting room had felt perfectly inviting...until now. The current inhabitant made Wynona want to run away and never return.

"Sister!" Celia Le Doux drawled with a smirk. She threw her shiny, waist-length hair over her shoulder. "How good it is to see you."

Wynona kept her chin high. "Hello, Celia. What brings you here?"

Celia let out a soft laugh that bordered on a cackle, a trademark of their kind, and let her dark eyes roam the room. "I see running away from home has been good for you." She raised a perfectly manicured eyebrow at Wynona, her own red lips a practiced smirk.

It would be easy to be jealous of her sister's looks. After all, Celia was what most would describe as drop dead gorgeous. No hair would ever dare be out of place and every stitch of her clothing was made to show off a figure most women envied. However, it wasn't looks that Wynona found herself coveting, since she, herself, looked very similar to Ceila, albeit less flashy... No, it was Celia's powers. The one thing Wynona wished for above all.

It was the very power that was sparking at Celia's fingertips as she wiggled her fingers in an unconscious pattern, dripping like diamonds onto the newly varnished hardwood floors before dissipating.

"I like it," Wynona said, her voice strong and steady. Despite her envy, Wynona vowed she would never show her family any weakness. Learning to control her emotions was the product of a lifetime of abuse.

"You would," Celia muttered under her breath. She began walking again, letting her fingers touch everything she passed. If Wynona didn't know any better, it would appear as if her sister were caressing the fabrics and flower petals. Instead, she was more than likely leaving hexes on the next person who would sit down.

Wynona made a mental note to make sure none of their future patrons got a nasty shock when the store opened next week.

"You missed Grandmother's funeral," Celia said off-handedly. She tsked her tongue. "For someone who claims to have loved the old hag, that wasn't very well-mannered."

Wynona counted to ten, just like Granny had taught her, when dealing with someone who was particularly difficult. Oh, how she wished her family was the type who gave hugs and baked cookies. Life would have been so different. But then again, maybe it was better this way. Maybe her freedom was worth being seen as an abomination for most of her life.

Her mother had actually used that word once. As if it were Wynona's fault that she had been cursed. Or that she had any control over the fact that she was born into the Le Doux family. Wynona had most assuredly not asked for any of that, yet it had happened.

"I said my goodbyes," Wynona said softly. She hoped her sister didn't hear the catch in her voice. Granny had been a unique and special woman, and Wynona would never forget her kindness. Even the servants had been afraid to be around Wynona, as if the curse was contagious. But Granny had rarely left Wynona's side.

When Granny knew it was her time to go, she'd quietly told Wynona to escape at midnight on the spring equinox. It wasn't until later that Wynona realized Granny had passed away at that exact moment, creating just enough of a diversion to allow Wynona to get out of their estate undetected.

Countless tears had already been shed, but Wynona hadn't dared go to the funeral. She was too afraid of what her mother would have done. Instead, she'd held her own vigil and said goodbye, hoping her granny's ghost could hear her. If she had half the power of her sister, Wynona could have summoned Granny and done it properly, but such was not her lot in life.

Celia gave a delicate snort, then wrinkled her nose. "What is..." She bent down slightly, then jerked backward with a screech.

"What?" Wynona asked, running forward just in time to see a dash of white scurry from one bookcase to the other.

"A mouse!" Celia shouted. She pointed a finger toward the area the mouse had darted and twirled it quickly.

"NO!" Wynona cried, holding out her hand as if to stop the spell. A flurry of sparks burst, forcing Wynona to shut her eyes or be blinded for the rest of her life, a handicap she did not need to add to her already lengthy list, only for the light to disappear as quickly as it had begun.

"There." Celia wiped her fingers against each other in satisfaction. She turned her pouty lips toward Wynona. "You're welcome!" The cheer in Celia's voice was like nails on a chalkboard and Wynona had to hold back tears.

She hated how little her family cared about life, whether a rodent or their own daughter's. If something wasn't useful to them in the political arena, it wasn't worth acknowledging. It was just one of the many reasons Wynona had made it her personal mission in life to be the exact opposite of everything the Le Doux family stood for.

She clenched her hands into fists, fighting the urge to teach her sister a lesson. It was times like these that her lack of magic hurt the most. She was helpless against the evils of her family and other witches.

"I'll ask again, Celia," Wynona said with forced calm. "What brought you here?"

Before Celia could answer, voices began trickling from the back of the small tea house. Someone must have come in through the kitchen entrance and Wynona needed to go greet them. She hoped it was Chef Droxon. She needed something to go smoothly right about now. She wasn't comfortable leaving her sister alone, though. Who knew what else the cruel sibling would get up to if Wynona wasn't watching?

Celia studied her nails. "Sounds like you have company." Her eyes darted to the kitchen door, then back to her fingers.

"They can wait," Wynona said easily. She folded her arms over her chest. Maybe the move would hide the chaotic beating of her heart against her rib cage.

"Well," Celia huffed. "While I'm glad to see family is a priority to you, I really must be going." She blew her sister a sarcastic kiss. "I'll just let you clean up that little mess," she said, pointing to the bookcase. "I'm sure you've had plenty of practice."

Wynona didn't answer as she waited to see her sister leave. A little magic to make the door smack that perfectly rounded derriere wouldn't go amiss right about now, but Wynona had to content herself with staring hard enough to bore a hole into her sister's back.

Once the witch was gone, Wynona quickly locked the door, then scurried to the back. She would indeed need to clean up her sister's mess, but right now it would have to wait. Dread filled Wynona's stomach as she walked past the bookcase, until a small sound caught her attention.

She paused and listened harder. The tiniest squeak could be heard and a smile crept across Wynona's face. "You survived," she breathed. A crashing in the kitchen drew her attention again and Wynona waffled. "I don't think I've got..." She stuffed her hands quickly into her pockets, searching for any kind of crumb she could find. The pickings were minimal, but hopefully they would be enough. Wynona carefully sprinkled the tiny bits of cracker onto the floor directly in front of the bookcase. "That should tide you over until I can find something else." Shouting ensued from the kitchen and Wynona cringed. "I'll be back later."

Straightening, she rushed to the kitchen to see Chef Droxon with half a dozen other workers swarming the small space. When Wynona had renovated, she hadn't bothered to put in a full commercial kitchen. After all, she really only needed room to store her teacups and equipment to make the tea. Everything else she planned to serve was being purchased ready made. But apparently Chef Droxon had other ideas.

"Where is stove?" he screeched, his tiny stature hiding him from Wynona's eyes. "No stove! No scones!"

Wynona gave an awkward smile to the first couple of workers she passed who were standing around looking lost. Each held large storage containers in their arms and didn't seem to know what to do with them.

"Good afternoon, Chef Droxon," Wynona said carefully. She hoped none of the hostility from seeing her sister bled into her tone.

Chef Droxon glared at her from waist high. His beady eyes could have melted steel and the mottled green of his skin was mixed with red. He, apparently, hadn't thought it necessary to dress to impress, since he still wore his work apron, complete with a large brown streak across the front. "I thought you had kitchen," he demanded.

Wynona looked around, keeping a pleasant smile on her face. "I do." She clasped her hands in front of her. "Perhaps I can show you around? But this won't be where your baked goods are displayed. Oh no." She winked. "I have something special in mind for that."

Chef Droxon huffed and folded his arms over his barrel chest. "Show."

Wynona nodded respectfully. "If you'll just follow me." She led the way out of the kitchen into a large butler's pantry. "You can leave the containers here," she said, giving her best smile to the employees. They probably could use a little kindness in their lives if they worked for the grumpy baker.

Each and every one of them looked extremely grateful as they set down the large containers on the long counters.

"And in here..." Wynona led them through a revolving door to the main tea room, "Is where your wonderful treats will be displayed." She indicated a glass counter she had had custom made right next to a stunning display of vintage teacups and specialty brews.

Chef Droxon glared and marched over to the space. He walked around it and studied it from every angle. With each step his eyebrows grew tighter and tighter. Wynona was sure he was about to have a tantrum when he finally looked at her and nodded. "It will do."

High praise indeed from the spoiled gnome. A breath she hadn't known she'd been holding slowly released and Wynona's heart rate went back to normal. "I'm so glad you approve," she said. The cabinet had been outfitted with the best lighting and display cases to show off his pastries to perfection. When she had planned this renovation and subsequent opening of her business, no detail had gone unplanned. Wynona wanted the best, so she had built for the best.

Doing so had cost her greatly, though, so if her business didn't turn a profit, Wynona knew she would find herself in trouble all too quickly.

Chef Droxon waved a hand in the air. "Enough," he spat. "You will see what I bake."

Only strict self control kept Wynona from rubbing her hands in glee. She had been waiting her whole life to try something from Droxon Bakeries. It was a luxury her family had indulged in often, but Wynona had never been included. Once she had managed to find a forgotten drip of icing in the bottom of a pastry box and that tiny amount had been enough to send her on a lifelong quest for more.

"Let's sit right here." She indicated a lovely preset table. "And you can show me all your delicacies."

Chef Droxon huffed his way to sitting across from Wynona, then snapped his fingers and shouted a few phrases in Gnomish. The workers he had brought with him jumped to obey and soon the table was laden with every baked good imaginable. It was far more than Wynona had asked to see and she began to worry about the dent this would put in her leftover savings. It seemed as if what she had managed to hold onto might not last quite as long as she had hoped.

"First." Chef Droxon held a stubby finger in the air. "The creme puff."

The next hour consisted of Wynona moaning her delight at every bite and fighting her inner child to keep from devouring everything within reach. She understood now, more than ever, why so many people believed that Chef Droxon baked magic into his goods. They were unlike anything she had ever tasted before, and that edge certainly made one question how it was done.

"It's all perfect," Wynona gushed, meaning every word. She could just imagine the women coming in for tea and staying for long periods of time simply so they could eat one more bite.

Chef Droxon looked smug in his too-large chair, but didn't speak. He was more than likely used to her reaction with every person he came in contact with.

"Let me just get the binder with our contract and we'll finish filling out the first order," Wynona said. She scooted away from the table and tried to walk, not waddle, to her office. The extra exercise necessary to work off what she'd just eaten would certainly be worth it. She giggled like a young girl once inside her small office. "We're going to make it, Granny," she whispered into the dark space. Her fingers went over her lips, but her too-wide smile remained. "We're going to make it!"

CHAPTER 3

Wynona put her game face back on and strutted confidently back to the sitting room where Chef Droxon was waiting. "I have it right here," she said with her best smile, the one Granny said could win over even the hardest of hearts. "I'm ready to sign for the cream puffs, the eclairs..." Wynona continued to rattle off a few more delicacies and ended with, "Plus, those magnificent scones."

Chef Droxon glared at her while he grabbed the paperwork and began to look it over. It took him a long time to read through it and Wynona mentally begged him to hurry. She was so eager to feel like it was all in the bag. After the arrival of her sister, she desperately wanted this to go right. Her family was probably waiting for any sign of weakness and would do their best to make her life a living purgatory if they sensed they could get to her. They weren't likely to forget how she had slipped through their fingers.

Chef Droxon grunted several times before holding out a hand and snapping his fingers. Wynona ignored the rudeness and dutifully handed him a pen, which he promptly used to scribble something illegible on the line at the bottom.

She swallowed her squeal, barely managing to hold onto her business persona as she collected the papers for her portfolio. "I'll provide a copy of this for you by tomorrow," Wynona said. She hurried to put her stuff away. The session had gone on longer than she'd expected and she had an appointment with her landlord in just a few minutes. She had yet to meet the elusive warlock, as all their communications had been through his secretary. She was eager to show him all the renovations she had done to the shop.

Chef Droxon continued glaring, despite Wynona's beauty pageant smile, and climbed down from his chair. His green skin kept flushing red with the effort it took to move his round body down to the ground. Wynona made a mental note that perhaps having some tables more suited to any smaller clientele would be a smart move in welcoming everyone to her shop.

"Thank you so much for your business," Wynona said, standing as well to follow him out.

Chef Droxon waved her off and began barking orders to his employees.

Pity swirled in Wynona's chest as they jumped to do their master's bidding. She knew exactly what it was like to have to kowtow to someone's every whim. Especially someone who enjoyed taking advantage of their power. She hoped they were compensated fairly for their difficult work environment, but odds weren't in their favor. She'd dealt with people like Droxon her entire life and Wynona knew their cruelness could extend to every aspect of their lives.

Determined to do something for them, she snatched up a packet of teas she had recently bagged. A little goodwill could certainly go a long way. "Thank you so much for bringing those delicious pastries," she said to the first one she saw. "You're a wonderful help." Wynona smiled and held out a bag to the lean man. If she was to guess, she would assume he was some kind of shifter, more than likely a prey type, not a predator. His fearful glances around the room reminded her of a rodent, but her gift made his eyes light up.

"Thank you," he muttered, quickly glancing toward his boss before accepting the gift.

"Be sure to steep it properly," she warned him, keeping her voice low as well. "This style of tea does best in a French press."

He nodded his understanding, stuffed the packet in his pocket and scurried around her. Doing her best to avoid Chef Droxon's angry gaze, Wynona worked her way around to all the employees. Each and every one of them looked shocked, then thrilled at her praise and present. It left Wynona feeling much better about them having to spend time with such a grumpy boss.

She started to take the few packets left back to the sitting room when she noticed one more worker skulking toward the door. Her eyebrows rose in surprise before she hurried over and blocked him before he could leave. "Excuse me!"

The man was of medium height and completely forgettable in looks. Brown hair, brown eyes, dark bags under his eyes and dry, chapped lips. There were absolutely no telltale signs of what his species was, but in the end it didn't matter. When Wynona caught his gaze, he backed into the counter, his eyes moving around as if searching for a way to escape. Unlike some of the other employees, the man was extremely quiet. His shoes didn't squeak at all on her tile floor.

"I just wanted to say thank you," Wynona said carefully, pausing a few feet away. She didn't want to frighten the man. Perhaps he was another shifter. She held out the tea bag and gave a gentle smile. "This is for you," she said, nodding toward the gift. "A little thank you for helping out today."

The man stared at her as if she had grown two heads, and it began to take some effort to keep her smile in place.

"THIEF!" Chef Droxon's booming voice rattled the few pots and pans in the kitchen and Wynona automatically covered her head as if the ceiling would collapse at such a sound.

"Out of the way," the employee in front of her growled before charging.

Wynona screamed as she went crashing to the ground in a tangle of limbs. The man was smaller than her and she pushed him off her, doing her best to scramble to her feet, but since he was doing the same, they only fell once more.

"STOP THE THIEF!" Chef Droxon screamed.

Over the man's shoulder, Wynona could see Chef Droxon standing in the kitchen doorway, pointing a finger at her and the man.

The baker's employees poured into the room, running into each other as they ran toward the pile of bodies on the floor. Another scream ripped from Wynona's throat as dozens of hands began grasping at her and the man. The space wasn't large enough for them all, so instead of an organized catch, it was a free for all. Her hair was pulled multiple times, along with her arms and feet. Someone accidentally kicked her back, causing Wynona to groan. When another foot landed on her rib cage, she used every bit of strength she had left to roll to her side and curl into a ball.

"ENOUGH!" A deep commanding voice finally brought the entire situation to a halt.

Strong arms went around Wynona and she sagged in relief as they pulled her to her feet. "Thank you," she said hoarsely. Her heart was still trying to leap out of her throat and her body ached from the beating she had just taken.

"Are you alright?"

She blinked and finally brought her rescuer into focus. Silvery grey eyes, almost the color of the stainless steel sink behind her, met hers. Right after she got hit with a bout of attraction, a sinking feeling hit her in the stomach. This was going to be far from a good first impression.

"Miss?"

Wynona finally found her tongue. "I-I'm fine, thank you," she whispered. Immediately embarrassed by her response, she cleared her throat and stepped back. "I'm fine, thank you," she said as she brushed off her clothes. "Just a little bruised."

Those penetrating eyes turned from her and glared daggers at the rest of the room. Only then did Wynona start to register the chaos that was still happening around her.

"Just what is going on here?" the man demanded. His blond hair was slicked back in a smooth business-style look and his suit was a perfect match for his eyes, looking custom tailored, if Wynona's guess was right. She had a sneaking suspicion that she had just met her landlord.

Chef Droxon was still screaming angrily as he marched toward the struggling thief and snatched something from his pocket. "How *dare* you take my recipes!" Chef Droxon shouted in the man's face. His green face flushed a weird brown as he screamed in anger. His words began to blur as Gnomish flooded through his thick lips until the cursing and shouts were completely unintelligible.

The man who arrived late grabbed the thief by his collar. "What do you have to say for yourself?"

The thief looked terrified and shook his head, refusing to speak.

"We should call the police," Wynona said in as soothing a voice as she could manage. "I'll be right back."

Though she was sure one of the employees had a cell she could use, Wynona decided they had their hands full holding onto the thief. She wiggled her way through the crowd and made her way to her office, where she quickly called in the emergency. Once that was done, she took a moment to redo her hair and make sure she didn't look quite so bedraggled before making her way back to the kitchen. "The police are on their..." She trailed off when she realized everyone was now yelling at each other.

"Where did he go?"

"Couldn't you hold onto him?"

"Did anyone look in the alley?"

Chef Droxon and the blond-haired man were speaking. Well, the blond was speaking, but Chef Droxon, as usual, was screaming at the top of his lungs.

Wynona stared, looking around the room in confusion until she realized a key aspect was missing. The thief. He was gone. She gasped and put her fingers over her mouth.

The blond jerked his head her way at the sound, then left an open-mouthed gnome and headed her way. "Are you sure you're alright?" he asked, his concern audible in his voice.

"Oh, yes," Wynona said, still flustered. "I'm fine. But...what happened to the man? The one who tried to steal Chef Droxon's black binder?"

The man sighed and brushed a manicured hand over his hair. "I'm not quite sure. I was speaking to Droxon when there was a rustle behind us. Next thing I knew, the thief was gone and the workers were all blaming each other."

Wynona frowned. "Did he use some kind of magic to escape?"

The man shrugged. "Not that I could feel, but I'll admit I wasn't paying much attention. I thought they had a good hold on him." He smiled. "Forgive me. I should have introduced myself earlier. Roderick Caligari. Warlock."

Once again a gasp escaped her lips. "Mr. Caligari, I'm sorry. I suspected that's who you were." She gave him a rueful smile and shook his outstretched hand. "Wynona Le Doux. I'm your tenant in this building."

"I assumed so." He nodded thoughtfully. "Good to meet you as well. I should have known from your fancy signature on the contract that you would be as beautiful in person."

Wynona smiled, but gave him a look. "Well, that wasn't cheesy at all."

He chuckled. "It worked, didn't it?"

"I guess that depends on what you were trying to accomplish."

"I was hoping to gain a smile from a beautiful woman," he explained casually.

Heat crept up her neck, but Wynona held her ground. "Thank you for the sweet compliment, but I think we have bigger things to deal with." She nodded over his shoulder. "It looks like the police have arrived."

Roderick spun. "Indeed." He glanced back with a bright smile. "But call me Roderick. Mr. Caligari is too formal."

Wynona gave him a soft smile. "If you want."

"I do."

"Then that's what I'll do." She followed him farther into the kitchen as the police were taking statements. She knew she'd have to do the same, though she wasn't looking forward to it. She hadn't even opened her shop yet and already the police were here. This didn't bode well for the future. She muttered a quick prayer that her landlord wouldn't kick her out, deeming her as trouble before she'd even had a chance to begin.

"And you are?" An officer stood in front of her with a pad of paper and a pencil. She appeared to be a vampire, if her almost translucent skin was a clue. The slight red ring around her pupils was the clencher.

"Wynona Le Doux," Wynona said, ignoring the officer's widened eyes at her last name. "I own this shop."

The officer nodded and wrote down a few notes. "Did you witness the incident?"

"I did," Wynona said. "But I'm not leaving any time soon. Why don't you take care of Chef Droxon and his workers, allowing them to leave. I'll wait here for you to have time for me."

The officer looked around uncertainly. "Are you sure, Ms. Le Doux? We can certainly take care of you first."

Wynona held back a sigh of frustration. She truly despised the hold her family had over the general public. "I'm fine. Really." She smiled as kindly as she could manage in her exhausted state. "Please take care of Chef Droxon and his employees. I'm sure they're all ready to leave."

The officer nodded sharply, then turned and did as Wynona suggested.

Propping the kitchen door open, Wynona walked into the dining area and dropped into a chair. She rested her head in her hands. This was not how she'd expected today to go, but at least it had a mostly happy ending. The Chef's black book was safe, and she still had a contract with the best baker in all of Hex Haven. She had even discovered that her landlord was extremely handsome, which was a bonus. At least, it was if he stayed her landlord after this.

Roderick walked in and sat across from her. "This wasn't exactly how I pictured us meeting for the first time."

Wynona smiled. "Me either. I had planned to have tea and leftover pastries at the ready."

His eyes flitted back to the kitchen door where a dozen voices continued to speak over each other. "Perhaps it's just as well. As tempting as those pastries sound, if we'd met under normal circumstances, I wouldn't have had the chance to hold you in my arms so quickly."

Wynona laughed quietly and tucked a piece of hair behind her ear. She'd never had anyone flirt with her so openly. Really, she'd never had anyone flirt with her like this at all. It was equal parts flattering and awkward. "You're quite the charmer."

He smirked. "I try to be."

Wynona laughed a little more. "Are you waiting to give your statement?" She wasn't quite ready to continue their current topic. Roderick was handsome, but she wasn't really looking for a relationship. Besides, when he found out she had no powers, odds were he would hightail it out of there before she could say Abracadabra.

"I am."

"I guess now is as good a time as any to have that tea. Give me a moment and I'll get us something to drink." Having something to do helped calm Wynona down and she was feeling decidedly better by the time she had steeped two cups. "Chamomile, lemon balm and passion flower," Wynona stated when she set down the cups. "It'll help us calm down."

"Thank you," Roderick said, dunking the infusion ball a few times. "It smells heavenly."

"Thanks," Wynona said. She grabbed a platter. "I even managed the leftovers I mentioned earlier." The eclairs still looked as fresh as the moment they'd been displayed. *There HAS to be some magic in these. But how?*

"I didn't expect to be so spoiled," Roderick said with a grin. He put the cup to his lips. "At this rate, you'll be able to use my glowing review to advertise your business."

Wynona wasn't sure when she'd laughed so much. "I'll look forward to it," she returned.

"Miss Le Doux?" The vampire officer from earlier was standing in the kitchen doorway.

"Yes?"

"Can I take your statement now?"

Wynona waved a hand at the table. "Have a seat and I'll tell you everything you need to know."

The officer frowned, then did as asked. "You're...are you related to President Le Doux?"

Wynona nodded, keeping her face perfectly pleasant. "I am."

"Huh." The officer shook her head. "You're not quite what I would have expected."

A wide, genuine smile graced Wynona's face. "Why, thank you Officer..."

"Nightshade. Amaris Nightshade."

Wynona nodded. "Officer Nightshade. I do believe that's the nicest thing anyone has ever said to me."

CHAPTER 4

Wynona hummed as she let herself into the shop through the back door and into the kitchen. She had stayed late last night and with the help of her new friend and landlord Roderick, they'd managed to put the kitchen back to rights before heading to their respective homes.

He had been the ultimate gentleman and Wynona found herself wishing things could be different. He was flirty and sweet and terribly handsome, but he was also a warlock. By trade, she knew that warlocks and witches were always looking for more power. This wasn't an attitude brought on by her skewed childhood. It was a statement of fact.

As soon as Roderick knew she was power*less,* he would more than likely stop speaking to her altogether. She sighed as she flipped on the lights. It was a sad situation, but one she needed to get used to. It's not like she could change her circumstances. Not to mention, she didn't want someone who was only interested in her magic.

"Having no powers just means you can be together with someone who wants you for you," she reassured herself. It was a line she told herself over and over, but on days like today, it felt especially important. Roderick seemed like the type of man who would have been fun to get to know.

After setting down the basket of tea leaves she had brought, Wynona headed out of the kitchen into the dining area, flipping on all the lights as she went. As she walked through the largest gathering room with all the tea tables, her eyes drifted to the spot on the floor where she had left the crumbs in front of the bookcase. When she realized that the space was empty, she paused midstep. Eyes widening, she hurried back to the kitchen and threw open the fridge. There was very little in it at this point, since she didn't plan to stock the perishables until the day before she opened, but there were a few takeout containers from her long nights decorating and cleaning.

She ripped one open and grabbed a crust of pizza from The Weeping Widow. It was a small pizzeria down the street, run by Mewla Wraithsong, a banshee. Apparently, the songs she screeched in the kitchen did something special to her creations and it had been voted the best pizza in the haven for three years running.

Breaking off a nice chunk, Wynona went back to the sitting room and carefully bent down in her heels and pencil skirt to leave the crust just in front of the bookcase. "I hope you're alright from my sister's hex," Wynona said, feeling only slightly foolish for speaking to a mouse. "Hopefully, this will help you recover."

She waited a moment, but there was no sign of the creature, so she stood and brushed off her fingers. It was time to get to work for the day. She'd check back later to see if her little houseguest had ventured out.

Wynona walked across the room and headed down the hallway, only to pause just outside her office door. A frown pulled on her lips as she stared at her door. It was slightly open, which shouldn't have been the case. Wynona was meticulous in the way she ran her life. Every door had been shut, every light turned off, and every deadbolt locked when she'd gone home last night.

An eerie foreboding crawled up her spine and her hands began to tremble. Her eyes darted around, looking for some kind of weapon, but unless she wanted to use a vintage teacup, there was nothing within reach. She made a mental note to get some kind of weapon to keep on hand. This was just another example of how having magic would have drastically changed her life. Celia would have marched in without a care in the world, knowing that nothing in the room would have been strong enough to hurt her. Once again, Wynona had to hold back harsh thoughts about whoever had cursed her. The culprit had never been found, but they'd left an indelible mark on her life.

Reaching out, she slowly began to push the door inward. The wary feeling grew the farther the door opened. "Hello?" she asked, leaning around so she could see inside. No one answered her call, which wasn't surprising. She scoffed in her mind. If an intruder was there, they weren't exactly going to announce themselves.

All was still...too still. She stepped fully into the room and frowned, putting her hands on her hips. Whoever had been there had obviously come and gone. A quick glance at her shelves showed nothing obvious missing.

Wynona huffed and the dust in the air floated into her eyes. Blinking rapidly, Wynona waved a hand in the air. "Ew. I need to..." Her words trailed off when she spotted something on the floor.

Without running a single step or lifting any kind of weight, Wynona's heart began to race and her stomach flipped. Her shaking hand rose to her lips. "Oh..."

On the floor lay a body. Or what was left of a body. The flesh had all been turned to ash, which was currently floating around Wynona's face, while the clothes lay perfectly on the floor, untouched by whatever hex had been thrown at the individual.

"Nona?"

Wynona jumped at the sound of her name and it spurred her into action. She rushed out of the door and ran down the hall as fast as her heels would allow. "PRIM!" she yelled.

Primrose was just coming through the kitchen door when Wynona ran over and grabbed her arm. "What are you doing?" Primrose asked.

"You need to come see this," Wynona said breathlessly. She pulled her friend forward. "Come on."

"I don't understand," Prim managed through her panting. She was still in her fairy form, making her much smaller than Wynona.

"You will in a minute."

"Nona, I—" Prim cut off and her face contorted before she screamed as if the reaper himself was swinging his scythe at her head.

Wynona ducked and covered her ears. "If they weren't already dead, I think you'd have finished the job," she said wryly.

Prim covered the rest of her scream with her hands. "Soidnge-orhewhrwek."

Wynona tugged on the fairy's hands. "I can't understand you."

"Who is...you know..." She pointed at the body from behind her other hand.

Wynona held back her eyeroll. "They can't hear you, Prim. It's okay to talk out loud."

Prim dropped her hands,but her shoulders remained bunched up near her ears. "Who is that? And what in the world happened?"

Wynona's eyes went back to the gruesome sight. She shook her head as she studied the scene. Nothing in her room seemed out of place, except for the dead body, of course. What in the world were they doing in her office of all places? "I'm not sure," Wynona said. "But if I had to guess..." She swallowed hard. "I think it might be Atherton Droxon."

"WHAT!" Prim's voice had risen again.

"Oh my word, Prim! I'm going to be deaf before the police get here."

"Sorry." Prim brought her voice back down, but it was still shaky, making Wynona feel bad about scolding her. It was clear the fairy was terrified. "What makes you think that's him?"

Wynona shook her head sadly and pointed. "The apron? See the brown streak? I saw him wearing that yesterday when he came over for the taste test."

Prim squeaked and she rose on her tiptoes. If she had wings, she'd have risen off the floor, but just like Wynona, Primrose was an outcast among her kind. She was a fairy born without wings.

Primrose, however, was not the type of personality to let something so mundane get her down. Although she kept her feet firmly planted on the ground, she'd let her dreams reach the clouds, and now Prim was the premiere flower farmer in the land.

She might have taken on the business world fearlessly, but apparently that attitude did not apply to murders.

"The ghost reporters are going to have a field day," Prim grumbled. She looked up, her pink eyes glassy with tears. "This is a disaster."

Wynona nodded. "I know." Not only was she sad that a man had died, but she couldn't help but mourn how this would change her tea shop as well. She had been so excited to have a contract with him. She shook her head. Her business definitely wasn't as important as a man's life. Not to mention his family was probably worried sick.

"Are the police on their way?"

"No. You arrived just as I found him," Wynona said softly. "Let me grab my phone." She walked back to the kitchen where her purse was sitting on the counter. After digging around, she found the device and punched in the number.

"Emergency services, what is your emergency?"

"I'd like to report a murder," Wynona said matter of factly. Her stomach was still doing flip-flops, but she figured being hysterical on the line wouldn't be very helpful.

"Excuse me, ma'am, but did you say a murder?" the voice clarified.

"Yes."

"Can I get your address, please?"

"I'm on Haven Main. The new tea shop. Saffron's Tea House." The name still made Wynona choke up, even when she wasn't already emotional. She hoped her granny knew the shop had been named in her honor. "Please have the officers come around back." After answering a few more questions and assuring the worker that there was no present danger, Wynona managed to hang up just as her back door opened. That was fast. "Oh, Roderick!"

He smiled. "Good morning, Wynona. I wanted to check on you to make sure there weren't any lasting problems from last night."

"Oh, no, I'm fine." She began to assure him when Prim barged into the room.

"Nona, I can't stay in that room any longer," Prim gushed. "That body gives me the creeps." Her mouth snapped shut when she spotted Roderick. Pink eyes darted back and forth between Wynona and Roderick multiple times before a mischievous smile pulled at Prim's thin, pink lips.

"Prim, this is Roderick Caligari," Wynona hurried to introduce them before Prim got the wrong idea. "He owns this building." The words were said very pointedly and Wynona raised her eyebrows at her friend.

"Ooooh!" Prim nodded slowly, her mouth still forming an "O". "Gotcha." Sticking her hand out, she sashayed toward the handsome warlock. "Nice to meet you, Mr. Caligari. I'm Primrose Meadows."

"The famous florist?" he asked with his usual charming grin.

"The one and only." Prim put her hands on her hips and stood as tall as her fairy stature allowed. It wasn't exactly impressive next to Roderick's height, but Prim definitely had the bigger attitude. She was taller in her human form, but Prim normally only used that in public. With Wynona, she was free to be herself.

Roderick frowned and turned away from Prim to look at Wynona again. "Did she say something about a body?"

Wynona slumped against the counter. "Yes. I found a body in my office this morning."

Sirens wailed in the distance and Wynona winced. She had hoped they would quietly show up and take care of matters without creating an undue scene. Apparently, she wasn't going to be that lucky.

Roderick glanced toward the sound, then looked at her again. "I think you better tell me what's going on."

"Atherton Droxon is dead in Nona's office. We can tell because of his apron, but we can also tell it was a murder because the body is nothing but ash." Prim fluttered her eyelashes at Roderick's astonished look. How she'd managed to sound so matter of fact when she'd nearly been a sobbing mess earlier, Wynona had no idea, but any second now, the police were going to break down her door.

"Excuse me," Wynona said softly, stepping around Roderick. She pulled open the door and Roderick grabbed her upper arm.

"Are you hurt?" he hissed, looking her up and down.

"No," Wynona said even as she blushed from his perusal. "I found the body when I arrived this morning. Whoever did the deed was long gone."

"But why did they kill him here?" he pressed. "Why was Atherton back at the shop?"

Wynona shrugged. "I wish I knew."

"Ms. Le Doux?"

Wynona looked out the door. "I'm she."

A tall, pale-faced man stepped into the kitchen. His dark hair was slicked and his red eyes pronounced him a vampire. He was tall and muscled with a hooked nose that should have dominated his face the way his presence dominated the kitchen, but instead it gave him a rough sort of attractiveness. "Chief Deverell Ligurio. Dispatch said you reported a body."

"I did." She stepped out of Roderick's hold. "I wasn't expecting the chief to show up," she said with half a smile. "It's in my office. I found the body when I arrived this morning. Judging from the clothing, I'm fairly sure it's Chef Atherton Droxon." She pursed her lips. "He was here for a business meeting yesterday and the clothes on the body are the same ones he was wearing." She turned and began walking. "This way." Wynona led her small entourage through the shop and down the hall. Instead of going in, she stood near the door and waved everyone inside. "To the right of the desk."

The chief stepped past her, followed by Roderick and a slew of officers. One in particular caught Wynona's eye when he winked as he walked into the room. His golden eyes and messy brown hair were as striking as his physique. He had to be a shifter. A flush rose up Wynona's cheeks before she could stop it. She wasn't used to so many men flirting with her.

"Ms. Le Doux?"

She snapped out of her thoughts and looked at the chief. "Yes, sir?"

"Mind telling me where you were last night?"

"I..." Wynona's jaw was slack. She hadn't even considered the fact that she would be a suspect. "I was at home," she choked out.

"Is there anyone who can corroborate your story?" the office pressed. His red eyes were intense.

"Come now, Chief Ligurio," Roderick said impatiently. "You just got here. Surely you aren't suggesting Wynona had something to do with this." His hand waved over the body.

The chief barely spared him a glance. "I've done this job a long time and I've found that usually the easiest explanation is the truth. We're in her office with a hexed body. She's a witch from an extremely powerful family." He tilted his head, staring at her like a naughty wood sprite. "Please answer the question."

Wynona knew this day would come, but she hadn't been prepared for it to be quite so soon. Knowing there was no way around it, she squared her shoulders and looked him in the eye. "No. I live alone. But I couldn't have done this anyway."

"Oh? And why is that?"

Ignoring the fact that an entire room full of officers and friends were staring at her, Wynona admitted, "Because I have no powers."

CHAPTER 5

The chief's hand slowly dropped from his notebook. "You...what?"

Wynona dropped his penetrating gaze and looked at the ground. She could feel the eyes of every person in that room boring into her head. She knew word would eventually get around about her handicap, but she hadn't wanted it to happen like this. "I was cursed as a baby," she explained, still not making eye contact. "I have no access to my powers. Never have. They were bound by an unknown entity." She forced herself to bring her head back up. Just like when she dealt with her family, this was not the time to act vulnerable and afraid. This wasn't her fault. It was the hand life had dealt her and she refused to be ashamed of it.

The chief pointed a pen at her. "You could have bought a spell."

"Chief." The man who'd winked at her stepped up and put his hand on the vampire's arm. "Let's get all the information from the scene before we make any assumptions."

The chief scowled, but nodded. "Right." He spared Wynona one last sharp glance before going back to the body.

Wynona sighed quietly in relief. Her eyes drifted to the golden ones who had saved her and she gave him a small smile of thanks. He gave her a curt nod, then turned away, effectively dismissing her.

The room broke into movement again as the officers wrote down clues and discussed what might have happened.

"Who would have wanted to kill Droxon?" one of the officers murmured.

Wynona kept her thoughts to herself. While she was devastated to lose the contract with the baker, she thought there could be many people who might have wanted a little revenge. He wasn't a nice gnome, and the tantrum he'd had in her shop yesterday had been clear proof. Heaven only knew how a disgruntled employee would feel after years of dealing with his vitriol.

"Have you ever tasted his lemongrass muffins?" another asked.

The officer he was speaking to shook his head.

The officer's white teeth glowed against his dark, bark-like skin. "I'm pretty sure I know what a cat on catnip feels like."

His friend snorted. "Invite me next time. We'll give it a whirl."

"There won't be a next time," the nature fairy grumbled. His eyes shot to Wynona and she stiffened, but didn't defend herself. She knew she was innocent. Nothing they said or did would change that.

Her eyes drifted down to the body and she considered the situation. Now that she was calm enough to pay attention, something seemed...off. Slowly, unconsciously, she walked farther into the room, her eyes never leaving the ash.

"Excuse me, Ms. Le Doux," Chief Ligurio said forcefully. "You'll need to wait outside the room."

Wynona snapped upright and shook her head slightly. "Sorry," she said with a smile. "Just curious." Spinning on her heel so she didn't have to look at his face and whatever emotion was aimed at her, she marched out, going back to the main dining room. Primrose was waiting at one of the tables, a freshly brewed tea in her hands. Wynona took a deep sniff. "Ah, I see you found the lemon balm."

Prim shivered and took another sip. "Can you blame me? There's someone dead just down the hall." She wrinkled her petite nose and made a disgusted face. She had shifted into her human body, allowing her to sit naturally at the table and not give away her wingless state to the police. "This better not interfere with your grand opening next week."

Wynona paused before sitting down. "Why would it? I've still got six days."

Prim gave her a look. "If this is still considered a crime scene, there's no way Chief Undead will let you open and bring customers all over his precious evidence."

"Prim!" Wynona scolded. "You can't talk like that."

Pink eyes rolled to the ceiling. "What's he going to do? It's not like it's illegal to not like him."

"Why don't you like him?"

Prim pursed her lips. "I heard what he asked you. He didn't even bother to gather any evidence or take your statement, just automatically accused. It was ridiculous."

Wynona slipped into her seat with a sigh. "Can you blame him?" she asked softly. "It's not like my family has a lot of friends."

Prim huffed. "You're nothing like your family."

"Thank you for that, but that doesn't mean the chief knows that."

Prim grunted. "Stop trying to talk me out of it. The man was rude. End of story."

Wynona laughed softly. "Alright. I'll stop defending him."

"Thank you," Prim said with her nose in the air.

Wynona shook her head with a smile. They grew quiet for a moment, though the voices from down the hall were still filtering into their space. The smell of Prim's tea met Wynona's nose and she took a deep breath, only to pause mid-sniff.

A quiet squeaking noise, the same one from the day before, could be heard if she strained. Twisting in her seat, Wynona ducked her head to look in the direction of the bookcase.

"What are you doing?" Prim asked, leaning sideways and essentially blocking Wynona's view.

Wynona put a finger to her lips, stood up and walked around to the bookcase. Squatting down carefully, she kept her ears peeled.

The noise happened again. "Did you enjoy the pizza?" Wynona whispered. She'd noticed immediately that the crust was gone.

More squeaking ensued and Wynona looked over her shoulder, grinning at Prim.

"What is it?" Prim mouthed.

"A mouse," Wynona whispered gleefully. "I thought Celia killed it, but it's still alive. I fed it some crumbs yesterday and a crust of pizza this morning..." She trailed off when she heard more noises and turned back to the spot under the bookcase. Her hands came up to cover her mouth when a nose peeked out from the dark space.

Black and twitching, the nose moved around, then slowly crept forward. The snout came next, then one paw and another.

Wynona frowned. She gasped when the whole head appeared.

"It's purple!" Prim squealed.

The mouse disappeared again.

"Prim!" Wynona scolded.

"Sorry," Prim whispered, locking her lips with a pretend key. The motion did nothing to stop her from speaking again. "How did it get purple?"

Wynona's eyes were wide as she shook her head. "I have no idea." She kept her eyes on the shadow. "Come on out," she said in a sweet tone. "We won't hurt you. Prim was just startled."

After a moment, the nose slowly worked its way out again. Wynona held as still as possible, though her calves were starting to scream from being crouched down in that position.

The creature emerged quicker this time, his entire body eventually coming into sight. Prim was right. The white tail Wynona had spotted yesterday was now a bright purple. "It had to have been my sister's spell," Wynona mused. "Something must have gone wrong."

"Huh." The clanking of a teacup let Wynona know that Prim had taken another drink. "I've never seen anything like it and we live in Hex Haven. Weird things happen every day."

The lavender rodent now stood on its hind legs, nose still twitching as it stared at Wynona with black, beady eyes.

"Hello," Wynona said softly. She smiled.

The creature squeaked as if answering her and Wynona's smile grew wider.

"Are you still hungry? Want me to bring you something from the kitchen?" Even more than it had yesterday, Wynona's heart went out to the tiny animal. Yesterday he'd been viewed as a nuisance. Today he had joined the outcast club. Just like Wynona and Prim, the purple mouse was one of a kind.

More squeaking and a head bob answered her question.

"Right. Give me a moment." Wynona bit back a groan as she stood up, the blood rushing through her cramped limbs.

"How do you know what it said?" Prim asked.

Wynona shook her head. "I don't," she said as she walked past. "But when is a mouse not hungry?" It just felt like the right thing to do, especially after it was almost killed yesterday. Grabbing a package of crackers from the cupboard, Wynona quickly made her way back out to the sitting room. She came to a screeching halt when she saw who had joined Prim.

Roderick stood up from where he'd sat down. "Wynona," he said, tilting his head to her. "Are you doing alright?"

Wynona held herself stiffly. She had no idea how Roderick was going to react to the news she'd shared earlier, but she wanted to be prepared. "Fine, thank you." Without another word, she headed back to the bookcase. The mouse had disappeared again, but Wynona knew it would take the cracker if she left it on the floor. She stacked three of the butter crackers on each other, left them strategically placed, then stood up and wiped her fingers together.

"What's that for?" Roderick asked. He was frowning and smiling at the same time, causing Wynona to relax just a little. As long as he wasn't going to be mean about her issues, she wouldn't need to defend herself.

"Nona has a new friend," Prim said right before another sip.

Roderick's eyebrows rose up. "Under the bookcase?"

Wynona shrugged. "He's...unique in size."

"Right." Roderick gave her one more look, then pulled back a chair. "Why don't you have a seat?"

Wynona walked over. "Thank you," she said softly, letting him push her in. He sat next to her and faced her direction.

"How are you holding up?" he asked. "After nearly being trampled yesterday, and now you've got a murder in your shop...you must be overwhelmed."

Wynona shrugged and drew a random pattern on the tablecloth. "I'm okay. Sad more than anything. It's hard to believe anyone would kill..." She paused. Something was tugging at her brain.

"Droxon?" Roderick scoffed. "Is that what you were going to say? I know the man could bake better than anyone else in the haven, but I don't think he had much in the way of friends."

Wynona nodded. "I know, but something is not quite right."

"What do you mean?" Prim asked. She reached over and stole the package of crackers, crunching into them immediately.

Wynona smiled. She loved how Prim was comfortable enough to just take advantage of Wynona's kindness. It made her feel like a true friend, something Wynona had never had before now. Except for Granny.

"Nona?"

"Oh, yeah..." Wynona cleared her throat. "I don't know, it's just...something is tickling at the back of my brain." Her eyes went to the hallway. "But the chief wouldn't let me look close enough to figure it out."

Roderick studied her for a moment, then jumped to his feet. "Come on," he said, reaching out and taking her hand.

"What?" Wynona said breathlessly as he pulled her along.

"If you think you have something to offer, then you should be given the chance to figure it out."

"Stop," Wynona said, pulling backward until he listened. "They think I killed him," she whispered. "I shouldn't go in there."

"We both know you had nothing to do with that murder," Roderick said with a shake of his head. His silver eyes held no doubt, and that helped her relax a little further. "They can't accuse you of anything without proof, so let's go in there and figure out what's bugging you."

Wynona pressed her lips together, then finally squeezed his hand. "Okay." She let him lead her inside. She'd learned long ago to stand on her own two feet, but it felt good to let Roderick help. She was still nervous about being accused of murder, so a friend at her side was helpful.

"Chief," Roderick said loudly as they walked into the office. "I think maybe you should let Ms. Le Doux take a look at things."

Chief Ligurio glared at them. "This is a crime scene," he snapped. "Please wait outside."

Roderick let go of Wynona's hand and folded his arms over his impressive chest in a stance that spoke of ease and confidence. "I think you'll like what she has to say."

Wynona almost choked. She didn't have anything to say! All she had was a funny feeling in the back of her mind that said something was not what it seemed.

The chief turned his glare directly on Wynona. "Is that so? What is it?"

Wynona swallowed hard, turning to Roderick first before going back to the chief. "May I look a little closer at the body?" she asked, her voice softer than she would have liked.

The chief looked heavenward as if sending a prayer to the Creator for help. "Sure. Why not?" he snapped, waving his arm at the ashes. "Let's see if a powerless witch can see more than a trained police crew."

Ignoring the jab, Wynona tentatively walked over. She could feel the eyes of the team on her again and it made her skin itch. The golden eyes were the worst. It was as if she could pick them out of all the others, probably because he'd winked at her and come to her defense earlier.

Clasping her hands behind her, she studied the ashes. Her frown grew the longer she looked.

"See anything interesting?"

Wynona jumped slightly and looked up into the face of the handsome officer with the messy hair.

"Do share," the chief drawled.

Wynona pinched her lips together, then decided things couldn't get any worse. "Well, I'm sure you already noticed, but the shape left behind with the ashes is of medium height and slim build."

"Of course," the chief said in an unimpressed tone.

"Atherton Droxon is a gnome."

The chief waved a hand in the air as if to say *And...*

"So, he's short and round," Wynona continued. She straightened. The more she thought about it, the more she knew she had to be correct. "Don't you think the ashes would be more in the shape of a circle if it was him?"

The chief took a moment to respond. He put his hand on his hips. "Are you telling me that you don't think this is Atherton Droxon? Wasn't it you who told me it was when I first arrived? You recognized the apron, right?"

Wynona nodded. "Yes. It's his apron, but I'm reasonably sure it's not his body."

"That doesn't make any sense," the wood fairy officer murmured.

"So, let me get this straight," Chief Ligurio said slowly, his eyes never leaving hers. "You think someone...dressed like Atherton Droxon...broke into your shop, got himself killed with a hex... but isn't actually Atherton Droxon?"

Wynona nodded firmly. "Yes."

The chief opened his mouth, but a shout from down the hall caught their attention. Wynona's eyebrows shot up. She knew that voice. Turning to the door, she waited.

"What is going on here?" Chef Droxon screeched as he burst into the office.

"But..." One of the officers started to argue.

"You're not dead," Chief Ligurio said, his tone almost disappointed.

"Dead?" Chef Droxon scoffed. "I not dead. I bake!" He glared at the room, Wynona included, then his black eyes landed on the ashes. "Who is that?" he demanded in his usual imperial tone.

"Not you, apparently," the handsome officer muttered under his breath.

Wynona glanced his way and met his stunning eyes again.

"Good work, Ms. Le Doux," he said, a note of admiration in his voice.

Heat infused her cheeks. "Thanks. But that still leaves us with a question."

"Yep." The officer turned and Wynona saw his nametag: *Officer Strongclaw*. "If this isn't Chef Droxon," he looked up at his chief, "who is it?"

CHAPTER 6

Wynona once again sat at a tea table and tried to control her breathing. Her face was buried in her hands and the loud voices around her all seemed to blur into complete chaos. She was ready to scream. How could this day have gone so horribly wrong? She'd been so excited. Her contract with Chef Droxon was in place, she was only six days from opening, the mouse hadn't been killed... For a split second, life had been good.

Now she had a dead body, an angry chef and a suspicious police chief. Though the chef had been sent home, the other two were still in her shop. It was all moving too fast for her to keep her head wrapped around it. A large, warm hand landed on her neck and began to massage.

"Oooh, that feels good," she moaned, letting her head hang forward.

"I thought it might."

Wynona let herself enjoy the touch just a moment longer, before she straightened and pulled away. Roderick was handsome, hadn't yet said anything about her lack of powers, and was extremely charming, but right now she had no desire to consider anything beyond a platonic relationship. "Thank you." She gave him a smile as she stood and moved out of his reach. Perhaps when this murder was taken care of, she could see if he wanted to come over for an afternoon tea and they could test out this spark, but not right now.

Roderick nodded. "Anytime."

"Ms. Le Doux?"

She spun. "Yes?" It was the officer with the delightfully messy hair. Once again, Wynona had the feeling the man was a shifter.

There was something inherently predatory about him, but not in a bad way. He just seemed strong and confident, and his movements were smooth and calculated.

"Would you mind stepping into the kitchen to answer a few questions?" he asked. His golden eyes were narrowed, making him look slightly intimidating, but Wynona realized he wasn't even looking at her.

Frowning, she glanced over her shoulder to see Roderick looking smug, staring right back at the officer. Shaking her head at the weirdness of it all, she began to walk his way. "Of course," she responded.

"Do you need me to come?" Roderick called.

Wynona waved him off. His presence was comforting, but it wasn't like she was afraid of the police. She knew she was innocent. Surely the truth would come out. "Thank you," she murmured as he held the door open for her. Stepping inside, she leaned her hip against a counter and folded her arms over her chest. "What can I do for you, Officer Strongclaw?"

He snorted. "Just call me Rascal."

Wynona couldn't help the bubble of laughter. "Rascal?"

The officer didn't look the least bit embarrassed. "Yeah. My parents cursed me with a *very* pretentious name, but my friends quickly nicknamed me Rascal." He shrugged his massive shoulders. "It stuck."

"I think the real question is, does it fit?" Wynona asked.

A slow smile spread across his delicious face. "I hate to admit it, but yeah...probably."

She laughed softly. "Good to know." A piece of hair fell across her face when she tilted her head. "But now I'm curious about your full name."

Rascal shook his head. "Nope." He made some notes in a small notebook. "That's privileged information. Plus, I'm the one supposed to be asking the questions here."

Wynona nodded slowly. "Ah...gotcha." She grinned. "I'll just have to ask around."

Rascal winked. "Good luck." He sobered. "You ready for me to ask some questions about the murder?"

All humor fled and Wynona nodded. "Yes. Go ahead."

"Before we start, I'm sorry about my boss. He's been around a long time and sometimes wants to jump to the end, rather than take all the necessary steps in between."

Wynona nodded her understanding. "I get it. I'm sure everyone gets a little burnt out in a job like this."

"We can," Rascal mumbled. He cleared his throat. "Okay. Let's start from the beginning. You said you were the last one to leave yesterday?"

She nodded. "Yes. I had a meeting with Chef Droxon where we had a taste test and picked out what pastries he was going to supply for the shop."

"Did you pick anything good?" His golden eyes sparkled with good humor.

Wynona barked a laugh, her hands automatically covering her mouth. "Aren't they all good?"

"Point taken." Rascal nodded. "Continue, please." His pen was poised above his notepad.

"I stayed here after everyone left..." Wynona's eyes shot open. "Oh my goodness. How could I have forgotten?"

Rascal gave her an expectant look.

Wynona tucked the stray hair back, eager to share her memory. "A man tried to steal Chef Droxon's little black book yesterday."

Rascal didn't move. "What?"

"Yes. A man was pretending to be one of Chef Droxon's employees. I was walking around giving out tea gift bags to everyone to say thank you, and the man panicked when I tried to give him one. Just as he ran me over, Chef Droxon came in screaming that someone had stolen his recipe book. Then Roderick arrived and saved me from the dog pile, but while I was calling the police, the man escaped."

Rascal closed his eyes for a moment and shook his head. "Let me get this straight. A thief tried to steal Chef Droxon's recipes. He ran you over?"

His eyes ran up and down Wynona's body as if to check on her story and she felt a flush rush up her neck. White skin was such a curse sometimes.

"Mr. Caligari played hero and saved the day." There was no mistaking the slight edge of resentment in his tone, though Wynona had no idea why. "The book was returned, but the thief escaped. Sound about right?"

Wynona nodded. "That's it in a nutshell."

Rascal nodded several times and scribbled on his notepad for a few moments, putting a finger in the air for her to wait. Grabbing the radio that was attached to his collar, Rascal relayed a message. "Chief. There was a robbery here yesterday. We need to get the paperwork on it." Rascal glanced her way. "You did say you called the police?"

"Yes," she clarified. "I spoke with Officer Nightshade."

"That explains it," Rascal muttered. "She's off duty today." He then told his chief the same information.

"I want that folder now," Chief Ligurio snapped.

Wynona gasped. She waited until Rascal was able to focus on her again. "Can I look at the body again?"

He narrowed his eyes. "Got another hunch?"

Wynona nodded. "I think maybe the body is the thief from yesterday."

"And how will you be able to tell that? It's nothing but ash."

"His shoes." Wynona took off walking. She couldn't believe she'd forgotten about yesterday's debacle, but as soon as she'd retold the story, the recollection of the man's non-squeaky shoes burst back into her mind with a vengeance.

Wynona could feel Rascal behind her as she dashed through the main room and down the hall. She stopped in the doorway, Rascal's large presence, warm and comforting behind her. "It's him," she whispered.

"What are you doing back here?" the chief asked, sounding exhausted. "Rascal, I thought you were interrogating her."

"She had a hunch," he said unapologetically.

"A hunch?" The chief didn't sound impressed. "Like the one about it not being Chef Droxon?" Red eyes turned to her.

"You could say that," Wynona said. "I'm sure you all have noticed the shoes, since none of the clothes were burnt."

"The point, Ms. Le Doux," Chief Ligurio demanded.

Wynona pointed to the rubber soled shoes. "I saw those on the thief from yesterday. I noticed because he wasn't wearing the same squeaky sneakers as the rest of Chef Droxon's employees. They all had on the kind meant to keep someone from slipping on a kitchen floor."

"And this guy didn't?" the chief mused as he looked down at the crime scene.

Wynona held her breath. She had poked her nose into this investigation too much. She just hoped it was enough to not only get her off the hook, but help the police get it solved quickly. She had a business to open.

"That doesn't help us figure out who this guy is," Rascal said from behind her. "He's wearing Chef Droxon's clothes."

"Yeah, that's strange," Wynona agreed.

"What? No hunches about why?" Chief Ligurio drawled.

"I have no doubt that you and your wonderful team will figure that out," Wynona said in her most polite voice.

The chief snorted, but went back to the paperwork he was looking at.

Slowly, Wynona backed out of the room. She'd pressed things enough for one day. Probably should let the chief forget about her for a while. "Do you have any more questions?" she asked as she and Rascal walked down the hallway.

"Just a good description of the morning's events," Rascal said, checking his notes. "And your alibi." He glanced her way. "I know you said you were home alone, but I need the official statement."

Wynona nodded. "Gladly." They paused before reaching the main room and Wynona told him everything he needed to know. "I think that's it," she finished. "I'm sorry I don't have more for you."

Rascal chuckled. "I think you've been very helpful, Ms. Le Doux."

"Wynona," she quickly corrected. Heat infused her cheeks once more when he raised his eyebrows at her. "If I'm calling you Rascal, it doesn't seem right to have you address me so formally."

Rascal nodded. "Sounds good. Thanks."

"Hey, Nona?"

Wynona turned to her friend, who was watching from the same table as before.

"What are we going to do about opening?"

Wynona frowned a little as she cleared the hallway and entered the main room. Roderick was leaning against the far wall as well. "What do you mean?"

"If the investigation is still going on, are they going to let you open the shop next week?" Prim asked, her eyes dancing between Rascal and Wynona.

Wynona froze. "Surely they won't be here that long?" She turned to Rascal, trying to keep her panic hidden. Prim had mentioned the possible problem earlier, but the conversation had taken a different turn and Wynona hadn't had a chance to consider the consequences of the case.

Rascal gave her sheepish look. "I don't know, but I doubt it."

Wynona felt her face fall. "Well, how long do you think it's going to take to get this wrapped up? I'm supposed to open in six days."

Rascal scratched the back of his head. "I don't know, but murders usually take a little longer than other crimes. Six days doesn't seem like a lot in the grand scheme of things."

Wynona rubbed her pulsing forehead. "I understand," she said softly. She did, she really did. But that didn't mean she had to like it. The idea of helping solve the mystery flitted through her mind, but Wynona pushed it away. This wasn't her problem, not to mention she was busy enough as it was. She'd already offered the police what she could. They could take it from here and Wynona would just hope they were quick workers.

Footsteps echoed through the room as Roderick came to stand by her side. "Don't worry," he said softly, bumping his shoulder against hers. "We'll get it all figured out."

Wynona smiled up at him. "Thanks," she said. It was nice to know she had friends in this situation. She'd only ever had Granny to rely on and that connection had been severed just a few months ago. Without any magic, it would stay that way.

"I'm sure the police will get it figured out quickly," Prim added, though her eyes still looked worried.

Wynona nodded. She felt the same as Prim. They didn't even know the victim's name. Or why he was dressed like Chef Droxon. Or why he was at the shop!

A sense of hopelessness tried to engulf her. She had put her entire future into this shop. What was going to happen if she had to postpone everything? She was booked solid with patrons for the first two months.

Closing her eyes, Wynona forced herself to breathe slowly. She had been through worse than this. She'd lived with a family who hated her for thirty years. There was no way that a murder in her shop was going to get her down.

Roderick's arm came around her shoulder and he gave her a side squeeze. "I meant it. We'll get through this."

Wynona opened her eyes and looked up gratefully. "Thanks," she responded. "I appreciate you sticking around."

If silver could be warm, that's exactly what his eyes were right now. "Anytime," he said.

There was an extra message in that, but Wynona let it go. She did, however, allow herself to relax against him. For just a moment, she would let someone else help hold her up. Then, like she always did, she'd pick herself up, brush off the dust and move on. Very little good came from living with her family, but the ability to push past negative situations was one of them.

"I'll let you know if we need anything else," Rascal said, bringing Wynona out of her mental pep talk. He snapped his notebook shut, gave her a polite nod, did the same for Prim, then turned and walked back to the office.

It wasn't lost on Wynona that he'd ignored Roderick, but it was of little importance at the moment.

Roderick glanced at his watch. "I have another meeting." He raised his eyebrows at her. "I can cancel. Do you need me to stay here?"

Wynona shook her head. "No, thank you. We'll be fine." Her smile was genuine, if a little sad. Not at his leaving, but at the situation. This wasn't what she had hoped for, but it was the hand she'd been dealt.

She walked Roderick out, then joined Prim at the table.

"Did you still want to go over flower arrangements?" Prim asked warily. "We don't have to do it now."

Wynona shook her head. "No. I'd like to." Her smile trembled slightly. "Until I know otherwise, I'm absolutely planning to open on time."

Prim made a face. "From the looks of it, they might need your help to do that." She gave Wynona a significant look.

"Don't tempt me," Wynona whispered. The thought still sat in the back of her mind, but she *really* didn't want to get involved. She was finally free from her horrible family, and now she just wanted to focus on making friends and opening her shop in her granny's name. That's it. She wanted nothing to do with murder.

CHAPTER 7

I t felt weird to enter the shop the next morning, but Wynona was determined not to let yesterday's setback slow down her progress. She now only had five days until opening and she had things to do.

The shop was dark as she walked into the kitchen and the first thing she did was quickly walk around, turning on all the lights. She paused at the entrance to the hallway, noting the police tape still covering her office door. It was off limits to anyone without a badge, though they had been kind enough to let Wynona grab her books and computer before they shut it down last night.

She sighed at the sight. It definitely didn't go with the rest of the decor and it would be much appreciated when they solved the crime and took it down.

Shaking her head, Wynona walked away from the sight, only to pause when her eyes flitted to the bookcases. She smiled. The mouse. She hadn't fed him this morning. Walking quickly back to the kitchen, she grabbed a few strawberries out of her lunchbox, placed them on a tea saucer and brought it out.

"I've got something a little healthier for you today," she said in a cajoling tone. She'd seen yesterday her guest was skittish, and though that was natural for a small rodent, Wynona had a strong desire to befriend the little creature. Maybe it had something to do with the fact that Granny had had an animal familiar and this was the closest someone without magic was going to get, or maybe it was because the messed up hex had left the animal an outcast, but whatever the case, Wynona just knew she wanted to be friends with it.

She squatted down and set the plate on the ground, the same place she had left the crust and crackers. Now she just had to wait.

It didn't take long.

The smell of fresh berries proved to be enough to pull the purple mouse from its hiding place within only a few seconds. That black nose emerged, twitching incessantly, quickly followed by a purple face with pink eyes and a soft, fluffy, purple body.

The mouse looked up and squeaked at Wynona a few times, as if in thanks, before stepping up and starting to nibble on the sweet breakfast.

"You're very well mannered for a mouse," Wynona whispered with a smile. "And you're welcome." She let herself watch for a few minutes before rising to her feet.. "I'll come get the plate when you're done," she said before heading back to the kitchen.

Once there, she unloaded the teas she was carrying with her, organizing her kitchen exactly how she wanted it to be. The silence of the space became a little claustrophobic, allowing Wynona's mind to wander to the dead body, which was all too fresh in her mind. Grabbing her phone, she turned on some soothing music and allowed it to cast the dark aura from the shop.

"A little incense wouldn't hurt either," she murmured. Dusting her hands on her skinny jeans, she walked to a cupboard and pulled out her sage and a plate. Ten minutes later, she felt much better and the sweet smell of herbs permeated the kitchen, feeling much more like home than it had earlier.

Once done, Wynona went back to organizing her tea blends, only to jump when the kitchen door opened with a bang. Her heart nearly leapt out of her throat and her hand fluttered as if it could stop it. "Who's there?" she asked, then winced internally. Letting an intruder know she was there was probably the last thing she should have done.

A shuffling sound came from the doorway and Wynona forced herself to walk out of the pantry to see who was there. She blinked several times when she spotted her visitor. "Hello," she said, a shaky smile on her lips. "Can I help you?"

The brownie glared up at her from under his large fedora, his long ears pointing straight out to the sides from the pressure of the hat. The red feather sticking out of the top of the chapeau should have looked quite dapper, but the wrinkled, scowling face ruined the effect. "Don't know why they sent me to a witch," he muttered, shaking his head. His beady black eyes dropped from hers and he peeled a dirty overcoat off an equally dusty button-up shirt. Bright red suspenders matched his feather and held up pants that had probably once been black, but were now more of a stale brown.

Wynona quickly glanced at her floor, and she was shocked to find it still clean. The small hobgoblin carried so much dirt, she was sure he left a trail anywhere he went. She tilted her head, keeping her smile in place. "Who sent you?" she asked. "I don't understand."

The brownie huffed and held up his coat. It floated into the air and rose high enough to attach itself to a small rack near the back door.

Wynona watched with wide eyes. That unwanted jealousy rose within her breast once more, but she pushed it back. It wasn't fair to be jealous of this man for being who he was. "I'm sorry," she choked out. "But I still don't know who you are."

"Lusgu Roich," the brownie grunted. He began walking around the kitchen, peering under tables and cabinet edges, grumbling under his breath with each step.

Large toes poked out from under his pants, caked with just as much dirt as hair, and Wynona caught herself staring before she put her manners back into place. She knew what a brownie was, of course, but they were fairly elusive creatures and she had yet to see one in person, only pictures. Why there was one inspecting her kitchen, she had no idea. "Nice to meet you, Mr. Roich," she said, following behind him to make sure he didn't touch anything he shouldn't. "But I still don't know why you're here."

If possible, his scowl grew even deeper. Not looking at Wynona, Lusgu stopped when he spotted some crumbs on the floor, reached his hand to the side and snapped his fingers.

Wynona was staring again. What did he want? Was he expecting her to hand him something? She didn't have anything to offer. Glancing around, she squeaked and ducked to the side when a broom came careening across the room. She stepped to the left just before it would have hit her, and it landed directly against his palm.

Instantly the brownie began sweeping the crumbs together. "Don't know how to keep things clean," he muttered. "No wonder you need help." He huffed. "Witches."

Wynona let out an exasperated huff of her own. "I'm sorry, Mr. Roich, but could you please—" Her words were cut off when there was a loud pounding coming from the front of the shop. "What now?" she muttered, turning to walk toward the sitting room. She glanced warily over her shoulder, but Mr. Roich seemed too caught up in catching every speck of dirt than her leaving. "I'll be right back," she said before ducking out the door.

The door rattled with another round of pounding and Wynona sped up her walk. The heeled boots she was wearing didn't allow for much running, but she adored how they looked with her jeans. She grabbed the door and quickly pulled it open. "Hello, Chief Ligurio," she said with a stiff smile. "How are you today?"

The vampire glared at her with dark red eyes. He must have fed recently for them to be so bright. "We need to talk," he said, pushing his way into the room.

"Oh, uh, come on in," Wynona said, opening the door wide. She did her best to keep smiling and nodded at each of the three officers who followed the chief inside. When Deputy Chief Strongclaw winked at her again, Wynona felt a flush creep up her neck. Her smile became a little easier after he walked past.

"Sorry about this," Officer Nightshade whispered with a grimace as she ended the line of officers.

"Officer Nightshade," Wynona said, her smiling widening. "How good to see you again."

The female vampire gave a small smile, but it fell when Chief Ligurio cleared his throat.

Flashes from outside caught Wynona's attention and she turned to see nothing but lights obscuring her vision. "Ms. Le Doux!" a voice shouted, seemingly out of midair. "What does your family think about your predicament?"

Wynona stepped back quickly, nearly stumbling to get away from the doorway.

"Ms. Le Doux! A statement, please!"

A warm presence came up behind her and a large arm reached over Wynona to slam the door shut. "Ghost reporters," Deputy Chief Strongclaw growled.

Wynona looked over her shoulder, still feeling slightly shell-shocked. The last thing she needed was bad press before she'd even opened, especially with her family. "Thank you," she whispered sincerely.

Those golden eyes twinkled with good humor. "Any time," he said.

Wynona realized she was still leaning against his chest and she immediately straightened. Good heavens, she was losing her head. Between Roderick and Deputy Chief Strongclaw, or Rascal, she was in way over her head. Good thing she had a business to focus on. Straightening her shirt to give herself time to pull herself together, she walked over to approach the Chief. "What can I do for you today, Chief Ligurio?"

"I want to hear more about this alibi of yours," he snapped, pulling out a notebook. "You said you were home...alone?" He glanced up from the papers and raised an imperious eyebrow.

Wynona nodded, folding her hands in front of her to keep them from shaking. "Yes."

"No neighbors or anyone to corroborate your story?"

Wynona shook her head. "No. Although someone might have seen me leave that night, I live at the edge of the forest in a small cabin. There's no one close enough to see me come and go."

The other eyebrow joined the first. "The forest? Do you mean The Grove of Secrets?"

Wynona nodded. She knew the forest had a reputation. You didn't go inside unless you didn't want to come back out. It was called the Grove of Secrets because it was a complete secret as to what was inside. Her house probably wasn't in the safest area, but it allowed her the peace and freedom she desired, and the price had been more than right. So far, she'd been just fine and she figured it would remain that way as long as she didn't do anything to upset whatever creatures resided inside.

The chief grunted and wrote something down.

A loud crash came from the kitchen and Wynona gasped. She automatically started to leave, but the chief stopped her with his hand. Not saying a word, he looked over her shoulder and jerked his head at one of his officers.

Wynona had no idea whom he sent. Her attention was completely caught by the deadly white hand in her vision.

"Not so fast," the vampire said. He dropped his palm. "I have a witness that places you here, at the scene of the crime, late on the night of the murder. Said they saw..." He consulted his notes. "A woman figure was seen skulking around to the back of the building around ten o'clock on the night of the murder."

Wynona gave him a distressed look. "That's great that you have some kind of witness, but how does that mean it was me?"

The chief consulted his notes again. "The witness said it appeared her hair was wound up in a bun on top of her head."

"You can't be serious." The cool, tenor tone took the attention of the entire room.

Wynona let out a little sigh of relief as Roderick walked out of the back, looking as confident and suave as ever.

"Now see here," the chief said, pointing a finger at Roderick. "You have no authority in this case. Being the owner of the building has nothing to do with investigating a murder."

"Maybe not," Roderick said casually, adjusting his cuff links as if he hadn't a care in the world. "But a vague description from a half blind mole shifter won't go very far in court and you know it." He glanced at Wynona, giving her a quick grin before turning back to the chief. "For all we know, that 'hair bun' could have been a hat of some kind." He smirked at the increasingly angry chief. "It's fairly dark at ten o'clock at night," Roderick continued. "How could she even tell the creature was female?"

The chief pressed his lips together and closed his notebook with a snap.

"Now, unless you have some concrete evidence," Roderick said, turning his attention to the other officers in the room, as if asking their permission, "I suggest you leave this beautiful woman to get her business ready for its opening and go search for a murderer."

The chief's nostrils were flaring, which was an interesting trick, since Wynona knew vampires didn't breathe. His eyes flashed between Roderick and herself. Wynona found herself holding her breath. She was grateful for her landlord's confidence in her innocence, but she wasn't sure that antagonizing the police was the best way to help her.

"You'll be lucky if this place ever opens," the chief spat. "RAS-CAL!" he shouted, causing Wynona to duck her head slightly at the anger in his tone.

"Yeah, chief?" Rascal was panting as he came skidding out of the back. There was a tear in his shirt, dirt was smeared across his face and his hair, which was already messy, stood up like he'd been shocked by a live wire.

"What the he—" The chief closed his eyes and pinched the bridge of his nose. "I don't want to know," he muttered.

Rascal shrugged. "Brownie," he said, as if that explained it all.

He looked at Wynona, who knew her eyes had to be as wide as tea saucers. Just what was Mr. Roich doing back there?

Rascal winked, a small smirk on his attractive mouth. When his eyes shifted to Roderick, the amusement fled and disdain appeared instead.

"Having trouble, Deputy Chief?" Roderick asked with a smile.

Wynona barely held back a groan. The testosterone in the room was going to choke her.

"Nope," Rascal said, fixing the collar of his shirt. "Everything is perfectly under control." He didn't even flinch when a spoon flew through the air and smacked him on the back of his head. It landed on the floor with a clang, drawing everyone's eye.

Roderick's smirk grew. "Looks that way."

"Rascal," Chief Ligurio ground out. "We're leaving. Now."

"Right away, Chief." Rascal didn't bother looking back. He did, however, take a route around the tables that brought him very close to Wynona and then gave her one last wink before following his group out the door. "Don't use the front," he said just before ducking out and shutting the door behind him.

"What's wrong with the front?" Roderick asked when they were left alone.

"Ghost reporters," Wynona said as she turned and scurried to the kitchen. "Thank you, by the way," she tossed over her shoulder. "I appreciate your help with the chief."

"You're welcome," Roderick said politely as he followed her.

Wynona scooped up the spoon from off the floor, then braced herself for what kind of condition she would find the kitchen in. From the sound of things, it couldn't be good.

"Oh my..." She felt her jaw drop open as she entered the space. If ever a kitchen sparkled, this was it. Her cabinets gleamed and her few dishes looked as if they were made of crystal with the way the light reflected off of them. The counters looked clean enough to eat off of and Wynona clasped her hands together. She was afraid to touch anything.

"Nobody keeps things clean anymore," Mr. Roich grumbled as he shuffled around the center island. "You young'uns have no sense of pride in your homes."

"How did you...?" Wynona shook her head. She had no idea where this man had come from, but she was grateful he was here.

"Wolves aren't allowed," the brownie continued. "Messy...hairy...no manners."

Wynona put her fingers over her lips and stifled a giggle. Rascal certainly seemed mischievous, but she doubted he was as bad as Mr. Roich said.

"We need to keep him around," Roderick whispered in her ear.

Wynona jumped. She had forgotten he was there and had no idea he had gotten so close. "He certainly knows how to keep things clean," she said, putting a little distance between her and Roderick. "Can I interest you in a cup of tea?" she asked, walking farther into the kitchen to get some cups and saucers.

"Will I have the privilege of your stunning company?" he prodded.

Wynona smiled over her shoulder. "Mr. Caligari, I do believe you're flirting with me."

"You just now noticed?" His grin was entirely too charming as he put a hand to his chest. "I'll have to up my game."

CHAPTER 8

"There you go." Wynona set down a saucer and cup in front of Roderick. The steam tickled her nose and made her want to take a deep breath. The touch of ginger in the tea was slightly spicy, with a peppery backend. It was one of Wynona's favorites.

"Thanks," he said, giving her a sultry smile as he picked up the cup and took a sip. Whistling under his breath, his silver eyes dropped to the tea. "I've never been much of a tea person, prefer coffee, but that's pretty good."

Wynona allowed herself to preen just a little under his praise. She might not have any magical powers, but she knew tea. Her granny made sure of that. "Thank you."

"So." Roderick set down his cup just as Wynona's phone buzzed. She held up a finger for him to wait, and answered. "Hello?"

"Ms. Le Doux?"

"Yes, that's me." Wynona snuck a sip as she waited for the person to speak again. Mmm...she loved this blend.

"This is Yukimi from Hex Haven Career Resource Center for Paranormals," the tinny voice said.

"Oh. Yes!" Wynona smiled as she thought of the tiny imp that she'd spoken to about finding a...Oh.

"We wanted to make sure that Mr. Roich had arrived and was behaving satisfactorily."

Wynona's eyes automatically went to the kitchen, where the brownie was now rearranging her entire pantry. She had no idea where anything was in the kitchen anymore. "Uh, yeah. He's great." As long as you weren't a wolf. Or you don't care where your stuff is.

"Good, good. Then we'll take your job listing out of the open files. I'm so glad to hear he's working out. Mr. Roich had a history... Well, I really shouldn't say anything more."

"Uh..." Wynona's eyes opened wide and she looked at Roderick as if he could help her.

"He needed a good home. Thank you so much for giving him a chance. Bye!"

Still feeling slightly shell-shocked, Wynona turned her head to look at the phone. That was definitely not what she had expected.

"What happened?" Roderick took another sip of his drink. "You don't exactly look happy."

"I'm fine," she said, still a little lost. "I figured out where Mr. Roich came from."

Roderick's blond eyebrows rose high.

"I completely forgot I'd put in an application at the HHCRC," she explained, using the acronym she heard around town. The name itself was just too long to say all the time.

"Ah. So, Mr. Pigpen is the answer to your query?"

Wynona gave him an unimpressed look. "Be nice," she scolded, though not very fiercely. She couldn't exactly blame Roderick for his description. Mr. Roich *was* covered in dirt, all except that fedora. He obviously took great pride in at least one part of his wardrobe.

Her companion only grinned. "So what seems to be the problem? You must have asked for a janitor, and it looks like that's exactly what he excels at."

"If the kitchen is anything to go by, he'll be great at the job," Wynona agreed. "I think I just need to make sure he doesn't interact with any of my patrons."

Roderick snickered, then rubbed his mouth as if to push away the humor. "I don't know. I can't really fault his intuition. Wolves can be quite...pesky."

Wynona kept her mouth shut on that front. It wasn't worth arguing over. Any idiot could see Roderick and Rascal didn't like each other. "Do you think—" Her phone buzzed again, interrupting their conversation, and Wynona sighed. "Sorry," she apologized, answering once more. "Hello?"

"Is this Saffron's Tea House?"

Wynona immediately straightened in her chair. This was a business call. "Yes, it is. This is Wynona speaking."

"Good," the feminine voice snapped.

Wynona's smile fell.

"This is Eytha Salmold. I have a tea appointment next week on Saturday." The voice sniffed. "Cancel it."

"I..." Wynona's mouth flopped open. "I'm sorry to hear you won't be able to make it," she choked out. "Is there another date that would work better?"

"I don't associate with murderers." After a sharp click, the line went dead.

Once again, Wynona was left staring at the small device. A trickle of worry began to work its way down her spine. How could this have happened? She wasn't a murderer. She hadn't been arrested or charged with a crime. How in the world did word even get out about the police chief's accusations?

Almost as soon as she thought it, Wynona answered her own question. "Ghost reporters," she said tightly.

"What was that?" Roderick was watching her intently and Wynona forced herself to calm down.

"Sorry," she said, quickly taking a long sip of her drink. She needed all the help she could get right now. "That was a...an appointment cancellation."

He nodded. "I know." His voice was soft and sympathetic. "I could hear loud and clear." He looked truly sympathetic. "I'm sorry."

Wynona didn't meet his gaze, but she nodded. "Thanks." Tapping her fingernails on the table, she forced herself to think. What if more people cancelled like Ms. Salmold? Would the selkie tell her friends that Wynona was a murderer? Or was it already running rampant through Hex Haven? Would her family use this embarrassment to force her back to the castle? The only reason her family had left her alone up to this point was because of the media uproar it would cause if she suddenly disappeared. As long as Wynona stayed under the radar, she was certain her parents would leave her be. Bringing down scandal on the family name would be another matter.

She slapped her hand on the table, causing the teacup and saucer to rattle. "Enough," she said out loud. "It's only one customer. There's no need to panic."

"You're right," Roderick said with a sage nod. "No need to worry. Business will always have cancellations." He raised his teacup in the air in a toast motion. "I have no doubt you'll fill the slot quickly."

Wynona smiled and lifted her own cup, then together they each drank the last of their tea.

No sooner had they finished when her phone buzzed again, this time with a text.

Wynona's heart fell as she read the words.

"Wynona?"

She looked up with a sigh, setting her phone aside. "Another cancellation."

Roderick shook his head. "Those da—" He looked sheepish and cleared his throat. "It's those ghost reporters. They sensationalize everything."

Wynona closed her eyes and rubbed her forehead, a headache suddenly coming on. Good thing she'd just had some ginger. Hopefully it would help curb the pain before it got too bad.

"What are you going to do?"

She made a face, dropping her hand. "I don't know. What can I do?"

"You could make a public statement," Roderick offered.

"No." Wynona shook her head. "I don't want my family to have an excuse to come here."

Roderick narrowed his gaze and tilted his head. "You don't get along with your family?"

Wynona pinched her lips together. Should she tell him? She didn't know him that well, and she wasn't the kind to air dirty laundry to anyone who would listen. "It doesn't matter," she finally said. "But I don't want to create a public spectacle."

He took in a deep breath, his chest puffing up before deflating in a long exhale. "I don't know. It seems to me the only real way for you to be seen as innocent is for the real killer to be caught."

She nodded, her fingernails tapping again. Prim had asked if Wynona wanted to get involved, but Wynona had said no. She wanted to let the police do their job. Just like she wanted to be able to do her own job by opening and succeeding at the tea shop. Pretending she knew anything about solving a crime just seemed ridiculous.

A squeaking and scuffling sound caught her ear and Wynona turned in her seat to see if she could see her new friend. A dash of purple came rushing across the floor in her direction. "Well, hello, little one," she said as the mouse stopped at the bottom of her chair.

"What is that?" Roderick asked with a chuckle, leaning around the side of the table in order to see.

"A hex gone wrong," Wynona explained.

Roderick frowned. "I thought you didn't have any powers."

That dang blush crept up her neck. "I don't. It was... Nevermind." If Celia knew Wynona had told someone her hex went wonky, she'd come back just to prove a point. "Suffice it to say that this little guy is a survivor and now we're becoming friends."

Roderick grunted, but didn't ask more questions.

The little mouse rose up on his back legs, nose twitching in Wynona's direction.

"Hungry again?" she asked with a soft laugh. "I have a couple of cookies up here. Want one?"

Without another squeak, the mouse scampered up the leg of the chair and into Wynona's lap.

Wynona held back her own squeak at its boldness. This was not quite what she had expected.

"Curious little thing," Roderick mused, watching intently.

The mouse rushed up Wynona's arm and nestled onto her shoulder, just barely in her peripheral vision.

"I think maybe I need to give you a name," Wynona said softly.

The creature squeaked and curled itself into a ball.

"Huh. You don't usually see that unless it's a familiar," Roderick said, his eyes once again intent. "What did you say happened to your powers?"

Wynona started to shrug, then immediately stopped. She didn't want to upset her buddy. "I was cursed as a baby. My powers were bound."

"And you don't know who did it?"

She shook her head. "Believe me, my family tried. They have fairly...vast resources."

He rubbed his chin thoughtfully. "I can imagine. And nothing was ever found?"

"Nope. Nada."

"Interesting."

Her new friend made a few noises. "Oh, right. A name." Wynona smiled at her shoulder. "First I suppose I ought to know...um...are you a boy or girl?"

The mouse chittered and opened its eyes wide.

"Boy?"

The chittering became angry.

Wynona held up her hand. "Sorry. I'm just guessing." She smiled. "That must mean you're a girl." Her eyes flitted over the bright purple fur. "How about Violet or Periwinkle?"

The air was filled with chattering, but Wynona had no idea what was being said.

"Uh...was that a yes? To which one?" She watched the mouse. "Periwinkle?"

If mice could frown, this one did, causing Wynona to laugh. "Violet?"

A purple head bobbed up and down.

"Alright. Violet it is."

"Sounds good to me," Prim drawled as she came through the kitchen entrance. She stopped in the middle of the room and jabbed a thumb over her shoulder. "Do I want to know why there's a brownie cursing out anyone who dares walk on his shiny floor?"

"He's the new janitor," Wynona said, relaxing into her seat slowly so as to not upset her new friend.

Prim huffed. "A possessive brownie janitor and a purple mouse named Violet." She winked at Wynona. "You're collecting quite the menagerie."

Wynona smiled back. "Doesn't sound too bad to me."

Prim finally acknowledged Roderick by nodding at him as she sat down at the table. "You might not think so, but your energy needs to go toward saving your reputation rather than collecting odd creatures." She turned to Violet. "No offense meant."

Violet chirped a couple of times, then settled back down for a nap.

"Why do you say that?" Wynona asked warily. She didn't need more bad news. The two cancellations were enough to have her head spinning.

Prim stood in the chair so she could be seen over the top, and pounded a fist on the table. "One of my customers today told me she planned to cancel her appointment here."

"Not another one!" Wynona cried in dismay. Violet jumped on her shoulder. "Sorry," Wynona said automatically, reaching up to soothe the creature.

"Another one?" Prim put her hands on her hips. "How many is this?"

"Your announcement makes three," Roderick supplied. He shook his head. "This isn't good."

"You can't let this happen," Prim said, her pink eyes trained on Wynona. "You haven't even opened the doors yet." She put her palms on the table and leaned in. "You have to do something."

"But what?" Wynona splayed her palms to the side. "There's nothing I can do."

Prim rolled her eyes. "I heard you picking up clues when you were looking at the body," she snapped. "You have a great eye for detail, not to mention you think outside the box." Prim smirked. "Something Mr. Stuffy Shirt Vampire could learn from."

"Prim," Wynona warned.

Prim waved her off, not the least bit concerned. "My point is, *you* should solve this."

Wynona was shaking her head before Prim even finished. "There's no way I can solve this. I'm not a detective. I have no skills outside of making tea." The next words almost choked her, but they were true nonetheless. "And I don't have one ounce of magic that would help me do a better job than the police will."

"Who says you need magic?" Prim cried. "Vampires barely have any magic at all. Their place on the food chain has more to do with how hard they are to kill, not their ability with spells."

"She has a point," Roderick said.

"Not you too." Wynona groaned, dropping her head back.

Roderick leaned forward, his forearms laying across the table. "We've already talked about how the chief only seems to be looking in your direction. If you want any chance of opening this place not only on time, but at all, you're going to need to help clear your name."

"I agree." Prim slapped the table again.

Wynona sighed. She could see their point, but it still felt like too much. She escaped her family in order to find peace and freedom, not to risk everything by rushing after a murderer.

Her phone buzzed and she closed her eyes, dropping her head. She didn't even want to look.

Prim grabbed it and opened the message. "Better hurry, Nona." The phone was carefully set back down. "They're falling fast."

A soft nose nuzzled into her neck, sending a barely there buzz across Wynona's skin. She reached up to pet Violet as a thank you. "You're right," she said hoarsely. "I don't like it, but I'm not ready to give up my dreams quite yet." She glanced up at the antique Victorian clock on the wall. "I'll start this afternoon."

CHAPTER 9

Wynona double checked the address she had entered in her phone. "This is it," she muttered to herself. Climbing off her scooter, she pushed down the kickstand and walked to the front door.

The house was quite grand, even for someone who grew up in Hex Haven's biggest castle. Wynona's eyes drifted up, up, up... She counted four stories in the mansion. Tall, with spires on the corners as if it wanted to channel a slightly Gothic vibe, but wasn't fully ready to commit, the house was certainly a show stopper.

The size and architectural style were not what drew the eye, however. It was the fact that the mansion was bright pink with yellow and blue shutters. From a distance, it reminded Wynona of a cupcake. "He probably did that on purpose," she whispered to no one in particular.

Shaking her head, Wynona forced herself to look away and continue to the door. The stairs felt endless with her heart beating harder against her chest with every single step. Wynona had never done something like this before, and she wasn't entirely sure what she was doing. She only knew she couldn't sit around on her hands all day.

Two more appointments had been cancelled since yesterday. She couldn't allow this to go on any longer. If the police weren't going to set the record straight, then Wynona would do it herself.

She had no idea why Chief Ligurio was so set on her being the killer, but Wynona knew the truth. "The truth shall set you free." Her hand shook as she knocked on the ten-foot door, but the sound was still strong and it gave Wynona's confidence a boost.

She threw back her shoulders and put her chin in the air. She could do this.

"May I help you?"

Or not.

"Uh..." Wynona blinked rapidly and cleared her throat as the giant of a butler glared down at her from the top of the doorway. Apparently, it was functional as well as decorative. "I would like to speak to Mrs. Droxon, please."

The giant's yellow eyes narrowed and his nostrils flared. "Do you have an appointment?"

Wynona shook her head. "No." Clasping her hands in front of her and appearing contrite, she lowered her chin a little. "My name is Wynona Le Doux. I know I should have called ahead, but there wasn't really time. I need to ask her a few questions about her husband."

If possible, the butler's eyes had gotten even smaller at the mention of her name. Wynona couldn't yet tell if that was a good sign or a bad one.

"One moment, please," the creature intoned.

As soon as the door closed, Wynona deflated. This was going to be harder than she'd expected, and she hadn't exactly thought it would be a walk in the park. She tucked a piece of her hair behind her ear. She'd worn it down today because it looked more formal, but the breeze was just enough to make it dance and mess up her look.

"You may come in."

The deep, gravelly tone made Wynona jump and she immediately felt a flush creep up her neck. "Thank you," she said with a polite smile before stepping out of the sun.

"This way."

She did her best to walk quickly in her heels, but the butler's long legs made it difficult to keep up.

"Mrs. Droxon is in the red room." The butler pushed open a door and waved an arm inside.

Again, Wynona gave her thanks, then walked past him. It took a minute for her eyes to adjust. If she thought the outside of the house was impressive, it had nothing on the red room.

Bright red, the shade of Christmas berries, dominated the space. The walls, the furniture and even Mrs. Droxon's dress as she lay on a fainting couch. The couch was the one black piece of furniture in the room and was the perfect foil to her Victorian style dress.

The wide skirt was spread across the black velvet, while Mrs. Droxon leaned precariously to the side. Wynona had to admit that the woman knew how to pay attention to detail. Every piece of the dress looked authentic, right down to how well Mrs. Droxon filled out the corset. Her sharp ears were the only thing that stood out in the picture as different and gave Wynona just a little bit of background. Mrs. Droxon was an elf.

"You're Ms. Le Doux?" she asked in a low, breathy tone.

Wynona figured the tone was because the woman could barely breathe, though maybe it was all part of the persona. "I am."

"And you have questions for me?"

Wynona did her best to smile. "I do."

Mrs. Droxon raised a perfectly manicured eyebrow. "Have a seat, please." She waved an elegantly pale hand toward a chair and Wynona took her weight off her heels.

"Thank you for seeing me without an appointment," she started, hoping to ingratiate herself a bit. If Mrs. Droxon was anything like her husband, she would wish to be pandered to.

Mrs. Droxon nodded regally, though her eyes seemed unfocused, as if she were a million miles away. "Gerall said you wished to ask about my husband."

Wynona nodded. "Yes. You see, someone wearing his clothes was murdered at my tea shop the other night." Wynona scooted forward slightly, leaning forward in her eagerness. "I was hoping to ask if you knew of anyone who would wish to kill Chef Droxon."

Mrs. Droxon blinked a couple of times, her face perfectly blank. Then with the flash of one second to the next, the breathless, simpleminded woman disappeared and a shrewd elf took her place. Rising from the couch in a truly amazing show of elegance, Mrs. Droxon walked across the room to a buffet filled with liquor bottles. She pulled the stopper off a crystal decanter and turned to Wynona, asking a silent question.

Wynona shook her head. She wasn't a fan of alcohol. It changed people and muddled her mind. She'd stick with her tea, thank you very much.

"You know..." Mrs. Droxon sipped her glass. "For a moment there, I thought you were simply another one of his fans coming to figure out if I would stand in your way."

Wynona jerked back. "Excuse me?"

Mrs. Droxon waved a hand in the air. "Don't misunderstand me." She looked Wynona over from head to toe. "You're not his usual type, but your looks can't be disputed."

Wynona folded her arms over her chest. "Thank you? I think."

Mrs. Droxon snorted. It was the first normal sound to come from the elf. "Atherton prefers his women a bit more...decorated." With a toss of her head, the glass was emptied and Mrs. Droxon was working her way around the room. "So you want to know if he had any enemies?"

"I do." Wynona rose to her feet. She didn't like feeling like the smallest person in the room, which she technically was, but she could pretend otherwise.

Mrs. Droxon stopped at a vase of flowers, fingering the petals. They were just as red as the rest of the room and Wynona recognized them as a mix of chrysanthemums and cockscomb. Both held their color well, but considering it was mid-spring, both flowers were out of season. They must have been spelled to bloom this early.

"I think the better question is, who wasn't his enemy?"

It took a moment for the words to penetrate. "He didn't have any friends at all?"

Mrs. Droxon grinned, but the look was malicious, not kind. "Not unless you count the endless string of mistresses." Her look shifted to one of nonchalance and she shrugged. "But considering how fast he goes through those, I doubt they'd claim that title either."

"I suppose being the best baker in Hex Haven means stepping on a few toes along the way," Wynona said carefully. Her eyes were caught on a shadow just beneath Mrs. Droxon's left eye. When Wynona had first arrived, she hadn't noticed anything odd, thanks to a superb makeup job, but now, at the angle she stood, she began questioning what she was really seeing.

"I suppose," Mrs. Droxon said dryly. She left the flowers behind and paced the large room.

"Do you think any of his...paramours would have wanted him dead?" The more Wynona watched, the more she felt bad for the woman. Mrs. Droxon put on an excellent facade. The breathless beauty was probably the face she presented to the world, a way of hiding what really went on in her home. And now with Wynona, Mrs. Droxon had gone with haughty. It was a protective effort.

Yet, Wynona felt sure that inside, the woman was crying. Lonely, hurt and obviously bitter, her name, unfortunately, went immediately to Wynona's mental suspect list. Who better than a jilted wife would wish to kill a husband?

A few odd questions remained though. If Mrs. Droxon did indeed try to kill her husband, why do it in Wynona's shop? And why couldn't she tell that the man she killed wasn't her husband? Surely Mrs. Droxon knew her husband's silhouette, even if they'd been in the dark.

"I'm sure many of them did," Mrs. Droxon continued.

Wynona pinched her lips. "Did you?"

The elf stopped, her eyes wide as she turned to face Wynona. "You're very direct."

Wynona clasped her hands. "I believe it's the best way to get a direct answer."

A slow smile crept across the elf's face. "You may call me Maeve."

Somehow it felt as if Wynona had just been handed a gift, although she wasn't exactly sure why. "Alright...Maeve. Were you mad enough to kill your husband?"

She grinned. "My husband isn't dead."

"No..." Wynona tilted her head. "But the man who was killed was wearing your husband's clothes. I believe the killer *thought* they were killing Chef Droxon."

Maeve nodded and sighed. "You're probably right." She walked back across the room and sat on the fainting couch with an audible *plop*, her skirts poofing before settling around her feet. "And while I admit I wish I had the courage to kill him, I'm afraid I don't."

Wynona took two steps to the right, putting her in just the right position to see the spot under Maeve's eye. It was exactly what Wynona feared. "There's places that can help women like you."

Maeve laughed harshly and put a thin fingertip to her eye. "Never trust makeup made by sprites."

"Would you like me to help you call them?" Wynona ignored her change of topic.

"No." The word was succinct but hoarse. "I'm afraid that isn't a good idea."

Wynona stepped closer. "Why not?"

"Because if I leave..." Her emerald green gaze met Wynona's. "It won't be my husband who dies next."

Wynona's next words faltered. "Surely we can get you protection—"

Maeve waved her off. "Don't worry about me," she said with a tight smile. "I made my bed long ago. Now, I have to lie in it."

Wynona didn't answer. She knew what it was like to feel as if you had no choices and could never break free. But because someone cared, she had, and now she was working to make a new life for herself. There was no reason Mrs. Droxon couldn't do the same. But it would only work if the woman wanted it to.

"And just because I know you're curious," Maeve clasped her fingers in her lap. "On the night of the murder, I was here." She nodded toward the door. "Gerall can vouch for my whereabouts."

Wynona looked over her shoulder. She hadn't been aware that the butler had followed her inside the room. From the way the man was watching Maeve, Wynona guessed the woman had at least a little more support than she had first supposed. Nodding, she turned back to Maeve. "Thank you for letting me intrude in your day."

Maeve rose up and nodded regally. "Good luck to you in your search." She arched an eyebrow. "My husband's pastries might be well liked, but he isn't. You're going to need all the help you can get."

After another round of thanks, Wynona headed outside to her Vespa. She rode down the road for a minute before pulling over and grabbing her phone from her pocket. She had missed three calls and fifteen texts.

"What in the world?" she muttered as listened to the messages.

"Nona?" Prim's voice was squeaky on the tiny speaker. "You've *got* to call me back, pronto!"

Each message was another iteration of the first, except the panic in Prim's tone grew exponentially by the end.

"NONA! Get your phone out of your pocket and call me! This is big, girlie! BIG!"

Wynona pulled the phone away from her ear and winced at the last shout. "Good grief," she murmured as she dialed Prim back.

"NONA!"

Wynona rolled her eyes. "Yes, it's me. What in the world happened in the last hour that has you in such a tizzy?"

Prim was panting on the other line. "I've got a hot tip for you, and you need to follow it up now."

"Why now?" Wynona pressed. "And who did you hear this tip from?"

"My sources aren't important," Prim said, brushing the question away. "But you have to go now because she's going to get away if you don't."

"Can you please start from the beginning? I have no idea who *she* is."

"Oh. Right." Prim took a deep breath. "Word on the street is that Chef Droxon's secretary nearly had a heart attack when word got out about the murder. She's been with him for five years now, longer than any other secretary, and news of the murder has her turning tail and running."

"Why would the death of a thief matter so much to her?" Wynona asked. "Did she know the man?"

"No idea," Prim answered. "All I know is that she's making a big fuss and there's got to be a reason for it."

Wynona pulled back her phone to glance at the time. "Do you know where she is now?"

"She should technically be at work," Prim said. "But my source said they saw her last heading into Shade Banking and Loan."

"Okay." Wynona shifted on her scooter seat. "I'll see what I can find out."

"Oh, and her name is Delila Caseis. She's a siren."

Wynona paused. "Oh, great."

"What?" Prim asked.

"Nothing," Wynona said quickly. "Talk to you soon, bye!" She shut off the phone and stuffed it back in her pocket with a sigh. That was all she needed was to confront another woman in Chef Droxon's life. From Mrs. Droxon's description and the fact that the baker obviously went through secretaries like he went through sugar, Wynona could only guess what kind of a relationship they'd had.

"Why can't people just be good and honest?" she grumbled while getting her Vespa going again. Her heels weren't the easiest thing to ride in, but the look had been important and Wynona was grateful she'd chosen to dress up a little when confronting Mrs. Droxon.

Wynona could only imagine what the secretary was going to look like. But Prim was right. Running scared because someone else died was an odd reaction. Wynona tilted her face up, enjoying the warm sunshine as she rode into town. She would just have to see what was going on with the siren. And maybe add another possible suspect to her list.

CHAPTER 10

I t took a good fifteen minutes for Wynona to get from the Droxon estate to the bank. If a human ever wandered into Hex Haven, at first it would look like a normal city with some unique residents. One look at Shade Banking and Loan, however, and every Halloween horror movie they'd ever seen would come to life.

The building was as Gothic as they came and had been around for centuries. Snarling gargoyles sat on every corner, ready to rip thieves into shreds at the slightest provocation, or at least they looked that way. The creatures were made of stone, but Wynona had a sneaking suspicion that they weren't quite what they seemed. Their eyes in particular, were a little too...alive.

The entire bank was surrounded by a stone wall and an iron gate, much to the consternation of Prim and every other fairy living in Hex Haven, since iron was poisonous to that particular species. The rest of the population were simply frustrated by the lack of doors.

Since the bank was run by shades, the ghostly creatures didn't require entrances into a building in order to go in or out, and apparently had felt to use that skill to their advantage when the bank was built.

In order for any person or creature to enter Shade Bank, they had to be spelled by the attending security, which was usually a low level warlock with more brawn than brains. The setup kept everyone's money extremely safe, but made it difficult for even the owner of the money to handle their accounts.

Parking her bike just outside the gates, Wynona stayed seated for a moment, eyeing the group waiting to go inside. She didn't want to wait in line unless she had to. If Ms. Caseis had gone in before Prim got a hold of Wynona, then odds were the siren should be coming out by now. If Wynona hadn't already missed her.

A loud catcall caught Wynona's attention and she whipped her head around to see a group of teenage dryads staring all in the same direction. With their tongues practically hanging out of their mouths, Wynona figured she had hit the jackpot.

Bingo.

A redhead strutted out of the bank, her every move designed to draw the male eye as she headed toward the gate. The guard practically tripped over himself as he let her out, tipping his hat at her in the process. "Come again, Ms. Caseis," the man stuttered.

Wynona had to admit the woman was aptly named. Delila always brought to mind a picture of a femme fatale and this woman was definitely an asset to her ancestors. "Thank you," she purred, touching the security guard's forearm.

Wynona shook her head when the man began nodding a little too vigorously. Sometimes living in a paranormal city was ridiculous.

Ms. Caseis winked at the teenagers still drooling over her, then turned smartly to her right and began walking down the street. Her actions brought her right past Wynona, whom she ignored.

"Apparently only men get her attention," Wynona muttered to herself. She hopped off her scooter and was about to call out the woman's name, when she paused. Ms. Caseis had changed. Her walk was less runway worthy and she ducked her head a little. Pausing in front of an alleyway, the siren glanced around, then darted into the darkness.

Wynona's interest was piqued. Scrambling quickly to lock her scooter, she hurried down the street and carefully peered around the corner. The alleyway looked deserted, but opened up on the far end into another street. Staying in the shadows helped give Wynona cover, but it also meant watching where she stepped.

"Someone needs to put together a street cleaning team," she muttered as she stepped over yet another pile of foul-smelling garbage. Such a venture would fall under the political leader of the land and Wynona snorted at the thought of her parents taking the time to worry about something so mundane.

She reached the other street and paused before walking out onto the sidewalk. Just like Haven Main, which she had left behind, Runes Road was busy. Haven held most of the shops, but Runes was home to businesses. Skyscrapers towered over her on both sides, making Wynona feel small and insignificant. A feeling she wished she wasn't so familiar with.

Pushing back her insecurities, she looked around, hunting for bright red hair. It couldn't be that hard to find. Just as she was about to give up, a flash of sunlight reflecting off a glass door caught Wynona's attention.

"There you are." Without another word, Wynona darted into the foot traffic and began working her way toward the large, almost solid glass building that Ms. Caseis had disappeared into.

It took a little maneuvering, but Wynona made it across the street and casually went to pull on the bar. The door rattled, but didn't budge. Frowning, Wynona pulled again. Still nothing. Glancing around, she looked to see if there was any sort of sign or instructions for visitors, but the front of the building was completely blank. Out of desperation, she tried pushing instead of pulling, but the door still didn't open.

Worried she was making a scene, Wynona tried to glance around, but luckily no one seemed to be paying attention to her. Stepping up to the glass, she tried to shade her eyes in order to look inside, but all she could see was darkness. "What is this place?" she whispered to herself. Her eyes wandered over the whole front, but there was no doorbell or otherwise in order to be allowed inside. Carefully, keeping an eye on the other people, she walked to the side of the building and darted around the corner.

The alley was slightly cleaner, but no less creepy than the one she had already wandered through. This time, however, her aim wasn't the other street. Slowly, Wynona ran her hand along the side of the building. There were no obvious doors or windows, since the entire building was glass. She began to wonder if there was a spell that protected it from outsiders.

About halfway down the building, Wynona grew frustrated and turned around. A group of businessmen were standing at the entrance to the alley and she decided to ask them about the building. She didn't come to this street very often, so perhaps these men knew what and who was inside.

"Excuse me!" Wynona waved and walked back to Runes Road. "Do you live around here?" Several of the men looked her way and Wynona immediately dropped her arm. As she drew nearer, Wynona realized that what she thought were business suits were actually dirty hand-me-downs. She stumbled backward a couple of steps as three of the men broke free from the group and began prowling in her direction.

There was something decidedly predatory about their movements, causing her heart to leap into her throat. This was not what she had expected at all.

"You know what? Never mind." Wynona spun and began speed walking toward the road at the back end of the alley. She wasn't sure what it would lead to, but hopefully there would at least be other people. Safety in numbers and all that.

As she walked, her ankle twisted in her high heel, and now she regretted dressing up for her meeting with Mrs. Droxon. Pain radiated with every step, but she didn't stop. At least not until a hand grabbed her arm and spun her around.

"Hello..." the man purred, looking her up and down. "What brings you to this side of the street?"

The other two men chuckled and Wynona swallowed hard. She was in serious trouble. How had it all gone so wrong? It seemed as if her curse extended to more than just binding her powers, which, subsequently, would have been extremely useful right now. "Please let go of me," she said through clenched teeth, pulling on her arm.

"Those are nice manners," the man sneered. His face was covered in stubble and dirt, and his yellow teeth matched his eyes. Wynona could tell he was some kind of shifter, but from the looks of it, he didn't mix in polite company very often.

It wasn't unheard of for a shifter to go feral, or at least, mostly feral. From the smell of decay and the state of his hygiene, Wynona guessed this man and his buddies were some of them.

"I said, let me go." She pulled harder, but his hold only tightened, increasing the pain in her arm.

"You asked us a question," the man said with a wide grin. "What was it?"

"It doesn't matter now."

"Oh, but it does." Her captor didn't look away, but addressed his question to one of the watchers. "What was it she asked, Sim?"

"I think she was curious about the building." The man called Sim wiped at the corner of his mouth, as if picking up drool, and Wynona had to look away.

Her stomach churned and she began to wonder if throwing up on the men would make them leave her alone.

"That's right. The building." The man holding her pulled her closer and Wynona turned her face away. "Just to be nice," he said, "we'll answer your question, and then you can help us with ours."

"I don't know anything," Wynona said automatically. Her eyes began searching the ground for anything that could be used as a weapon. She might be able to hurt one of them with her heel, but getting it off and then stumbling around barefoot probably wasn't going to be very efficient. There had to be something else in this dirty alley.

"Oh, I'll bet you do." The man took in a long sniff of her hair and Wynona cringed away. "That there behind you is the Droxon Headquarters." His yellow eyes flashed. "It's said the gnome keeps his little black book inside."

Wynona stopped struggling. "You mean his recipe book?"

A bushy eyebrow rose high. "That's right," he drawled. "His office and test kitchen are all inside, which is why it's so hard to get in." He chuckled. "Not that you'll be needing in after we're done with you."

Wynona's neck instantly broke out in a heavy sweat. She needed to get away from these men, and she needed to do it now. Slowly, using every bit of control she had, she forced herself to relax. "What question did you have that I can answer?" she asked, trying to keep her shaky voice calm.

The man barked a laugh. "I didn't have a question, sweetheart."

She frowned. "Oh, but I thought you said I could return the favor." She gave him an innocent smile. Right on cue, his hand relaxed slightly on her arm. Wynona didn't wait another heartbeat. She quickly wrenched her arm free and stepped back, grabbing a broken piece of wood from the ground.

She wielded it in front of her like a knife, knowing it would do little good, but all she needed was to buy herself some time. If she could just get close enough to the street to scream, surely someone would come help. "It's been fun, gentlemen," she said tightly. "But I think it's time I go home."

The three men were openly glaring at her, their arms spread out to the side as they tried to herd her toward the building.

"I don't think so, sweetheart," the leader sneered. "We helped you. Now it's your turn."

"I offered," Wynona said. "But now I really must go." She swung her weapon around, trying to keep all three men in her sights and walk toward the street at the same time. She'd only made it a few steps when a growling sound caught their attention.

Her attackers froze, ears perking up like the animals they were. "Get her and let's go," the leader snapped, pointing to Wynona.

Sim nodded and lunged.

Wynona screamed and swung the piece of wood blindly, her eyes closing as she prepared herself for the impact of his body.

The alley filled with shouts of anger and pain and Wynona realized no one had grabbed her. Carefully she opened her eyes, only to have them shoot open like saucers and her jaw nearly hit the ground.

Two of her attackers were lying on the ground, unconscious, with their hands cuffed behind their backs, while Rascal sat on another and was finishing locking the handcuffs while his captive squirmed. "Don't make me knock you out," Rascal growled at the man, giving his head a shove while he stood up.

"What did you—? How—?" Wynona shook her head. She had only had her eyes shut for a few seconds. How in the world had he managed to subdue three men in that time? And where in the world did Rascal even come from?

"Are you alright?" he asked, walking toward her carefully. He held his hands out as if to keep her from bolting, but Wynona wasn't about to leave the protection that had just arrived. Maybe she wasn't cursed after all.

She rubbed her upper arm. "Bruised and coming down from a heart attack, but fine," she managed.

Rascal's lips twitched. "Do you mind if I take a look?"

Wynona frowned. "Are you trained in medicine as well as police work?"

He shrugged. "I used to be a first responder. I know enough to keep someone alive."

Wynona shrugged. "Sure, but I really am fine. I just need a cup of Rose Petal and Matcha, a long nap and I'll be as good as new."

"How about we start with your arm?" he asked, closing the distance between them.

Wynona allowed Rascal to slip off her suit jacket. She would be burning it when she got home anyway, along with the pants and boots... Well...maybe she'd keep the boots. She just knew she wanted to get rid of any reminders of what had just happened.

"That's gonna be rough for a few days," he murmured, feeling around at the darkening ring on her arm.

"Ouch," she whispered as he touched a particularly tender spot. "I thought you said you had training."

"Guess I'm out of practice." Rascal winked at her. He seemed to do that a lot. "Sorry."

"It's fine," Wynona said with a sigh. She rubbed her forehead. "I'm sorry. I'm not trying to be rude, but I really would like to go home. Can I do that now?"

Rascal's playful look turned to one of sympathy. "I'm afraid not, Ms. Le Doux. You're going to have to come with me."

"Oh? Why?"

He jabbed his thumb over his shoulder. "I need to book these guys at the station and I'm afraid I'll need your statement to do that."

Wynona groaned. "Just what I needed." She was losing time. Her shop was set to open in five days and if she didn't get this murder solved, she could kiss it all goodbye. And that was if she could solve it before all of her customers cancelled because they thought she was a murderer.

Rascal put his hand on her mid-back. "Don't worry," he said. "It won't take too long." Gently, he led her to the street, where a blue truck was sitting on the curb.

"That's quite the parking job," Wynona said with a laugh.

That wink came at her again as he helped her buckle up in the passenger seat. "Perks of the job," he teased.

Closing the door, he disappeared back down the alley, leaving Wynona to her thoughts. A soft tingling sensation in the middle of her back held most of her attention, however. It was pleasant and soothing, a far cry from the rioting emotions of earlier.

When she watched Rascal emerge from the alleyway, a man thrown over his shoulder and his muscles bulging, that same heat traveled to her chest, neck and face. Wynona forced herself to look away. "Murder," she reminded herself. "You've got a murder to solve. Then a business to open. And *then,* if things are going well, you can think about men. But not before."

She couldn't help but glance at those wide shoulders one more time. "Definitely not before."

CHAPTER 11

"You still haven't explained *why* you were at the Droxon Headquarters," the chief of police snapped, tapping his pen on his desk. He leaned forward, incisors flashing in his irritation. "You were wandering around, in broad daylight, at the building of a man who is possibility a target in a murder that occured in your own shop." He tilted his head and gave her a penetrating stare. "Does that not sound suspicious to you?"

"Why is walking around town suspicious?" Wynona argued. "Is it against the law to walk? I hadn't heard that. I'm sorry."

A growl emerged from between his pale lips. "You're playing with what little patience I have left, Ms. Le Doux."

Wynona wanted to ask him what patience he was referring to, but she kept her mouth shut. Just because she thought it, didn't mean she needed to say it. A skill she had lots of practice in. "Look, Chief Ligurio. I'm sorry that we keep running into each other, but I promise I wasn't doing anything nefarious. I'm just looking for answers."

"What answers?" he asked carefully.

"Answers as to who tried to kill Chef Droxon," Wynona explained. "And what they plan to do now that they failed."

"Those are police matters," he snarled, jabbing his pen in her direction.

"Yes," she said slowly, nodding her head in agreement. "But there's no law that says I can't ask a few questions."

His palms slammed against his desk and he leaned forward. "Don't make me lock you up, Ms. Le Doux. Prison doesn't agree with rich, spoiled women like yourself."

Her eyes widened. "Excuse me? I've broken no law."

"You still don't have an alibi for the night of the murder."

"I absolutely do," Wynona argued. "I told you, I was home that night."

"With no witnesses."

"No witness, you are correct," she agreed. "But until you can prove otherwise, I'm considered innocent."

"And yet you've just admitted to poking your nose into police business," Chief Ligurio snapped.

"I said I asked questions," Wynona corrected. "I haven't broken into anything and I haven't bothered anybody." She paused. "Speaking of which, did you know Chef Droxon is abusing his wife? If ever someone had a motive to kill, it's a wounded woman."

"Chief?"

Wynona almost breathed a sigh of relief when Rascal poked his head in. He'd dropped her off at the chief's office while he booked her attackers, but the time had been far from pleasant. She was ready to see the face of someone who didn't want to strangle her.

"What?" Chief Ligurio grumbled. Rascal had opened the door just before he could go off on Wynona and while she was grateful, it was obvious the vampire was pouting.

"The guys are all already in the system, so it won't take much to put them back behind bars." Rascal stepped farther into the room. "If you want, I can take Ms. Le Doux's statement and then see her home."

"See her home and then see that she stays there," Chief Ligurio said tightly. "She needs to keep her nose out of our business." He pointed a long, slender finger at Rascal. "If she interferes again, I'll count you personally responsible."

"Yes, sir." Rascal gave his chief a salute, then smiled at Wynona and offered his arm. "Ms. Le Doux. If you'll just follow me."

Wynona smiled back. "Thank you, Deputy Chief Strongclaw." She slipped her hand into his elbow and they walked out into the busy police station. Wynona whistled low under her breath. "You certainly are hopping in here."

"Today is a rough day," Rascal agreed. "Everyone is still going crazy about the murder, and Chief is acting like he hasn't fed in months rather than days."

Wynona nodded as they walked into a much quieter office. "Yes, about that." She sat and then leaned toward Rascal. "What in the world have I done to make him hate me so much? Or is it just witches in general he can't stand?"

Rascal snorted as he sat behind his desk. "As far as I know, Chief doesn't have anything against you, but even I have to admit that he's been on edge lately." He furrowed his thick brows. "Despite our eyewitness, which I'm very aware is not even close to being reliable, we don't have anything to pin you with and yet Chief can't seem to open his eyes to any other possibility." His look became sympathetic. "I'm sorry. I really don't know why he's in such a mood."

Wynona shrugged and looked down at her slacks, smoothing them out. They were a mess and there was a hole in one knee. "It's no big deal." She was used to people not liking her. She didn't enjoy it, but it was a common enough response in her life.

"Wynona."

She looked up at the tender tone in his voice.

"Are you alright?" he asked, his eyes searching all over her.

She smiled, feeling very tired all of a sudden. "As well as I can be. I hadn't exactly planned for my day to include a near mugging and a trip to the police station."

Rascal chuckled. "Nobody does." He raised his eyebrows and tilted down his chin. "But you're sure?"

She nodded. "Yes. I'm sure."

"Okay." He opened his computer and began typing. "Let's start at the beginning and you can tell me why you were in that alley."

Wynona sighed and leaned back in her seat. Deceit wasn't in her nature, so she explained her whole morning to Rascal. She knew Chief Ligurio wasn't going to be happy about it, but she hadn't broken any laws. Mrs. Droxon had seen and spoken to Wynona of her own free will.

Rascal leaned back in his chair. "You're going to get yourself in trouble if you keep it up."

Wynona nodded curtly. "I'm aware of the dangers. Thank you, Deputy Chief Strongclaw."

"Rascal," he corrected. That playful grin crossed his face. "We've been through this."

"That we have," she agreed, returning his smile. "Forgive me."

"No need," he said breezily. "But we do need to talk about you trying to solve this murder."

Wynona sighed and pushed a hand through her hair. "My entire business is relying on this being solved," she explained. "I've got customers calling and cancelling because your chief refuses to admit to the media that I'm innocent. And in five days, I've got a grand opening that has been planned down to the very last detail in order to help me start a new life." She leaned forward, pleading with him to understand. "I'm not trying to step on toes or get in anyone's way, but while this is all in the line of duty for you and your coworkers, this is my life. This is the only chance I've got to make a go of it."

Rascal tilted his head, studying her. "Why do I sense there's more to your story than you're sharing? How come no one even knew you existed until a couple of months ago when you bought that rundown shop and started renovating it?"

Wynona groaned. She didn't want to dredge up her past. She wanted to move forward. "I don't think my family and their choices have anything to do with our situation now," she said, slowly sitting up straighter.

Rascal blew out a breath and nodded. "Fine. If that's the way you want it."

"I do."

He didn't look happy, but he nodded again and went back to his computer.

The silence stretched uncomfortably while Wynona waited for Rascal to tell her she could go. Twiddling her thumbs, she let her eyes wander around the office. Behind her the window blinds were open and she could see the rest of the precinct bustling around their normal activities.

Several of the workers stopped in their tracks and Wynona couldn't see why until she spun in her seat to see Delila Caseis waltzing through the desks, chatting with one of the officers. "What is Chef Droxon's secretary doing here?" she murmured.

"We brought her in for questioning."

Wynona whipped around, feeling slightly guilty. "Oh?" She tried to act nonchalant. "About?"

Rascal gave her a look that said he wasn't buying her act. "About who might want to kill her boss."

Wynona waited, but Rascal went back to his computer. "And?" she prodded, slightly impatient.

Rascal looked up and grinned at her. "It's killing you, isn't it?"

Wynona scowled at him. "I know you don't have to share what you know, but I did come here offering my own information."

"Her statement is part of an ongoing investigation, Ms. Le Doux."

She rolled her eyes. "Please call me Wynona." She gave him a smile. "We've been through this before."

He chuckled. "Okay, okay." His eyes went out to the rest of the building, then back with her. "I can't give you specifics, but I can say she has an alibi."

"No clues as to what it is?"

"Can't tell you that...Wynona," he said pointedly.

She quickly picked up her purse. "You don't mind if I run an errand, do you?"

"I promised the chief I'd take you home."

"And I appreciate that, but first there's something I need to do." She held her breath.

Rascal pinched the bridge of his nose and sighed. "I'll meet you out front in ten." He pointed at her. "No more."

"That's fine," Wynona sang out as she dashed out the door toward the front of the station. She just hoped Ms. Caseis was still around.

If the crowd out front was any indication, Wynona wasn't too late.

She poked her way through all the police uniforms. "Excuse me? Ms. Caseis?"

The siren turned from her admirers to find Wynona. "Yes?"

Wynona finished wiggling her way into the center. She dropped her voice. "My name is Wynona. I was wondering if I could ask you a few questions?"

The secretary's look could only be described as disdain. "Are you a reporter?"

"Oh, no." Wynona waved off the notion. "This is all strictly confidential."

Delila peered more narrowly at her. "What did you say your name was again?"

"Wynona." She swallowed hard. "Le Doux."

Delila's eyes widened. Without speaking, she waved off the men, who disappeared grudgingly, but obediently.

"You're related to President Le Doux?"

Wynona nodded. "Yes. But that's not why I'm here."

Delila crossed her arms over her chest. "Then by all means, explain."

"The man who was murdered two days ago, the one dressed like Chef Droxon, was killed in my tea shop." Wynona stood a little taller. "I'm trying to piece some things together that don't make very much sense."

"Such as?"

"Such as where you were on the night of the murder?"

Delila scowled, but even that couldn't take away the stunningness of her face. "Are you accusing me of trying to kill my boss?"

Wynona shook her head. "No. I'm just covering all the angles. Mrs. Droxon informed me that you worked for the chef longer than any other secretary."

"And you think that means I was sleeping with him?" Delila snapped.

Wynona gave her a sad smile. "Actually, I'm hoping that means the exact opposite."

Some of the tight defensiveness in Delila's shoulders melted away. "What makes you say that?"

"Well, from what I've heard, Chef Droxon went through women rather regularly." Wynona shrugged one shoulder. "If you were one of his lovers, odds are you wouldn't have stuck around so long because he would have moved on to someone else."

Delila's arms fell to her side. "Thank you," she said softly. "You're the first one to believe me when I say there was nothing between us."

Wynona nodded. "Despite that, I'd still like to know where you were."

"I already told the police, but I was working late that night." Delila's deep hazel eyes darted away from Wynona. "I was catching up on paperwork." She looked back, understanding in her face.

"You're the one with the contract starting next week for the tea shop."

Wynona nodded. "Yes, that's me."

The siren smiled. "It sounds like a delightful place. I plan to visit."

Rascal stepped out of the police station and Wynona stepped back. "I'd like that, Ms. Caseis. I'll look forward to seeing you again." Before the secretary could say anything more, Wynona spun and walked to Rascal's side.

"Get what you needed?" he asked wryly.

Wynona grinned and shouldered her purse. "Yep."

He shook his head. "Come on. My truck is out back."

"Do you mind if we pick up my scooter on the way home?"

Rascal shook his head. "Where did you leave it?"

"Near Shade Banking and Loan."

"If it's still there, we'll get it."

Wynona relaxed in her seat. She was glad Rascal was taking her home. She needed time to think and to put all her new information together. She'd gathered several pieces today, but most of them still didn't make sense. Hopefully a good shower, a warm cup of lavender with honey and a chat with Prim would help her figure out what she was still missing.

CHAPTER 12

The next morning, Wynona set out bright and early on her scooter for town. It felt like time was slipping away from her and she was still a long way from figuring out the murderer.

Last night had been peaceful, if not just a little lonely. Prim hadn't been available, so Wynona had spent the evening by herself, writing down every piece of information she had gathered and trying desperately to put it all together.

She was just as clueless this morning, however, as she had been last night. The wife, obviously, had a motive, but also an alibi. One which she had a witness to. And why kill rather than just leave? Yes, Maeve had mentioned that Chef Droxon was possessive, but was that enough of a motive to kill him?

She shook her head. "Probably not," she murmured, answering her thoughts out loud.

Then there was the secretary. She also had an alibi, but it was flimsy at best. No one could corroborate it, but that wasn't the biggest problem. "Why?" Wynona parked her scooter and climbed off, the question still swirling through her head. What reason would the secretary have to kill her boss?

Wynona believed Ms. Caseis when she said they weren't having an affair. So why ruin a good thing? All it would do is leave her unemployed. "Unless he was harassing her and she was desperate." Again, she shook her head. That didn't sit right either. But there was something definitely fishy about the way Ms. Caseis had refused to meet Wynona's eyes.

Pushing the glass door inward, Wynona headed inside Roderick's office building. She needed an outside opinion on her information and had hoped he was available to do some brainstorming with her.

She checked the signage on the first floor and noticed his office was at the top of the building. "Of course it is," Wynona murmured to herself with a smirk. Roderick was a charmer, for sure, but he was also a man of power. It exuded from him with every movement and look.

Luckily, the elevator wasn't overly full and she was able to ride up immediately. Stepping off, she came directly into the lobby area, but there was no one seated at the front desk to greet her. Wynona stood there for a moment, unsure if she should push on or not, before a voice caught her attention.

She glanced down the hall and noticed a door slightly ajar, and Roderick's voice was coming out. With a smile, she walked toward it.

"Of course."

She paused before knocking. Maybe interrupting his meeting wasn't the best thing in the world. Should she wait in the lobby until the secretary came back?

"The package is to be picked up and delivered within the next two days. No later."

When no one responded to him, Wynona sighed in relief. He had to be on the phone. With his door ajar, surely he wouldn't mind her coming in and waiting him out. Knocking lightly, she poked her head inside. "Roderick?"

His chair spun around and blond eyebrows shot high on his forehead. "Wynona! What a pleasant surprise!" The businessman mumbled something into the phone, then hung it up and stood with his arms outstretched. "I heard about what happened down at Chef Droxon's building." After a quick hug, he stood back, holding onto her upper arms, and looked her over.

Wynona couldn't help her blush when the perusal took a little longer than she thought it should.

"Are you alright?" he asked, his voice soft and concerned.

She nodded and stepped out of his hold. Charming, yes. But Wynona still wasn't ready to send any signals that she would welcome anything more than his normal flirtation. "I'm fine. Just a few bruises and wounded pride."

He guided her to a seat. "We need to find some way for you to protect yourself," he said as he walked back around to his own chair. He paused before sitting down. "Unless you would consider always having me at your side?"

Wynona laughed, as intended, and nervously tucked a piece of hair behind her ear. "I think that might be a bit much, don't you?"

Roderick shrugged and sat the rest of the way down. "Perhaps...for now." He gave her a grin. "What brings you by my office this morning?"

Wynona waved at the phone. "I didn't mean to interrupt your business."

He pursed his lips and shook his head. "You didn't. It was simply a phone call about a delivery for my sister. It's her birthday and I'm sending a present since I can't celebrate with her in person."

"That's nice of you," Wynona said. What would it be like to have a family you actually *wanted* to be around?

He shrugged. "We were always close as children." He leaned forward, clasping his hands together. "Now...your turn."

Wynona nodded, scooting to the edge of her chair. "I was hoping you might find some time to brainstorm with me. After yesterday, I've got a couple of new suspects, but I have no idea where to go from here." She splayed her hands to the side.

Roderick nodded. "Indeed. Tell me what you learned."

"You sure you have time for this?"

Instead of answering right away, Roderick pressed a button on his phone. "Amelia?"

"Yes, Mr. Caligari?"

Wynona didn't miss the breathless tone to the secretary's voice. Apparently, she was back at her desk and eager to serve. A small pin-prick of jealousy stabbed Wynona in the sternum, but she shoved it away. It wasn't like she had anything to be jealous about. She and Roderick weren't a couple, and he more than likely flirted with every woman the way he did with her.

"Please hold all my calls for the rest of the morning." His silver eyes were intense as he looked at Wynona. "I have an important meeting to attend to."

Heat flushed up Wynona's neck and face. Okay...so hopefully he didn't flirt like this with everyone.

He was chuckling when he pressed the end button, then leaned back and folded his arms over his stomach. "Wynona...you're a de-lightful breath of fresh air."

She could use some fresh air right about now. "And you're a sea-soned flirt."

He smirked and gave her a slow nod. "I can't say I haven't been called that before." He shrugged. "But you'll also find I've been called singularly focused and loyal to a fault."

Wynona followed his example and leaned back, trying to appear completely at ease with the heaviness of this conversation. "Ad-mirable qualities."

"When used correctly, yes." Roderick tilted his head, as if exam-ining her. "Now. Were you going to share something with me?"

Wynona immediately straightened, leaning forward again. So much for acting nonchalant. This whole situation had her wound tighter than a spring and it wasn't worth the effort to pretend other-wise. "I spoke to Mrs. Droxon yesterday."

"Ah, yes. Sweet Maeve," Roderick drawled, his tone in complete contrast to his words. "How is the viper?"

Wynona jerked back slightly. "You're familiar with her?"

He shrugged. "Anyone who runs in the upper circles is." His eyes narrowed. "I'm surprised you'd never met her before. Between her marriage to Atherton and her family background, she graces even the Le Doux ballrooms."

This time the heat in Wynona's face was anything but pleasant. She dropped her gaze and studied her intertwined fingers. "Then I'm sure my family knows her well."

It only took moments for Roderick to sit in the chair next to her, his cool hand covering hers. "I'm sorry," he whispered.

Wynona played it off. "It's not your fault." She shook her head and straightened her shoulders, giving him a practiced, but far from sincere smile. "We all have our secrets, I suppose."

He nodded, his thumb caressing her knuckles. "We do. But that doesn't make them easier to bear."

"I suppose not/" She deflated just a little. "Still...this isn't about my family ties or lack thereof." Taking a deep breath, Wynona pushed on. "Mrs. Droxon said she was home the night of the murder and her butler..." Wynona huffed in amusement. "Or bodyguard, because I think they're the same thing, stands ready to corroborate her story."

After a final squeeze, Roderick released her hands and leaned back, resting his arms on the sides of the chair. "So it couldn't have been her?"

Wynona pursed her lips. "I don't...know. She obviously holds no love for her husband, and if her claim of his extramarital affairs is only half true, he views her as nothing more than a trophy." Wynona scrunched her nose. "I think he's actually hurting her, but she refuses to leave him." She turned to Roderick. "I don't understand why. My family never hit me, but life can be made miserable in many other ways without being manhandled. Why would she stay if she wasn't happy?"

Roderick shrugged, raising one leg to rest on the other. "I don't know. Perhaps her family won't take her back? Perhaps she doesn't want to lose the lifestyle?"

Wynona scoffed. "Money isn't worth that heartache."

"Says you," Roderick pointed out. "Not all people are willing to take that chance."

She sighed. "I suppose. Still...I feel bad for her."

He nodded but didn't add more to the topic. "You said you had more than one suspect?"

"Oh, yes." Wynona shifted in her seat. "Maeve hinted that Chef Droxon had a thing for his secretaries. So when I discovered his secretary was a siren, well..." Wynona drifted off.

"I believe most people think Atherton and Ms. Caseis are more than boss and secretary," Roderick said wryly.

Wynona laughed quietly. "You know everybody, don't you?"

He shrugged one shoulder. "A fair number of them. We're all in the business world together."

She nodded, thinking. "That makes sense. Perhaps I should have just come to you instead of bothering to poke my nose around. Might have saved me a bit of trouble."

"My dear Wynona." He leaned forward, capturing one of her hands and holding it between his own. "I am always available to answer your questions." He smiled. "My time is yours."

"You're doing it again."

He raised his eyebrows innocently.

"Flirting outrageously with me." Wynona made a pointed look at their hands.

"Can you blame me?" he asked, caressing the back of her hand.

Unable to wipe the smile off her face, Wynona slowly pulled her hand free. She couldn't think straight when he was being so sweet. She needed to keep their contact as professional as possible. Maybe after this was solved and her shop was open...

"What did you learn from Ms. Caseis?" Roderick pressed.

Wynona brought her mind back to the present. "She said there was nothing between her and Chef Droxon."

Roderick frowned and leaned back again. "Do you believe her?"

Wynona nodded. "I do."

"What makes you say that?"

Wynona pinched her lips together. "Mostly a gut feeling. Delila has been with him for five years, longer than any other secretary." Her eyes turned to Roderick. "His wife made it sound like he went through women quickly. I can't imagine he'd keep a secretary around that long if his tastes were always for the new and shiny."

Roderick scratched his chin, a few sparks of magic jumping into the air. "I can see your point." He frowned. "But Ms. Caseis is exceedingly lovely, even for a siren. Perhaps he was content with her?"

Wynona's brows furrowed. "Possible, but unlikely."

"Okay. They weren't having an affair. What's her alibi?"

"Now that's the thing," Wynona said quickly, anticipation bleeding into her tone. "She says she was working late at the office, alone."

"But you don't believe her." It was a statement, not a question.

Wynona shook her head, answering anyway. "No."

"And why is that?"

"Again, it's mostly a gut instinct, but she had been very direct with me when we were talking and suddenly her eyes couldn't meet mine." Wynona turned away with a huff. "However, I also fail to see what she would gain from it. Mrs. Droxon would get freedom and the whole estate, I'm assuming. But Delila?" Wynona shook her head. "I just can't figure out what her motive would be. At the same time, why would she lie about her alibi?"

"It is a bit of a conundrum," Roderick murmured. "It sounds to me like we need more information."

Wynona nodded. "Yes. But I'm not sure where to try now."

A slow, delicious smile grew on Roderick's handsome face and all too soon, the temperature in the room was once again uncomfortable. "When in doubt," Roderick said in a low tone, "always start with a cup of tea."

CHAPTER 13

With a couple of hours before Roderick and Prim would come over for tea, Wynona decided to go by the police station again. If she could slip around the chief and speak directly to Rascal, she had a feeling she could learn a little bit more about the case.

Chief Ligurio might want her to leave things alone, but Rascal had already proven to be helpful by turning the other way to allow Wynona time to question Delila. As Wynona pulled open the front door, she hoped it hadn't been a fluke. Though it wouldn't exactly be a hardship to spend time with the handsome Deputy Chief.

"Hello," Wynona said with her best smile as she approached the front desk.

The officer looked up. "Oh! Ms. Le Doux!"

"Officer Nightshade." Wynona's enjoyment became immediately more genuine. "How're you doing today?"

The female officer looked up. "I'm well, thank you." She tilted her head to the side, her short dark hair falling across her forehead. "What can I do for you today?"

"I was hoping to speak to Deputy Chief Strongclaw," Wynona replied, lowering her voice just a touch. She resisted the urge to look around, not wanting to appear suspicious in any way. "Does he happen to be in?"

Officer Nightshade shook her head. "No, I'm sorry. He's off today."

"Oh." Wynona chewed on her bottom lip. Geez, it was hard being without powers. Her mother or sister would be able to track him down with a simple spell. Wynona, unfortunately, had to use old fashioned tactics. "You wouldn't happen to have a phone book, would you?"

The officer grinned. "He's unlisted," she said, knowing exactly what Wynona was getting at.

Wynona's shoulders drooped. "Oh, well...thank you." She started to turn around. "Have a nice day." There had to be a way to get his information. Wynona wasn't about to interrogate Officer Nightshade. If the vampire had wanted to share, she would have. It was probably against regulations to give out that kind of information.

"Ms. Le Doux?"

Wynona spun. "Did you need something, Officer Nightshade?"

Officer Nightshade smiled and her teeth gleamed under the fluorescent lighting. "I need to run and get more blood coffee. Would you mind keeping an eye on the desk for me?"

Wynona jerked back slightly. "Me?"

The officer nodded, her grin growing.

Wynona looked around, trying to determine if this was a joke, but no one seemed to be paying any attention to them. "Um...okay. If I can help."

"Oh, you can." Officer Nightshade stood up and indicated for Wynona to take her chair. "Just sit here and make sure no one digs around in my stuff while I'm gone."

"Gotcha." Wynona nodded and looked up seriously. "You can count on me."

The officer chuckled. "And make double sure other visitors don't look in that black binder to the left. It contains information on all our officers and we wouldn't want it to get into the wrong hands."

Wynona froze. Ooohhhhh....She nodded more slowly. "Right. Keep *others* out of the binder." She held her breath.

"Right." Officer Nightshade turned around and was gone before Wynona could blink.

"One of these days I'm going to have to become a little more sneaky," Wynona muttered to herself. Once again making sure no one was paying her any mind, she quickly pulled out the binder and flipped to the 'S' section. "Strongclaw..." Her finger stopped. "Gotcha."

Thinking fast, Wynona snapped a picture of his information, worried writing it down would take too long, and quickly put all the evidence away. She was swinging from side to side in the chair by the time Officer Nightshade came back, calmly sipping her brew.

"Ah, nothing like a warm, fresh cup," she said, saluting Wynona with her mug. "Thank you so much for helping out. I think I can take it from here."

Wynona stood up and backed away, suddenly feeling extremely guilty. "Right. You've got it. I mean, of course you've got it. You're an officer." She promptly snapped her mouth shut. Not only was she not sneaky, but she apparently was also a rambler when she got nervous. Who knew?

"Thanks for stopping by." Officer Nightshade effectively dismissed Wynona.

"Thanks, you too!" Wynona stumbled when she realized what she had said. Shaking her head, she mentally scolded herself for being such a nincompoop. This was not how an investigator would act. They would be cool under pressure.

Wynona had learned how to stay calm when others were going crazy, but she'd never learned how to stay calm when she was breaking the law. She wasn't sure it was something she should get used to.

Hopping on her Vespa, she glanced at her phone and memorized the address. His apartment was on the other side of town and it would take her a good twenty minutes to ride over there. She glanced at her phone, double checking the time. If she was going to have tea ready for everyone by two, she needed to get this errand going.

With a deep breath and a push, Wynona took off, weaving seamlessly into traffic. Rascal's apartment building must have been a family affair, because children and adults who looked like they were also shifters were pouring out of the place as if it was a pack den.

Wynona frowned and checked the address once more. Nope. No mistake. This was it. Pasting on her best smile, she nodded politely and greeted everyone she walked past, doing her best to ignore the fact that every single one of them stopped and stared. It would appear that witches were not common in this community.

Putting her head high, Wynona tried to pretend like she belonged, but as the noise gradually died down, leaving a pregnant silence in its wake, she felt her knees begin to tremble. Marching up to Rascal's door, she raised her hand, clenching her fist tight to keep it from shaking, and gave a firm knock.

Rocking back on her heels, Wynona waited, but no one came to the door. She raised her hand to knock again, but suddenly felt foolish. What was she doing? Chasing down a police officer in his own home, just to see if there were any updates on the case? Rascal was going to think she was crazy. She was crazy!

Spinning on her heel, Wynona was determined to get out of there before someone could figure out who she was.

A door opened behind her and voices filtered into the hallway. One in particular made Wynona pick up her pace.

"Wynona?"

She hesitated, but didn't turn around.

"Ms. Le Doux?"

Crud. Wynona stopped and squeezed her eyes shut. Taking a deep breath, she turned and smiled. "Hello, Officer Strongclaw."

He was grinning at her as if he could see exactly how embarrassed she was. "Funny seeing you here," he said, wiping his hands on a paper towel. He turned back to the tiny, older woman beside him. "Just let me know if that drain gives you any more trouble, alright?"

The woman stopped glaring at Wynona just long enough to look up at Rascal adoringly. "You're such a good wolf," she said, patting his cheek. "Don't be a stranger." With one last glare at Wynona, she slammed the door, leaving Rascal in the hallway.

He continued to grin while sauntering toward her, only to stop at his door. "Would you like to come in?"

Wynona opened her mouth to say "no", but forced herself to stop. She wasn't some young teenage girl. She was an adult and perfectly capable of doing hard things....like asking police officers for help. Nodding instead, she walked back. "Yes, thank you. I was hoping to ask you a few questions."

Rascal chuckled as he opened his door and ushered her in. "For you to hunt me down at home, I have a feeling it's more than a few."

Wynona shot him a look, but that only seemed to amuse him more.

"Have a seat," he said, indicating the couch.

Wynona sat down gingerly, doing her best to maintain proper decorum.

He headed to the kitchen. "Drink?"

"No, thank you."

Coming back with a glass of water, Rascal apparently hadn't had the same manners tutor as Wynona and threw himself into an arm chair sideways, so his legs were hanging off the side. He drained the glass and set it aside. "Now, Ms. Le Doux—"

"Wynona."

He nodded. "Of course. We've played this game before." He smiled. "Wynona. What brings you here?" He frowned. "And how did you even know where I live?"

Wynona pursed her lips. "I probably shouldn't tell you that."

"What? Why you're here? Or how you knew to come here?"

Wynona tried to hide her smile, but she was pretty darn sure Rascal could see it anyway. "I'm here because I'm hoping we can discuss notes on the case."

One thick eyebrow went up. "You really don't plan to give up, do you?"

She shook her head. "No. I need to see this through."

He brought his legs forward and then leaned with his elbows on his knees. "Why is this so important to you? Why are you willing to risk getting hurt in order to solve the case?"

Wynona considered her answer. She didn't want to dig into everything, but so far Rascal had proven that he was trustworthy. Perhaps she could level with him a bit. Copying his stance, she leaned forward onto her knees. "I need to open my tea shop," she said softly. "I've already had trouble with patrons cancelling appointments because they think I'm a murderer. And if the shop doesn't open on its planned date, the odds of it ever happening are slim." Her hands intertwined and she wrung her fingers. "This is all I have, Deputy Chief Strongclaw. If I don't make this work, I won't have anything. I barely managed to break ties with my family as it was and going back would be the worst thing I can do, so before you suggest that, just know it's not an option. I'd rather be homeless and living at the creature shelter than deal with them again."

He narrowed his eyes, studying her, and Wynona held still for the look. This wasn't a man sizing up a woman, it was an officer sizing up the truth. Finally he nodded. "You realize we don't usually let civilians help us?"

Wynona nodded in return. "Yes. And as much as I hate to ask for exceptions, your boss seems in no hurry to help clear my name."

Rascal scratched his chin. "Yeah...I'm not quite sure what he has against you. Although, it's not like your family doesn't have enemies."

She splayed her hands to the side. "I know, and believe me, I understand why, but he's never even met me." She sighed and leaned back. "It's probably hate based on association and for that, I'm sorry. But I can't help who I was born to."

"True enough." Rascal relaxed against his seat as well. "So, you spoke to the wife?"

Wynona shrugged. "Yes. But since then I've come up with more questions."

"Such as?"

"Such as what's in the will? I didn't particularly feel like she was the killer, but I think it's possible she had the most to gain."

Rascal grinned and shook his head. "And there's where you'd be wrong."

Wynona's eyebrows shot up.

"The wife doesn't get a thing if her husband is killed."

Wynona gasped. "Are you serious?"

Rascal nodded. "It's all in the prenup. He was wealthy when he married her and it says she doesn't get a dime. Basically, she's free to go back to her family, but that's about it."

"Oh my goodness..." Wynona's gaze moved around the room, but she wasn't seeing any of it. Her mind whirled. Without the will, there was no reason for Mrs. Droxon to kill her husband. None. Except for the abuse, but the question still was, why not just leave? "Who does the money go to?" she asked, refocusing herself on Rascal.

A slight reddish tinge crept into the shifter's brown skin. "Well...now...we don't actually know."

"What?" Wynona jerked upright. "You just said it doesn't go to the wife. How would you know that if you haven't seen the will?"

He gave her a look. "Because we *have* seen the prenuptial agreement. The conditions were very clear that she wouldn't get anything."

"Then why haven't you seen the will?"

"Because no one can find it."

"No one can find it?" Wynona repeated the words, trying to make sure she was hearing correctly. "Rascal, excuse me if I'm wrong, but Chef Droxon is still very much alive. The murder might have been aimed at him, but he's still living. Why not ask him where the will is?"

"We have," he said defensively.

"And he just refuses to share it?"

Rascal shook his head. "No. He said it's not in the safe where it's supposed to be."

"It's...missing?"

Rascal nodded slowly. "Yep."

"Oh my..." Wynona deflated into her seat a little. "That does put a kink in things, doesn't it?" She quickly leaned forward. "Did you ask Chef Droxon *who* the will talks about?"

Rascal chuckled. "Boy, you're tenacious."

She grinned back at him. "Sorry. But I've told you more than once that my entire life is hanging on this murder being solved."

"Yeah...I get it."

Screaming children from outside his window caught Wynona's attention and she automatically turned at the sound.

"Ignore them," Rascal said easily. "It's always noisy around here."

"And that doesn't bother you?"

He shrugged. "Shifters, especially wolf shifters, tend to like being in groups. Our animals are social creatures."

Wynona made a mental note to someday ask about his wolf. She was fascinated by the idea of shifting and if she and Rascal remained friends, maybe she could ask him some personal questions about it. Of course, if she had her powers, she might be able to shift herself. That was the beauty of being a witch. They could do almost all the same magic as the other magical creatures, but with fewer consequences, like being pulled by a full moon. "Good to know," she responded.

He grinned. "Not a fan?"

She shrugged. "I like my quiet house, but then again, this is the first time I've actually owned my own space, so that might have something to do with it." Or the fact that she grew up alone and it was what she was used to. Glancing at the clock on the wall, Wynona jumped to her feet. She needed to get to the tea shop. "Thank you so much for answering my questions," she said in a rush. "I have an appointment, but I hope to chat with you again."

Rascal stood and escorted her across the room to the door. "Anytime," he said, pulling on the handle. "Now that you know where I live, feel free to come get updates whenever you need." He winked, a move Wynona was coming to realize was his signature, but that didn't stop her from blushing.

He really was very handsome. Maybe even more so than Roderick, though they were on complete opposite ends of the spectrum from each other. It probably just depended on one's preference.

"Thank you," she said. "I appreciate that."

"And I'll be waiting." Still grinning, he closed the door and Wynona headed down the hall.

It wasn't until she was on her scooter that she realized she'd never gotten the answer to her last question. Squinting up at the building, she smiled and shook her head. She had a strange feeling he did that on purpose. Well, if he wanted her to come back, she just might take him up on the invitation.

CHAPTER 14

"Yerba. For concentration. Careful," Wynona warned as she set a cup of steaming tea in front of Prim. "It's hot."

Prim rolled her pink eyes. "No kidding?"

Wynona huffed. "Sorry."

Prim grinned. "It's fine. You just have a nurturing spirit."

"Indeed," Roderick said into his tea cup.

That blasted flush heated up Wynona's cheeks and she quickly raised her own cup, hoping it would look like the steam was causing her to overheat instead of the compliment.

"What good is nurturing if you can't keep your house clean?" Lusgu muttered as he walked by, guiding a broom around the table they sat at.

Wynona ignored his complaint, something she was getting quite good at, but she couldn't help looking longingly at the way his fingers danced, making the broom do his bidding. It must be so nice to have such easy access to powers.

Roderick cleared his throat and Wynona blinked herself back into the present. She smiled. "Looks like we're all..." Her voice trailed off when she felt something shift against her leg. She stiffened and her eyes widened. Was Roderick playing footsies with her? Seriously?

"Oh my goodness!" Prim squealed, bouncing in her seat and pointing at Wynona. "Now our circle is complete!"

Wynona relaxed when she realized the movement on her leg had been Violet.

"You look stunning today, Violet," Prim gushed.

If Wynona didn't know any better, she would say the purple mouse now sitting on her shoulder was preening. The thought, however, was entirely ridiculous. After cleaning her face, Violet turned her twitching nose toward Wynona.

"Hungry?"

Violet squeaked.

Picking up a bit of biscuit, Wynona handed it to the small rodent, who took it and settled in for a nice snack.

Prim put her face in her hand. "Do you think she's your familiar?" the fairy asked.

Wynona shook her head, careful not to knock off her guest. "I don't have powers, remember? A familiar would be attracted to the magic since that's how they connect with their masters."

"True." Prim sighed. "Still, I can't believe you tamed a mouse."

The thought made Wynona pause. Really, she hadn't tamed Violet at all. A few crumbs shouldn't have been enough to tame any wild animal, but nonetheless, there was no denying Violet's friendly personality.

"Why don't we jump to why we're here?" Wynona said, changing the subject. She didn't have answers as to why she was suddenly friends with a mouse and her head couldn't take more than one mystery at a time.

"Oh, yes," Prim said quickly, straightening her tutu. She was in her human form at the moment, which meant the tuft of tulle was quite short, but Prim loved to dress dramatically. "Do tell us everything you've learned."

Roderick had been sitting quietly the whole time, but his eyes had followed the conversation...and the mouse.

"I already told Roderick a few things earlier, but I now have more information, which changes what I already knew." Wynona spent the next twenty minutes going over what she knew and the added information from Rascal. Knowing Mrs. Droxon gained nothing from the baker's death put a massive shift in her direction.

"So, the wife would gain nothing? Not even a penny?" Prim said in disbelief. She crossed her slim legs and sipped her tea. "That seems rather harsh."

Wynona shrugged. "I agree, but apparently it's been that way since the beginning. She signed the prenuptial agreement." Wynona paused. "Or at least someone in her family had her do so."

"She does come from a rather wealthy background," Roderick added. "I suppose it was a way to make sure she wasn't marrying Atherton for his money."

"And yet, that's exactly why I believe she married him," Wynona mused.

Prim shivered delicately. "Lifestyles of the rich and famous. I just don't see the appeal. Give me a bed of roses and I'm happy."

Wynona smiled at her sweet friend.

"But what about the son?" Roderick asked, looking back to Wynona.

Wynona sat up straight. "Son?"

The landlord nodded. "Yes. Mrs. and Chef Droxon have a son. What does the will say about him?"

Wynona pinched her lips together. No wonder Rascal had been so smug. He'd held back more information than he'd let on. If this wasn't a one and done thing on the solving mystery front, Wynona knew she would need to become much better at picking people's brains. "I didn't even know there was a son."

Prim's pink eyes gleamed with intelligence as she leaned forward in a conspiratorial manner. "Funny you should ask that." One side of her pale pink lips pulled up into a grin. "The Curl and Die was buzzing with his name today."

"What were they saying?" Wynona asked, passing another bit of biscuit to Violet.

"That dear Kayne had been cut out of Daddy's will."

Wynona paused. "How would they know that?" That seemed like a bit too much of a coincidence, but it did add to her list of suspects. Both the wife *and* the son were cut off? Would Mrs. Droxon have killed in order to preserve her son's standing as heir? Possibly before Chef Droxon could change the will? Would this Kayne have killed for his own sake?

Prim shrugged one delicate shoulder. "I'm not quite sure, but Gypsy is never wrong."

Wynona worked to hold back her smile. She adored Prim, but her penchant for gossip was amusing at times.

Roderick raised a skeptical eyebrow. "Never?"

Prim glared at him in challenge. "Never."

He nodded and turned to Wynona. "While I don't necessarily have quite as much confidence in everything that filters through those doors, I do have to admit that the ladies there have an uncanny ability to know the pulse of the town."

Wynona crumbled a cookie as she considered the situation. "Did anyone know why he was cutting Kayne off? Did they just have a falling out? How old is Kayne?"

Prim tapped her lips. "I believe he's in his early twenties." She grinned. "Awfully handsome, that one."

Wynona's eyebrows went up. Chef Droxon was anything but handsome. Another gnome might find his short, bulbous features attractive, but they weren't anything Wynona would fawn over.

As if knowing exactly what Wynona was thinking, Prim waved a dismissive hand through the air. "Don't worry, he takes after his mother."

"Ah." Wynona understood the appeal now. Elves could be very attractive indeed. The few males Wynona had run into since being free all held a sense of mystery about them that was quite alluring, even if their magic level was quite a bit less than a warlock's. Not to mention, Maeve had been exceedingly lovely. Which was more than likely why she was Chef Droxon's wife. He could afford the best.

"Anyway, as the only child of our famed chef, Kayne Droxon grew up...how to put it nicely..." Prim ticked her head back and forth. "Spoiled?"

Wynona laughed softly. "That's putting it nicely?"

"It was the only word that worked," Prim said with an unrepentant grin.

"I can imagine he was the apple of his mother's eye," Roderick added, setting his teacup down. He reached for a cookie. "Especially since her marriage was apparently not a happy one."

Wynona nodded. "Yes. It would make sense. But still, most fathers don't cut off their sons just for being spoiled."

"Unless the spoiled child acts out against the father," Prim offered.

"Maybe." Was it as simple as that? Right now, Wynona wasn't sure. Mostly, the information gave her an added suspect and a new motive. Instead of bringing clarity, it seemed as if her work was getting harder.

"So we have the neglected wife, the prodigal son and the secretary, right?" Prim asked.

"Yes. Ms. Caseis," Wynona reminded her friend. "You mentioned she'd had a bad reaction to news of the murder."

Prim pursed her lips and nodded vigorously. "Oh, yes. My informant said she nearly threw a tantrum when the police spoke to her."

"She was calm when I managed a few minutes of her time," Wynona said with a frown.

Prim shrugged and tucked a piece of neon pink hair behind her ear. "She must have calmed down by then. But they said her screech could be heard two blocks over." She raised an eyebrow. "You know how sirens can be when they're upset."

"I thought that was banshees," Wynona said with a small laugh.

Prim's tinkling giggle filled the room and Violet stirred from the nap she had slipped into.

"Anyway," Wynona said, pressing forward. "That leaves me a list of three suspects, including the secretary." She scowled. "But I can't for the life of me figure out a motive. Mrs. Droxon and Kayne have motives. Mrs. Droxon has an alibi, but I haven't met the son yet." She took a sip of tea. "Since the police haven't arrested him, I'm going to assume he has one as well."

"Didn't Delila have an alibi?" Prim asked. She had picked a flower from the vase in the middle of the tea table and was rubbing the petals. A sweet, floral fragrance floated through the air and the flower itself seemed to lean into Prim's touch.

Wynona held back a sigh of resignation. She just couldn't seem to get away from envying all the magic going on around her. It was beautiful, most of the time, but it was never going to be her life. That might have been the one thing that being locked up in the castle had done for her. Seeing what she would never have made it much more difficult not to be jealous. "Yes, Ms. Caseis says she was working late."

"And yet you told me you don't believe her," Roderick pointed out. He drummed his fingers on the tabletop. "Said she was shifty when she answered you."

"Yes..." Wynona frowned. "There was something...off...about her answer, but I have no way to prove my theory. Having a gut feeling wouldn't hold up in court."

"It sounds to me like we just need more information," Prim suggested.

Wynona sighed and drank the last of her tea. It was cooler than she liked it by now, but still tasty. "I suppose I'll have to do some more digging." This detective work wasn't exactly something that came naturally to her, but when it came to saving her business, it would be worth it. At least it would as long as she could help the police figure out the real murderer.

"Might be best to start with the son," Roderick mused thoughtfully. "It seems to me his motive is more than likely the strongest. I agree that Ms. Caseis doesn't seem to have a true reason for attempting to kill her boss. Not unless she is holding back information."

"Which we think she is," Prim pointed out.

"True enough," Wynona agreed. "I might just need to make the rounds again. With this new information, I'm more prepared to ask the right questions of everyone, including Mrs. Droxon."

"Is there anyone else we think might have committed the murder?" Prim inserted. She held her hand out toward Wynona's shoulder, eyes eager.

Violet squeaked a few times, but nuzzled into Wynona's neck, obviously not wanting to take the invitation.

Prim's lips pursed into a pout.

Inside, Wynona couldn't help but feel slightly relieved, though she worked hard to hide it. For some reason, she was a little protective of the tiny scamp and it was nice to know Violet returned her affection. Reaching up, she rubbed the top of the rodent's soft head.

"I certainly hope not." Wynona huffed. "Having three is already too many in the time frame I've got left."

Roderick gave her a sympathetic look. "How many days until the opening?"

"Well, provided I actually open, it's only four," Wynona replied. "I really need this situation done and gone, but it seems the more I learn, the more I realize I'm missing."

Prim patted Wynona's hand. "Don't worry. I have complete faith in you. You'll figure this out."

Wynona gave her friend a grateful smile. "Thanks, Prim. What would I do without you?"

"Hear less gossip?" Prim asked with a wink.

Wynona and Roderick both laughed as intended. "Maybe so, but if your gossip is correct, it could help me solve the case."

"And that's why I'm here." Prim stood, leaned over to kiss Wynona on the cheek and headed toward the door. "Thanks for the tea! I need to get back to my flowers, but when you learn more, be sure to let me know."

Wynona watched her friend go, feeling slightly melancholy. How she wished life was less complicated. That she could share a cup of tea not because of necessity, but because they were simply two friends enjoying each other's company.

Someday.

Roderick cleared his throat.

Wynona turned back to him. "Have a meeting you need to get to?" she asked with a smile.

He returned the gesture. "As a matter of fact, I do, but I wanted to leave a little advice before I left."

"Oh?" Wynona raised her eyebrows in anticipation of his words.

"Be careful," he said in a low tone. He held up a hand to stave off her automatic response. "I know you're not the reckless kind, but this town isn't always as safe as your family would have us believe."

Wynona felt her cheeks heat at the reminder of her family and her folly in the alley. Violet rubbed against her cheek. Whether enjoying the heat or trying to comfort, Wynona was unsure, but the soft gesture felt nice.

"We don't yet know if your attack was random or planned, and until we do, I think you should be on your guard." He went to stand but paused when Wynona spoke.

"You think someone targeted me?" she asked, her jaw going slack. It was an angle she hadn't considered before. They had just seemed like street thugs and she had been easy prey.

He finished standing, then shrugged as he adjusted his suit. "I don't know, but I don't want you to underestimate anyone or anything." His eyes turned into warm, liquid silver as he looked at her. "You're a special woman, Wynona. It would be a shame to see anything happen to you. And we both know that when we're talking about money in the amount Chef Droxon has, people will do outrageous things to keep it."

Wynona had dropped his gaze when he spoke about her. A small fluttering in her stomach began from the tenderness in his voice. She was wholly unprepared for a man such as him to make those types of remarks about her, but also couldn't deny how good it felt.

She could feel his large presence move around the table and stop at her side before long fingers tucked under her chin, forcing her to look up at him.

"Promise you won't put yourself in danger?" he asked, his thumb caressing her jawline.

Wynona swallowed hard. "I promise to do my best." It was all she could offer. She didn't like empty words and she wouldn't purposefully look for trouble, but if yesterday was any indication, it might find her whether she was careful or not.

His half smile was deliciously charming. "That will be enough." With one last rub of his thumb, he nodded goodbye and sailed out the door.

Wynona slumped in her seat after he was gone, nearly upsetting Violet from her shoulder. "Sorry," she whispered, reaching up to pet the creature again. "That man has me all discombobulated, Vi."

Violet squeaked animatedly and Wynona wished she spoke mouse, but in her magicless state, she had no such luck.

Laying her palm flat, she invited Violet to climb on, then moved the mouse to the table. While doing so, a flash of golden eyes and messy brown hair passed through her mind. Another shot of warmth hit Wynona's chest, but she pushed it away and shook her head.

"I don't have time for men," Wynona said to Violet, who was now devouring a cookie. "I have a murder to solve."

"Men are messy," Lusgu grumbled, walking by with a dustpan in his hand. "Don't ever learn any manners."

Wynona smiled. She didn't quite agree on the manners part, but messy? Absolutely. Two handsome men were messing up her life at the moment and Wynona had no patience for it. Her shop needed to come first. "Well," she said to Violet, "looks like I'm back to the drawing board." Standing up from her seat, Wynona went to grab her purse. Another round of interviews was in the works.

CHAPTER 15

Since Wynona had no idea how to find Kayne Droxon, she decided her best bet was to go back to the Droxon bakeries and try to talk to Delila Caseis. There was something nagging Wynona about her alibi. The woman had been strong and defensive, up until that moment, and it brought up a red flag in Wynona's mind.

The darting eyes and failure to make eye contact all screamed that the woman was lying. But how to prove it? Or how to get the woman to confess?

Ideas, none of them good, swirled through Wynona's brain as she rode her scooter through the town. A small amount of trepidation churned in her belly as she rode down to Runes Road. She wasn't going through an alley this time, but she had still been attacked here only yesterday and the feelings of fear and helplessness were close to the surface.

As she drove closer, however, everything drained away, except for the fear. The front of the building was completely blocked with police vehicles. Sirens had been turned off, but the lights flashed across the side of the building and onto the cars that slowly passed by.

Getting as close as she dared, Wynona parked her scooter and hurried over, slinging her purse across her chest as she went. "What happened?" she asked the officer standing guard in the doorway.

The man scowled. "Move along, please," he said gruffly. His height, combined with the gravel in his tone, left Wynona assuming he was some kind of troll. The angles of his face were sharp and the muscles beneath his uniform bulged. A rock troll. The problem here was that they were known for being as stubborn as they were strong. She would have to handle this delicately.

"I'm Wynona Le Doux," she said carefully, making sure her last name was clear. Oh, how she hated using it to gain advantage, but in times such as this, it was a blessing in disguise. "I have business with Chef Droxon and his secretary, Ms. Caseis. Please let me inside."

Large arms folded over an equally large chest. It was no wonder they put this guy at the door. He filled up the entire entryway, which happened to be two glass doors wide. "No one goes in."

"Deputy Chief Strongclaw is expecting me." The little white lie nearly got stuck in her throat, but she knew Rascal would back her up.

The guard's eyebrows furrowed. He stared her down, but Wynona stood tall. She needed to know what was going on. That same gut instinct that told her Ms. Caseis had been lying was saying that whatever was going on had to do with the murder in her shop.

Reaching toward his shoulder, the officer pressed a walkie-talkie and spoke into it for a minute. It crackled to life and the distinctive honeyed tones of Chief Ligurio came pouring out. "By all means. Let her up."

Wynona swallowed hard. She didn't like the way the chief had said that. He had almost sounded gleeful that she had arrived.

The guard moved to the side and waved an arm toward the entrance. "Tenth floor, Ms. Le Doux," he said in his harsh tone.

"Thank you," Wynona said politely. "I appreciate you letting me through."

The officer gave her an unimpressed look as she walked past and turned back to the front once she had gone inside.

Sighing in relief, Wynona made her way to the elevator. The bottom floor seemed deserted and she guessed the building had been evacuated. The elevator was straight ahead and Wynona hurried over. She didn't like the heavy, depressive feel of the abandoned area.

Luckily, it only took a few moments for the elevator to open and soon she was on her way up. Soft music played in the background, which seemed in direct contrast to her pounding heart. Something bad was going to happen. A heavy sense of doom weighed her down, but Wynona forced herself to stay upright.

She watched the digital numbers at the top of the elevator. The closer she got to the top floor, the thicker the air became until it was difficult to breathe. The door dinged, then opened, shocking Wynona out of her near hyperventilation.

Sucking in a much needed lungful of air, she pushed her legs into action, stepping out before the doors closed on her again. Whereas the bottom level has been silent, floor ten was buzzing with activity. It was like a hive of sprites, all dressed in blue uniforms.

"Ah, Ms. Le Doux." Chief Ligurio's voice was as smooth as ever. Those darn vampires and their charm magic. It seemed in complete odds with his grumpy personality.

Wynona smiled. "Hello, Chief. Thank you for allowing me to come up."

He curled a long, white finger at her. "Perhaps you would like to see what brought us here?" His black eyebrow rose. "Or perhaps you already know."

Wynona shook her head. "I have no idea what's going on."

"Ms. Le Doux!" Rascal came up behind his boss's shoulder. Wynona was grateful he was on duty this afternoon and had only been off for the morning shift. She'd need a friendly face in this crowd. "I heard you were coming." He gave her an apologetic grin. "Come on back and I'll show you where it happened."

Wynona looked back and forth between the chief and his deputy. "Where what happened?"

Chief Ligurio sighed and pinched the bridge of his nose. "Where were you between twelve and two o'clock, Ms. Le Doux?"

"Having tea with friends." She folded her arms over her chest. "Now will you please explain why you feel the need to ask me that? I still don't understand what's going on."

"Chef Droxon is dead."

Wynona's arms fell to her sides. "What?"

"You said friends," the chief continued. "I'm assuming they'll corroborate your story?"

"Of course they will," Wynona sputtered. She stepped forward, her mind still reeling. "Chief, I don't know why you are so dead set on this being my fault, but this is the first time I've ever been in this building. Ever. I had nothing to do with the chef's death and nothing to do with the man's death in my shop."

The chief eyed her with clear disdain. "Time will tell, I suppose." Turning on his heel, he led the way through the crowded space.

Wynona rushed over to Rascal and together they followed. "He's really dead?" she asked, putting a hand on her churning stomach. She *knew* something bad was going to happen.

Rascal nodded. "Yep. Just like before. Turned to ash."

"Are we sure it's really the chef?" Wynona asked. "Last time we were fooled as well."

"Coroner has already examined the ash and confirmed it," Rascal whispered. "We've been here for over an hour collecting evidence and questioning the entire building."

"And it happened in broad daylight?" Wynona asked, looking around at all the open windows.

"Sort of. Middle of the day, yes. But you can only see one way through these windows, so no one in a neighboring building would have noticed a thing." He stepped aside and let her walk through a doorway first. "And Droxon's office, as you can see, is closed off from the rest of the floor."

Wynona looked around, noting that Rascal was right. The office space was quite large, with a full kitchen off to one side and sitting area on the other. If it weren't for the oak desk and massive wall of filing cabinets, it would have looked like they had entered someone's home. Her eyes finally settled on the outline of a body. Apparently,

Chef Droxon's remains had already been removed, but the police had used tape to mark where it had been.

She noted that the shape, this time, was correct. Short and round. Exactly right for a gnome. "I would have thought the department was keeping an eye on him," Wynona whispered, glancing up at Rascal.

He scratched his chin. "We were. No one saw anything unusual. No struggle, no fight, no shouting for help."

"Then how did this happen?"

Rascal shook his head. "We're not sure. Ms. Caseis called it in. She had tried to call him over the intercom, but Droxon didn't answer. After a while, she went to check on him and found...this." He waved his hand toward the markings.

Back to Ms. Caseis. She seemed to show up a lot. "Is she still around?"

Rascal raised one of his thick eyebrows. "Why? Want to ask her some more questions?"

Wynona nodded. "Please," she added when Rascal didn't respond right away.

He sighed and tilted his head toward the front of the office. "Come on. She's in one of the other offices."

"Thank you," Wynona said softly.

He grinned. "We'll be lucky if I don't end up fired after this case."

Wynona stopped. "Do you really mean that?" she asked. "I wouldn't want to do anything that might cost you your job."

Rascal shook his head quickly. "Nah. I'm joking." His grin grew. "But it's nice that you're worried about it."

That dang blush. There was simply no hiding it and when it shot up her cheeks, Rascal's eyes were immediately drawn to the color. Wynona cleared her throat. "Um, which office is she in?" A change in subject was her only defense at the moment.

Rascal never stopped grinning as he led her to the far corner. He knocked twice on the door and poked his head inside, speaking to someone before opening it fully. "Go on in."

"Thank you," Wynona said softly, slipping past him. Rascal didn't leave her much room, so her shoulder brushed against his chest. It was a good thing her cheeks were already on fire, because getting even the smallest feel of his muscles was enough to send her temperature through the roof. "Ms. Caseis?"

Delila looked up from dabbing her eyes with a soggy handkerchief. "Ms. Le Doux?"

Wynona gave her a kind smile. "Wynona, please."

Ms. Caseis nodded. "Delila."

Walking over, Wynona put her hand on the siren's shoulder. Even grieving, she was stunning. A slight red rim on her eyes was the only true sign that she had been crying. Well, that and the garbage full of tissues at her feet. "I'm so sorry for your loss."

Delila nodded. "Thank you." She shrugged. "He wasn't the best boss, but I'd been with him for several years." She dabbed delicately at her eye again. "I just can't imagine who would do something like this."

"May I?" Wynona pointed to the chair next to hers.

Delila nodded. "Please."

Wynona sat down, taking her purse off and tucking it at her side. "Deputy Chief Strongclaw told me you found the body."

Delila nodded. "Yes. It was awful." Her bottom lip began to tremble along with her voice. "Just a pile of ash. His clothes were normal, but his body was gone." She sniffled and reached for another tissue, blowing it softly before dumping it in the trash.

"It must have been an awful shock for you," Wynona prodded.

"It was." Delila wiped a stray tear. "I've never seen the results of a hex before. It's something you think only happens on the television, you know?"

"Yes," Wynona agreed. "What were you doing when it happened?" There was no way to ask the question delicately, but luckily, Ms Caseis was too caught up in her grief to get upset about it.

"Working out front, at my desk." Her eyes grew wide. "The whole office can vouch for me."

Wynona reached out and patted the woman's knee. "I'm sure they can. I'm just trying to get a mental picture, is all."

Delila tilted her head. "Are you a detective or something? I thought you were a Le Doux."

"I am," Wynona responded. "If you recall from our meeting the other day, I own a tea shop, but ended up getting caught up in..." She waved her hands around. "This."

Delila nodded, though it was clear she didn't exactly understand. Which was fine. Wynona didn't want to break it all down anyway.

"Can you think of anyone who might have visited Chef Droxon during the time frame the police are looking at?" Delila's eyes skittered away and Wynona immediately grew suspicious. She had seen this look before.

"No one out of the ordinary," the secretary said. She wrung the handkerchief in her hands, nearly tearing the fabric.

"Can you tell me even the ordinary ones?" Wynona started a mental checklist in her head, ready to remember each and every name. She was sure Rascal already had it written down, but she wanted the information for herself.

Delila's eyes fell to her lap. "Just his...family, a couple of business associates."

"Family? Do you mean his wife, or his son?"

Delila's head jerked ever so slightly, but she played it off by stretching her neck. "Both. They had a family meeting during lunch."

"I see. And his business associates? Can you tell me their names?"

The siren sighed, exasperation leaking into her tone. "I really don't see what all this has to do with you, Ms. Le Doux."

Wynona fought to keep from arguing. This had everything to do with her. Whoever had mistakenly killed that thief back at her shop had finished the plot by killing Chef Droxon in his office. And despite having an alibi, she could tell the chief still didn't believe her. Her shop was doomed if she couldn't clear her name.

Jerking upright, Wynona turned to Rascal, who was chatting with another officer nearby. "Deputy Chief Strongclaw. Did anyone check for Chef Droxon's little black book?"

Rascal huffed. "We checked. But nobody can find it."

"And the will? Is it still missing?"

Rascal nodded. "Yep."

Wynona sagged in her seat. More than ever, she needed to find Chef Droxon's son and confront him. Something just wasn't adding up, and until she figured it out, she knew her entire future was in jeopardy.

CHAPTER 16

"**M**s. Le Doux?"

Wynona wasn't sure she enjoyed them having to be so formal. She preferred when Rascal called her Wynona, but she couldn't exactly scold him when they were in public and he was on the job. She gave Delila one last comforting pat, then stood and walked over, raising her eyebrows in question.

"Find out anything interesting?" he asked in a low tone.

"Nothing you probably don't already know," Wynona said. "Why?"

Rascal sighed and pushed a hand through his thick hair. "She wasn't exactly forthcoming about everything and I was hoping speaking to another woman might help her open up a little."

Wynona pursed her lips. "She told me Mrs. Droxon and her son, Kayne, were here. And that some business associates came by, but she didn't seem keen to name any of them."

Rascal nodded. "Yeah...that's about all we got." He wrinkled his nose. "I'm not sure if she's scared one of them did it and will target her next, or if she's got something going on with one of the visitors and is trying to protect them."

"She's hiding something for sure," Wynona mused, tapping her bottom lip. "But I'm not sure what."

"Do you think she's the killer?"

Wynona shook her head. "No. I don't. Do you?"

Rascal responded in kind. "No. She doesn't seem the type. I mean, she's a siren and all, but she's not exactly trying to charm every man on the force." He gave Wynona a rueful grin. "Not that she would have to try hard. I think half my men started drooling the second they saw her."

"And you? Did you drool?" Wynona snapped her mouth shut. She shouldn't have asked that. It wasn't any of her business whether Rascal thought Ms. Caseis was attractive or not. She and Rascal were only friends and most of that was on a professional level. The fact that she found him attractive was irrelevant.

A slow, boyish grin spread across his face. "I can't say that I did," he said, his tone slightly huskier than before. "I prefer my women a little less...high maintenance."

Wynona nodded jerkily, dropping her face to the floor in an effort to hide her ridiculous blush. "Good to know," she responded in as much of a business tone as she could. She cleared her throat yet again. Rascal was going to think she had allergies if this kept up.

"So, if you don't think Ms. Caseis is the killer," Rascal began, "who do you suspect?"

Wynona pinched her lips together. "I'm not sure. None of the clues make sense."

"Such as?" he prodded.

"Such as the missing will." She turned to face him fully. "Speaking of, you deliberately never told me what was in that will." She glared at him, though there was no heat behind the look. "I have a sneaking suspicion you did that on purpose."

Rascal grinned and shrugged. "I'll never tell."

"What was in the will? Or whether or not you withheld information on purpose?"

"Wouldn't you like to know?" he taunted.

Wynona fought the urge to roll her eyes. "What are we? Toddlers?"

He chuckled. A deep rich sound that resonated through Wynona's chest. "The will said his son Kayne would inherit everything. However, Chef Droxon told us he had plans to change the will. Planned to cut off Kayne completely." Rascal squished his lips to one side. "I'm guessing that didn't happen before he died. If the will ever shows up, it should show that Kayne inherited everything."

"Hmmm..."

"What are you thinking?" Rascal asked, eyeing her. "I'm starting to recognize your looks, and this one means you've discovered something."

"What?" Wynona blinked several times. "Oh. I was just thinking how convenient that was for Kayne. He was supposed to be cut off, but his dad couldn't change the will before he died? Don't you find that suspicious?"

Rascal nodded. "I do. Except that Kayne has an alibi."

Wynona's shoulders drooped. "Everybody has an alibi."

He grinned. "True."

"Which means that someone, or multiple someones have to be lying," Wynona continued. She looked up into Rascal's golden orbs. "But who?"

He scrunched up one side of his face. "I don't know." He scratched behind his ear. "Who would have reason to?"

Wynona tapped her bottom lip. "All of them, I suppose." She glanced over to Delila. The woman was still sniffling and wiping tears, but when an officer handed her a cup of coffee, she gave him a grateful smile that disappeared as quickly as it had arrived. She shifted continually in her seat, telling Wynona the woman was nervous. But why? That was the biggest question. There just didn't seem to be a good reason for the secretary to kill her boss. Or kill someone else in his place.

"The recipes," Wynona breathed. "Obviously they were after the recipes the whole time." She frowned. "But why kill for them? When that man tried to steal them at my shop, he wasn't attempting murder. He was just a thief."

"Joksac Skinflayer."

Wynona paused. "What?"

Rascal scrambled for a notebook in his pocket and flipped through its pages. "Joksac Skinflayer. The thief you were talking about." He snapped the notebook closed. "He was a doppelganger."

"Ah. That explains why someone thought he was the chef when they killed him," Wynona mused, tucking the bit of information away.

Rascal nodded. "Yeah. That's what we thought too. Though when he was killed, he reverted back to his original form."

"Letting the killer know they had the wrong man," Wynona finished for him.

"Exactly." Rascal's eyes gleamed with pride and Wynona couldn't help but smile at him.

"That still doesn't tell us why the person tried to kill the chef. Thievery doesn't lend itself to murder."

"Unless it's in self defense," Rascal offered.

"Coming back to kill the chef would dispel that theory. If they killed in self defense, why come back for him?"

"Perhaps they were still after the recipe book," Rascal said. "Both burglary attempts could have been botched."

"That seems unlikely." Wynona scrunched her nose. "And why were they looking for the book in my office that night? I don't have it. It was in Chef Droxon's pocket."

Rascal blew out a long breath. "Guess that doesn't work."

"None of it does," Wynona complained. "I feel like everything just turns in circles. If the recipe booklet was the real reason for the crimes, none of our suspects seem likely to want it. His wife certainly had no reason to want it. She already had access to his money, as long as he was alive. His son was out of the will, but how would stealing the recipes help that? And his secretary had been working here for years. If she wanted the recipe booklet, there's no way she would have had to kill for it. She knew this building, and more than likely knew his office and schedule. Of any of them, she would have the best chance of getting away with stealing it without having to commit murder." Wynona rubbed her temples. "I'm missing something," she murmured. "Something important. And when I find it, everything will become clear."

Rascal put his hand on her shoulder, creating a hotspot, which traveled down her arm. "Don't stress about it," he encouraged. "These things have a way of coming to light. If people are lying, we'll eventually figure it out."

Although she appreciated the sentiment, Wynona didn't have time to wait it out. Her shop was set to open in just a couple of days. She couldn't afford to relax about the matter.

"Ms. Le Doux." Chief Ligurio was scowling deeply as he approached them.

Rascal's hand dropped from her shoulder and Wynona felt slightly colder from the loss. "Sir," he said in a serious tone.

Wynona lifted her chin slightly. "Chief Ligurio. What can I do for you?"

His red eyes were menacing as he glared at her. "I came to warn you not to leave town."

Wynona huffed and folded her arms over her chest. "Not that I had plans to, but would you care to tell me why I'm being warned in such a way?"

He stepped a little closer and Wynona had to fight to hold her ground. She knew she was innocent, and nothing this man could do would change that. But without any powers to protect herself, she couldn't help but be a little intimidated by him. "Because I have every intention of proving that you're lying," he said in a low tone. "And when I do, you and your family will have nowhere to hide."

Wynona stood, stunned, as the police chief stalked away. She was fully aware that her family's power made them targets and not everyone liked the way the Le Doux's or other witch families ruled Hex Haven, but this was being taken to an extreme.

"I'm sorry," Rascal said from behind her.

Wynona turned just enough to look at him. He looked exhausted as he scrubbed his face with his palms. "It's not your fault that he's such a jerk," she said before stopping herself. She blew out a breath. "Now I'm sorry. I shouldn't have said that."

Rascal shook his head. "Under the circumstances, I think you had every right."

"I just don't understand why he's so determined to see me go to jail. I'd never even met him before you all showed up at my shop."

Rascal shook his head. "I don't know. I've never seen him like this." He made a face. "I mean, Chief has always been kinda hard-nosed. I think it comes from living so long, but he's also usually pretty good about digging for the truth, instead of jumping to conclusions."

That headache was pounding against her forehead again and Wynona rubbed the spot. "Maybe I better go. I don't think there's anything else I can learn from here anyway."

Warm fingertips brushed her upper arm. "Be careful out there, huh? I don't like the fact that we've had two dead bodies in as many days."

Wynona nodded, grateful for his concern. "Thank you, I will be."

"In fact..." Rascal began searching his pockets until he handed her a small tube. "Keep this on you."

Wynona frowned and studied it. "What is it?"

"A Banshee Scream," Rascal explained. "The container is spelled to hit whoever the container is aimed at." He grinned. "So don't mix up the front and back."

Wynona gave him a look. "I think I can handle that."

"Anyway, it'll incapacitate whoever it hits." His golden eyes turned warm. "Maybe it'll help keep you safe since you don't have, uh..." He trailed off, obviously worried about offending her.

"Since I don't have powers?" Wynona said plainly. There was no use beating around the bush. She wasn't happy about it, but she couldn't exactly hide it either. "Thank you," she said softly. "That's very thoughtful of you."

Rascal gave her his signature wink. "Anytime."

Holding the container up with a little shake, she gave him a smile and left the building. Once outside, Wynona shot off a group text to Roderick and Prim. After what she had just learned, it appeared that true to her landlord's claim, more tea was in order.

CHAPTER 17

"Wynona Le Doux to see Mrs. Droxon," Wynona said to Gerall, the Droxons' butler. She wasn't really very excited to be back at the Droxon manor, but she was hoping to use giving her condolences to Mrs. Droxon as an excuse to see if Kayne was home. So far he had managed to evade her at every turn. Her time was running out and if she didn't catch a break in this case soon, it was going to be too late.

"The family is in mourning," Gerall said crisply. "They aren't taking callers."

Wynona did her best to keep her smile in place. "I understand that, but I believe Mrs. Droxon will see me. Please announce me anyway."

Gerall's lip curled at the edge. His yellow eyes pinned Wynona in place. He was certainly willing to give her a dirty look, but apparently looking was all he could offer because with a sniff, he turned and disappeared behind the large door.

Wynona glanced at her watch. She had to be back at the shop in time to host an early dinner with Roderick and Prim. Now that Chef Droxon was dead, they needed to brainstorm all over again, since the game seemed to have changed...again.

"Mrs. Droxon will see you," Gerall said in a low tone. Slowly, he stepped back, opening the door enough for her to enter.

Wynona put a hand on his forearm and his head snapped toward her. "I appreciate that you're protective of Mrs. Droxon," she said in a soft voice. "Thank you for taking care of her."

Gerall hesitated before nodding his head. His stiff demeanor softened the tiniest bit as he led the way farther into the mansion.

Wynona was sincere in her praise. She felt bad for Mrs. Droxon, even if staying in an abusive relationship was her own choice. No woman should feel it necessary to condemn herself to such a life. While Wynona had had her grandmother, she was glad that Maeve had Gerall.

"Ms. Le Doux," Gerall intoned, announcing Wynona at the door of the same room as before.

Wynona walked inside and gave Maeve a sad smile. "Just Wynona," she reminded her new acquaintance.

Maeve nodded, her face pale and free from makeup. Her clothes were much subdued as well. Gone was the large historical dress and in its place were slim lounge pants that appeared to be made of silk. She was draped just as artfully across the fainting couch, however, and Wynona assumed Maeve didn't know how to be anything but elegant.

"I'm so sorry for your loss, Maeve."

Maeve nodded again and dabbed at her eyes. "Thank you," she said thickly. Her eyes went to the far corner of the room. "Have you met my son? Kayne?"

Wynona held back the squeal of excitement that wanted to break free, and the sigh of relief that wished to follow. Finally, she had caught the prodigal son. Turning slowly, she inclined her head. "Kayne. Good to meet you at last. I'm sorry it's under such terrible circumstances."

Prim had been right. The son definitely took after his mother, which was definitely to his credit. Tall and lean, his features would have suited a lord of old time England. Blond hair was cut neatly at his shoulders and his ears poked delicately through the silky strands. His eyes were as blue as the ocean and sharp as ice. Slowly, he returned her greeting, never taking his eyes from hers. "Ms. Le Doux. Mother told me you visited the other day." He tilted his head. "Why exactly are you looking into all this? The first murder and now the second? What do you have to do with them?"

It took some effort, but Wynona held her ground. She clasped her hands in front of her waist to keep them from giving away her nerves. "Let's just say I'm working with the police to put a killer behind bars."

"No...let's not," Kayne said. He came out from the corner, his walk almost leonine in style. If he had chosen to wear a bow and arrow and said he was hunting for prey, Wynona wouldn't have batted an eye. The fact that she was his intended target at the moment, however, made it harder to appreciate his fluidity. "Let's try answering the question again." He stopped only a few feet away, the hostility in him pulsing forth like a living entity. "Why are you here?"

"Dear," Mrs. Droxon started.

Kayne held up his hand. "No, Mother. I don't care that she's related to our president. She's in our house, at a time when only close friends and family should be. And unless I'm mistaken, she's here to ask more questions, similar to what she did before." Even as he spoke to his mother, Kayne kept his eyes on Wynona, like he was studying an insect under a microscope. "Please answer my question."

Wynona calmed herself with a deep breath. What she wouldn't give for a cup of chamomile right now. "Since the first murder happened in my tea shop, I have a personal stake in seeing the killer brought to justice," she said honestly. "My grand opening is in just a couple of days and the police still have it marked off as a crime scene." She held back an eye roll. "Not to mention, the chief has put me at the top of his suspect list." Shrugging, Wynona walked as calmly as she could to the nearest couch, pretending Kayne's presence didn't bother her. "I've bet my entire future on this shop and if I can't open, I'll be in serious trouble."

"With your family?" Kayne pressed.

Wynona shook her head. "No. My family would like nothing better than to see me fail." She hoped that by showing she also had a difficult relationship with her relatives, she could appeal to the fact that Kayne held no true love for his father.

It worked.

Grinning in a way that Wynona was sure melted unsuspecting ladies into gooey puddles, Kayne walked around the chair he'd been standing by and draped himself into it. "So your shop is your rebellion? No intention of going into the family business?"

"I suppose you could call it that," Wynona responded. "And definitely not."

Kayne looked over his shoulder at his mother. "I can see why you like her."

Maeve made an amused noise, then dabbed at her nose. "How can we help you, Wynona?"

Wynona smiled, but there was no joy in it. "I'm sorry to start this way, but first I need to know where you were when Chef Droxon was killed. Ms. Caseis mentioned you both came to see the chef during his lunch."

Kayne's eyes flared at the mention of the secretary, but his body stayed still.

Wynona made a mental note of the reaction. She would have to test it again and figure out exactly what emotion it was stemming from.

"Like you or not," Kayne leaned forward, resting his elbows on his knees, "you don't have the right to ask us that."

"You're right," Wynona said coolly. "But I'm asking anyway."

Kayne grinned again and leaned back once more. "Mother dragged me to the office, trying to invite Father to lunch." He raised a slim eyebrow. "You see, she had the notion stuck in her head that if she could get us talking again, Father would take me back into his will."

"And?"

"And what?"

"Did it work?" Wynona clarified.

"No," Kayne snapped. He schooled his features from the short outburst. "But after that, we left." He grinned. "And ate lunch together." His hands splayed to the side. "He was quite alive when we left, so there was no way we could have killed him. Since he walked, or rather stormed us to the door, the entire office can attest that we left him completely intact."

"And Ms. Caseis?"

"What about her?" Kayne's features tightened.

"She saw you all leave as well?" Wynona said carefully, watching his every move.

"She did. I have no doubt she will corroborate our story." Kayne looked away as if he'd suddenly lost interest in the conversation.

Wynona knew that was her cue to leave. Other questions could wait. She had some ideas churning in her head and needed to think on them. She arose from the sofa. "Thank you so much for your time, and again...I'm very sorry for your loss."

Kayne snorted, but Maeve managed a wave goodbye as Wynona headed out of the salon and house. Jumping on her scooter, she pressed the gas pedal as fast as it would go. She wouldn't have very much time to prepare for her friends coming over. It was a good thing Prim had offered to grab takeout. There would barely be enough time to put the tea on to steep before they arrived at the shop.

Half an hour later, Prim slowly shook her head. "I just...can't believe he was killed."

Wynona nodded, wiping her mouth with a napkin before grabbing her teacup. She took a sip of the soothing chamomile. It was exactly what she'd been craving ever since her run-in with Kayne Droxon. "I know. I was completely shocked."

Roderick huffed and set down his sandwich. "So where does this put us in regards to the first murder? Do they suspect it's the same person?"

A sarcastic snort broke free and Wynona had to stop herself from following it up with a sharp retort. "Yes," she said. "In fact, Chief Ligurio is still convinced I'm his number one suspect."

"What!" Prim sat up taller. "You were with us yesterday," she argued. "You have witnesses."

"And according to him, he'll be calling to check up on those witnesses," Wynona said with a sigh. She shook her head. "I don't know what his problem is, but he's completely convinced this is all my fault."

Roderick reached over and patted her hand. "Don't let it worry you. We all know you're innocent. He can look all he wants, but he's not going to be able to pin anything on you."

Wynona gave him a grateful smile. He had been so supportive of her from the beginning. Even when it had come out that she didn't have powers, his belief in her innocence had never faltered. It was extremely flattering and helpful. "Thanks," she said. "It's annoying, but I know it'll turn out okay." She frowned and looked down at her lunch. "The biggest problem I see, though, is if he's got his gaze turned on me, then the real killer is probably going to go free."

Prim huffed in annoyance. "Vampires are supposed to be good at details. I can't believe that jerk doesn't believe the evidence that's right in front of his eyes."

Wynona broke off a piece of bread and set it down next to Violet. The tiny creature squeaked and dug right in, not paying any attention to the solemn mood of the group.

"Cops," Lusgu grunted as he walked past. "Werewolves. Nothing but trouble."

Roderick smirked. "Can't say he's wrong."

Wynona tsked her tongue. "They're all doing the best they can and Rascal, uh...Deputy Chief Officer Strongclaw has been extremely helpful during the entire investigation."

"So what exactly did you learn from your visit with Kayne and Mrs. Droxon?" Prim asked over her teacup rim.

"Enough to have me putting him at the top of my list," Wynona said. "What throws me off, however, is the recipes." She tucked a piece of hair behind her ear. "If he's not interested in taking over the family business, then why bother taking the recipes? All he had to do was follow his dad around, learn the art and it would have all gone to him."

Prim tapped her long, butter-yellow fingernail on the white tablecloth. "That's true. What would he gain from killing his father that he couldn't have if his father were alive?"

"His inheritance, of course," Roderick said. "He had been cut out of the will."

"Yes, but since the killer stole the recipe book, we have to assume that's what they were after in the first place," Wynona pointed out. "The man who was killed first, Joksac Skinflayer, tried to steal the book, remember? That's more than likely how he ended up dead."

"That would imply Chef Droxon killed him," Roderick said. "But then, who would have killed Atherton?"

"Oooh." Wynona rubbed at her temples. "Every time I think I've got some kind of breakthrough, the facts end up muddled again. I'm still missing something."

Prim patted Wynona's head. "Don't worry," she encouraged. "It'll all get figured out soon, I'm sure."

"Meanwhile, I'm still a suspect and my shop is under quarantine," Wynona moaned, covering her face with her hands. She needed to snap out of it. This kind of behavior wasn't going to fix anything, but it was hard to stay positive when she felt like she was constantly chasing her tail. She decided then and there that if she ever made a career change, it would *not* include becoming a police officer.

Long, cool fingers gently took one of her hands and brought it down so he could cradle it between his own. "Chin up, Wynona," he said softly. His silver eyes should have looked cold, but somehow there was enough heat in them to warm her from the inside out. "Truth always wins," he said. "You are a remarkable woman and you haven't come this far only to come this far." He tilted his chin down a little and gave her that dazzling smile she was growing fond of. "Your ability to see and take care of the people around you attracts even the most cynical creatures to your side." He nodded toward Lusgu as he stomped by once more, the dustpan trailing in his wake.

Wynona had no idea how there was any dust left in the entire building, but the brownie obviously felt differently, since he never stopped cleaning. Ever. She gave Roderick a tremulous smile. "Thank you," she said. "That's very kind."

"It's the truth," he pressed. "From the moment I saw you, I knew you were special."

Her blush was starting to become a permanent accessory.

"I've seen you handle police accusations with aplomb and cranky suspects with elegance. You have a knack for seeing to the heart of a person, and no matter what day this shop opens, I have no doubt that every customer who enters these doors will leave feeling satisfied." He made a point of looking around at her shop. "The fact that you create custom teas tells us that you have a keen eye for detail, and I'm sure that will extend to each patron. Whether it's taking care of a patron with severe allergies or other unique issues, your care will keep them happy, but your kindness will have them coming back for more."

Prim's hand fluttered against her chest. "I do believe that's the sweetest thing I've ever heard," she gushed.

Wynona's blush flamed hotter than ever. "Thank you, Roderick," she whispered. "That means a lot to me. I mean it."

Roderick's smile could melt butter. "Anytime." He caressed her fingers, keeping eye contact until Wynona slowly pulled away, wanting yet not wanting to give the wrong impression.

She was thoroughly enjoying Roderick's attention and apparent admiration, but once again, the case stopped her from pursuing anything more. She needed it gone. Then, and only then, could she entertain the idea of a social life. With the way Roderick was looking at her, she just hoped it didn't take too long.

CHAPTER 18

"So what's the plan now?" Prim asked, settling back in her seat. Since she was among friends, she was in her fairy form and her head barely reached the top of the table, but Wynona didn't need to see her friend's face to hear the concern in her voice.

A loud grunt came from behind them and Wynona looked back to see Lusgu directing a duster along the top of the bookshelves. She couldn't tell if his grunt had to do with their conversation or his work. "Lusgu," she began, "would you like to come have a cup of tea?"

The brownie's shoulders hunched and he glared over his shoulder.

"I'm so grateful for how hard you work," Wynona said, trying to ease his obvious tension. "Perhaps you could take a break?"

"Take a break?" He snorted again and went back to directing the duster. "How can a body take a break when everything's so dirty?"

Wynona sighed and turned back to the table. "I tried," she said softly, shrugging.

Roderick was chuckling. "I think I can understand why the agency had a bit of trouble placing him."

Wynona couldn't help but crack a smile as well. "I suppose so, but everyone deserves a chance, don't they? Even if they're a little different than the norm." Those words were second only to her vow to be the opposite of her family's reputation.

Prim stood up and placed her elbows on the table, then cradled her chin in her hands. "Other than Mr. Handsome over here," she tilted her head to Roderick, "we're all sore thumbs." Her pink eyes gleamed. "I suppose that's why we all stick together so well."

Wynona laughed softly. "I suppose so," she responded. Her eyes darted to Roderick, who was studiously drinking tea and ignoring the fact that Prim had called him attractive.

"But that doesn't help us in this case," Prim continued, standing up straight. She whacked a child-sized fist on the table. "What are we going to do?"

Wynona pinched her lips together and shook her head. "I'm not sure. I feel like I need a new...plan of attack, as it were. I've run around asking questions and have only come out with more questions."

Roderick set down his teacup. "It's a possibility that we should let the police handle it," he said gently. His brows were slightly furrowed as if he worried about how Wynona would react to his words.

Despite his concerns, she wasn't upset at the suggestion. It had run through her own mind so many times it was ridiculous. She really had no idea what she was doing and part of her worried that if she kept going, she was going to get hurt or ruin something in the investigation.

But during those dark moments, she'd walk through her greenhouse or her shop and look at everything she had accomplished. Granny got her started, but it was Wynona who had grown all the plants at her little cottage home. It was Wynona who had stored dozens upon dozens of tea mixtures for her customers. It was Wynona who had renovated this shop into a cozy, welcoming place where acquaintances could become friends and friends could become family.

The thought of letting that all fall to the side, possibly to never rise again, made her ill. No...she'd come too far and fought too hard. This had to happen. Saffron's Tea House was going to be a hit, Wynona just knew it. She just needed to be able to open her doors in three days.

She gave Roderick an understanding smile. "I'm grateful for your concern," she said, "but I need to do this. I *need* this shop to open. Even though we've had some cancellations, I still have a lot of people counting on me to provide a unique experience they can't find anywhere else." She straightened in her seat. "I don't have any magic powers, but I do have good old fashioned ingenuity and a determination to succeed." She playfully stuck her chin in the air. "That'll have to be enough."

Prim buffed her fingernails on her sundress. "Plus, you have friends."

Wynona smiled. "Yes. I also have good friends. No one makes it far without that."

Preening, Prim drained her cup, then poofed into her human form. Dusting off the glitter that always accompanied her change, she stepped over to give Wynona a kiss on the cheek. "I can hear the daffodils crying for me," she said. "But don't forget to call if you need help."

Wynona waved her off. "I'll be fine. I just need to find that little detail I'm missing. I know it's there somewhere, lost in all the useless information I've gathered over the last couple of days."

Prim nodded, sent a wink to Roderick, then flounced out of the shop.

Both Wynona and Roderick watched her go, not moving until the door slammed shut behind her.

"Well..." Roderick slapped his knees and stood, adjusting his cufflinks. "I suppose that's my cue to go as well." He followed Prim's example and left a light kiss on Wynona's cheek.

A severe chattering came from where Violet was hiding under Wynona's chair. She spun, grateful for the chance to hide her blush. "I wonder what's wrong with Violet," she mused.

"Likely wanted to offer her support as well," Roderick said easily. He sauntered to the door. "Remember, I'm just a call away," he said, then pinned her with a hard look. "And please...be careful."

"I will," Wynona reassured him.

With a final nod, he too disappeared, leaving Wynona to her own thoughts. Violet had quieted down again, so she didn't bother to call out the creature. If there was trouble, Violet would let Wynona know.

Now that her friends had left, Wynona began to clean up from lunch. Her heart was still pounding from Roderick's kiss and declaration of his admiration, and she wasn't quite sure how to handle it. This had never been an issue when she lived with her family.

His interest was flattering, but the timing was terrible. "Why couldn't he have shown up when I wasn't being accused of murder?" Wynona grumbled. She carefully set the teacups in the sink, then headed back into the other room.

Violet stood on the edge of the table, her nose twitching rapidly.

Wynona smiled. "Feeling better?" She put her hand out and let the rodent climb on. Carefully, Wynona walked over to the bookcase and set Violet down on the ground. "Now that we're both full, I think we should take a nap, don't you?"

Violet stood on her hind legs and squeaked.

Wynona nodded as if she understood. "Yes...I don't have time for one either." She stood up and brushed off her pants. "I'll see you soon," she offered as the purple mouse disappeared under the shelves.

Back at the table, Wynona began to gather the tablecloth. It would need to be laundered before opening day. She paused. "If there is an opening day."

Despite Roderick's encouragement, Wynona still found herself feeling depressed. It felt as if her whole life had been on hold until Granny helped her escape, and now that she was away from her family, Wynona felt like a failure.

She plopped down in a seat, the tablecloth squished in her lap. "Three months is all it took, Granny," Wynona said to the empty room. "Three months for me to ruin everything."

She sighed in despair, her stomach feeling sick as she tucked a piece of hair behind her ear. Her ponytail just didn't seem capable of holding her thick head of hair, and right now it was driving her crazy. Everything was driving her crazy. Even the small sounds trickling in from the street were setting her nerves on edge. Self pity was settling on her like a blanket and it was smothering.

Where was the determination she had pulled on when Roderick suggested she leave things be? She should be feeling gung-ho right about now, with her friends all supporting her and wishing her well. Instead, Wynona found the voice of worry in the back of her head growing louder. Three days just wasn't much time. How in the world was she supposed to clear her name and open a business in a mere seventy-two hours?

"This isn't the way it was supposed to be," Wynona murmured to herself. How she wished she could talk to her granny. Granny would know exactly what to do in a situation like this. In fact, with as sharp as the older woman was, Wynona had no doubt that Saffron Le Doux would have had this case solved already.

The bell above her door tinkled and Wynona jerked upright. She wasn't expecting anyone and she wasn't open yet, so who in the world would be coming in? "Hello?" She set the tablecloth down in a wadded up ball and moved to the front entryway. "Hello....oh! Ms. Caseis."

The secretary stood in the doorway, her eyes darting around and her hands wringing against each other so hard Wynona could practically hear the woman's knuckles creaking.

"Can I help you?" Wynona asked, stepping a little closer.

"I..." Delila bit her lip. "I just thought..." She held out a hand. "I mean, you were so kind to me the other day and believed me when I said that I wasn't involved with Chef Droxon..."

Wynona frowned. "What is it, Ms. Caseis? What's wrong?"

The siren shook her head. "Delila, please."

"Alright," Wynona said carefully. "Delila. But that still doesn't explain why you're here."

Every time Wynona saw her, Delila looked ethereally beautiful. Her hair was pulled back in a low bun, but the hairdo only brought attention to her perfect features, letting her pouty lips take center stage, along with those large brown eyes. Eyes which were filled with tears at the moment.

Wynona tried very hard not to be jealous. She bet Delila never had to deal with unwanted blushes or having her face turn bright red in front of a handsome gentleman. The woman's tears, however, proved to be just the thing to help Wynona move past her own insecurities and jump into action.

"Why don't you have a seat," Wynona said, waving a hand at Delila, beckoning her into the dining room.

Delila nodded her thanks and followed Wynona to a table.

"Relax a moment and I'll grab you something to drink."

"You don't have to go to the trouble," Delila argued.

Wynona smiled kindly and put her hand on Delila's shoulder. "It's no trouble," she said softly. "This is what I do." Taking just a moment, Wynona studied the woman, letting the energies and emotions spill over her. Once she had settled on just the right mix of herbs, Wynona gave Delila one final pat, then headed to her cupboard. Luckily, she had everything she needed.

Tossing in three different herbs, Wynona quickly and efficiently filled an infuser with ginseng, sage and thyme. Her percolator whistled that it was ready and Wynona filled a cup, dunking the star-shaped infuser inside. "There now," she said, setting the cup and saucer down on the table in front of her guest. "Let that have three minutes and then it'll be ready."

Delila leaned down and took a long inhale. "Mmm...what is it?"

"Ginseng for clarity, sage for wisdom and thyme for courage," Wynona explained.

Delila's perfectly shaped eyebrows rose. "What made you pick those herbs?"

Wynona shrugged. "I don't know. It's just a knack I have."

"Is that part of your magical heritage?" The siren pulled the cup up closer for another sniff.

Wynona shook her head. "No, actually I..." She hesitated, but just as before, decided that in the end, it really didn't matter. "I don't have any magical powers."

The cup rattled on the saucer. "But I thought you were a Le Doux?"

If Wynona had a dime for every time someone said that... "I am," Wynona said patiently. "But I was cursed at birth."

"Oh my goodness, how awful," Delila gushed. "Do you know why? Or who did it? Don't you miss having magic?"

Wynona shrugged. "They never found the culprit, no one knows why, and you can't really miss something you've never had." Lament, yes. Miss, no. "But we're not here to talk about me." She smiled. "What brought you to my shop this afternoon?"

Delila stared at the cup for several long seconds. "I didn't know where else to turn." She looked up from under her lashes.

The look had probably brought many men to their knees at Delila's mercy. "For what?" Wynona pressed.

"I..." Delila paused yet again, to Wynona's frustration. "The police believe I killed Chef Droxon."

That's funny, Wynona wanted to say. *That makes two of us.* "How do you know they suspect you?" Wynona tilted her head, pushing that errant strand back yet again.

"Chief Ligurio is convinced that Chef Droxon and I were a...thing," Delila said, her eyes back on her lap. "How can I prove to him it's not true?"

Wynona made a face. She just couldn't keep up with the chief. His thought process was completely different from hers. "What do you gain by his death?" Wynona asked. "What do the police think your motive was?"

"They think I was after his recipes," Delila said with a delicate sniff.

"And why would they think that?" Wynona pressed. "Surely something had to give them the idea?"

Delila blinked rapidly, a few tears spilling down her cheeks. Her large, hazel eyes pinned Wynona in place. "Chef Droxon and I didn't always get along very well."

Wynona handed the woman a napkin, but otherwise waited.

"You see...even though we *weren't* a thing, it doesn't mean he didn't try."

"Ah." Wynona nodded. "Your work environment must have been a little difficult."

Delila nodded and dabbed at the corner of her eyes. "Oh, it was. He was very forceful sometimes, but the pay and benefits made it all worth it." Her eyes skittered away, like they had when Wynona had first met her, sending an immediate red flag up in Wynona's mind...again.

"Are you sure that's all it was?" Wynona asked, leaning back in what she hoped was a casual manner. "That's all the police have on you?"

Delila shook her head. "No. The real reason they're looking for me is because I lied."

CHAPTER 19

"You lied?" Wynona asked, her mouth gaping open. Before she could say anything more, the front door opened and loud voices infiltrated the entire shop.

"Delila Caseis!" a deep voice shouted. "We know you're in here!"

Delila stiffened, but made no attempt to flee. Wynona, however, jumped to her feet, not sure what was happening.

When Rascal's face appeared first around the corner from the front entry, Wynona blew out a breath and started to relax, but the look on his face said she should do otherwise.

"I'm sorry," he mouthed, the entryway behind him filling with officers. "Ms. Caseis?" Those golden eyes turned to Delila.

Delila's head hung down, and she didn't respond to his call.

"You're under arrest for the murder of Chef Atherton Droxon." Stepping to the side, Rascal allowed the men with him to come inside.

One of the officers grabbed Delila's upper arm and pulled her to her feet before turning her around and winding a glowing thread around her hands.

"Is that really necessary?" Wynona asked. She started to step forward, but a shake of Rascal's head had her backing up instead. Even without magic, it was clear to see the thread being used was enchanted, and Wynona worried it was painful.

None of this was right. Yes, Wynona had suspected that Delila was lying from the beginning, but deep down, she just didn't feel like the secretary had killed her boss, uncomfortable workplace or not. Taking the chef's recipes didn't seem like something the woman would do. What would she do with them? And what about the thief, Joksac? Even if the doppleganger had been in Chef Droxon's form, why would Delila have been at the tea shop? From the way the woman looked around when she first arrived, it was clear she had never been in the building before.

"They won't hurt her unless she tries to escape," Rascal said softly.

Wynona snapped her head in his direction. She had been so caught up in watching Delila's reluctant form that she hadn't heard the shifter approach. Or maybe his wolf side was simply that light on its feet. "What won't? The thread?"

He nodded. "It's an old hag hex," he explained. "As long as she cooperates, she'll be fine." For the first time since Wynona had met him, the twinkling humor was gone from Rascal's face. He looked weary and upset and Wynona felt a pang of concern mixed with pity. It must be hard to have a job where a person saw the worst in humanity at every turn.

"While I'm glad of that," Wynona whispered, "I think you have the wrong killer."

The other officers were now ushering the secretary out of the room. Those wide hazel eyes caught Wynona's before she was gone and Delila shook her head slightly.

No words needed to be exchanged for Wynona to know that Delila was saying she was innocent. Somehow the siren had known this was coming, but that didn't stop it from being wrong.

"She lied to us about her alibi," Rascal responded just as quietly, breaking the staredown between Wynona and Delila.

Wynona looked up, resting her hand on Rascal's arm. "That doesn't mean she killed him."

Rascal sighed and pushed a hand through his thick hair. Wynona found her fingertips itching to comb down the strands. There was something so appealing about a man's messy head, but the sensation was new to Wynona and slightly worrisome. All these new feelings and desires between Roderick and Rascal just reminded Wynona of how inexperienced she was with men.

A loud squeaking sound came from the bookcases and a purple streak darted across the floor. Wynona barely managed to keep herself from jumping when Violet climbed her pants and shirt, coming to rest on Wynona's shoulder.

The tiny creature nuzzled Wynona's neck, as if offering comfort, all while chattering in a soft tone.

Rascal grinned. "I'm glad to know you're not alone around here."

Wynona rolled her eyes. "I'm starting to feel like I'm *never* alone."

"Do you want to be?"

The question stopped her short. While peace and quiet were nice, Wynona knew that the chaotic life she was living with her friends was much better than the outcast lifestyle she had had with her family. She shook her head. "No. I shouldn't have complained."

He gave her a half grin. "You weren't, and I was just curious." His large hand came up, waiting in the air near her shoulder.

"Oh, she probably won't—" Wynona's eyes widened when Violet jumped from her shoulder to Rascal's outstretched hand.

Rascal chuckled, though the laugh still sounded tired. "I'd ask what happened to you, but the color looks good."

Violet stood on her hind legs and smoothed down her fur as if it were a fine dress.

Wynona's eyes widened. Somehow, her little mouse was not only acting a little too human, but it was *flirting* with Rascal.

Rascal caught Wynona's astonishment and gave her his usual wink. "It's the animal in me."

"But you're a predator," Wynona stammered.

"Maybe so, but she can see I'm not a threat." He looked back at Violet. "Can't you?"

Violet chittered and curled around herself until she lay in a small pile of fluff in his hand.

"Deputy Chief, sir?"

Rascal looked up.

"We've got the suspect in the car."

If Rascal was embarrassed at having been caught with a purple mouse in his hand and chatting with Wynona, he didn't show it, though his face did drop the humor from a moment ago. "Good work, Officer Heskill. I'll be there momentarily."

Wynona almost smiled at the official way Rascal spoke. He was normally so casual, but she bit back the temptation.

Carefully, he set Violet back on Wynona's shoulder. "Lucky mouse," he muttered with a soft smile.

Wynona's cheeks answered him immediately. She really was going to have to find a way to keep from blushing so often. Maybe another witch could make her a spell? "What are you going to do with Delila?" she asked, changing the subject and keeping herself from fangirling.

"She'll go through interrogation first," Rascal said, his smile gone once more.

Wynona mourned its loss. "And then what?"

He shrugged. "That'll depend on her. We have evidence that puts her at the scene of the crime."

Wynona didn't bother pointing out that Delila worked there, so evidence shouldn't have been hard to come by. "And her motive?"

Rascal rubbed the back of his head. "Look, I gotta go, but you're welcome to follow if you want."

Wynona pinched her lips. That was probably a good idea, but she hated being gone from the shop so much. She really should be here getting things ready.

"Wolves."

The darkly muttered word caused them both to turn. Lusgu was glaring at Rascal from the doorway to the kitchen.

"Lu!" Rascal said loudly, opening his arms wide. "Good to see you, buddy!"

Lusgu shook his head. "Messy, messy, messy." Spinning on his heel, he was gone before Wynona could say anything.

Rascal laughed. "One of these days, that brownie and I are going to be best friends."

Wynona rubbed her forehead. Why did it seem like everywhere she turned, she was out of her element?

Rascal stepped away. "You coming?" he asked.

Wynona sighed and nodded. "Yes. If only to talk to your chief about why Delila is innocent."

Rascal shrugged. "Good luck. Evidence is against her."

Wynona chose to take her scooter rather than ride in the police vehicle and they were all inside when she arrived.

"Hello, Officer Nightshade," Wynona said pleasantly. "How are you today?"

The vampire smiled, her white teeth gleaming in the fluorescent lighting of the office. "Good to see you again, Ms. Le Doux," she said pleasantly. "It appears that this time you have permission to be around." The officer shuffled some notes. "Deputy Chief Strongclaw said you were to be sent back, no questions asked."

Wynona felt her neck heat at the sly look Officer Nightshade gave her. "He brought in a friend of mine," she said, hedging the truth just a little. Delila wasn't exactly a friend, but acquaintance didn't have the same ring to it.

Officer Nightshade nodded. "They're at the end of the hall, last door on the right."

"Thank you." Wynona smiled as she walked away, but the pleasantness melted away as she drew closer to the interrogation room. If only she could figure out what she was missing. Delila had mentioned she had lied, but about what? Her alibi? Wynona had already suspected that.

But why lie? And to what extent did she lie? The idea of the secretary taking the recipes still didn't make any sense. And what about the will? What would Delila gain by taking the will? That was a family matter that had nothing to do with her. Plus, there was the fact that the siren had shown up at Wynona's tea shop. Again...why? What did Delila think Wynona could help her with? And why was she so insistent that she hadn't carried on any kind of a relationship with her boss?

Wynona paused with her hand on the doorknob, pulling in a deep breath and forcing her mind to calm. She wouldn't be any good to anyone if her thought processes were so chaotic she couldn't see straight.

She had a bunch of bits and pieces, but none of the reasons. Hopefully, if she listened to what was *and wasn't* being said, she could start to put tags on what she knew. Then they could figure out that key piece that was keeping them from solving the whole case.

"Knock, knock," Wynona said in her most polite tone as she pushed open the door.

"Wynona!" Delila cried, jumping up from her chair.

Rascal gave Wynona a welcome look, though the rest of the officers appeared confused by her presence.

She hurried over, grabbing a chair along the way, and sat down, pulling Delila with her. "Now...catch me up on what I missed."

"I told you they think I killed Atherton." Delila sniffled.

Three handkerchiefs were thrust in the siren's face.

"Thank you," she murmured, grabbing one without looking at the officer who was handing it to her. She wiped her eyes and nose.

Wynona glanced at Rascal, who was seated across the desk from them. When he gave her a subtle nod, she began to ask questions. "Delila, you told me you lied. Tell me what you lied about."

The siren blinked repeatedly. "I lied about my alibi. I wasn't at the office the night of the first murder."

"Where were you?" Wynona tilted her head, trying to meet the other woman's gaze, but Delila refused to give in.

She shook her head. "I can't."

"Can't or won't?" Rascal interrupted. He set out some papers on the desk. "Your security footage shows us the building was empty all night." He raised his eyebrows. "Ms. Caseis, we can't help you if you don't cooperate."

Delila dropped her hands to her lap in a huff. "Help? You're accusing me of murder! Why would I help you?"

"Delila," Wynona said, trying to bring down the tension in the room. "Why won't you tell us where you were?"

Mournful, but determined eyes met Wynona's and she had to blink a couple of times to keep from getting pulled in. No wonder men made such fools of themselves around sirens. "I wasn't at your tea shop," Delila whispered thickly. "I didn't even know the place existed yet." She looked pained. "I'm sorry."

Wynona shook her head. "That doesn't matter. Can't you tell us what you were doing?" A thought occurred to Wynona. "Or with whom?"

By the stiff set of Delila's shoulder, Wynona knew she had hit a nerve.

Her mind churned. Who would Delila have been spending time with? A family member? A boyfriend? The boyfriend seemed likely, but why hide it? Sirens were known for being attractive. It shouldn't have been a big deal for her to be in a relationship.

Unless the relationship was forbidden.

Saving the thought for another time, Wynona turned back to Rascal. "You said you have evidence against her. Her not being at the office isn't exactly condemning. Is there something else?"

Rascal sighed and nodded. "Yes." His eyes flickered between Wynona and Delila, as if he were sorry to have to bring it up. "A search of her home brought us this." He opened a drawer and set a small black binder on the desk, then pushed it closer to the women.

Delila gasped and Wynona's eyes widened. She'd seen that before. In the fat fingers of a baker who was trying to protect his legacy.

"I didn't take that," Delila cried, her voice shaking. She pointed at the object. "I don't know how that got in my apartment, but I didn't put it there."

Despite being fairly sure herself, Wynona had to ask. "Are you sure that's Chef Droxon's binder?"

Without speaking, Rascal opened up the small binder. Inside was a ripped page with what appeared to be a list of ingredients on it, only it was cut off before Wynona could tell exactly what all it contained.

"Delila," Wynona said breathlessly, shaking her head. "You've got to tell them the truth."

"The *truth* is that I didn't kill Atherton," Delila said through clenched teeth. "I didn't put that in my apartment. I'm being framed."

"Where were you?" Wynona asked more forcefully. She had a feeling that Delila's real alibi would reveal everything, but the woman was being exceedingly stubborn.

Before Delila could respond, the door to Rascal's office slammed open. "You," Chief Ligurio snarled, looking at Wynona. He crooked a slim, white finger. "Come with me." His eyes shifted to Rascal. "You too, Deputy Chief, if you value your job."

Without another word, the vampire turned and was gone, his footsteps a whisper in the noisy office.

Wynona pinched her lips together and gripped the arm rests on her chair to push herself into standing. She'd really stepped in it now.

Before she could get all the way up, a clammy hand gripped hers. Wynona looked down to see Delila holding her tightly. "I didn't do it," Delila pleaded one last time. "You have to believe me."

Holding back what felt like her millionth sigh, Wynona nodded and patted the siren's hand. "We'll get this figured out. Don't you worry."

"Ms. Le Doux?" Rascal waited by the door, his face drawn and serious.

Wynona clenched her fists as she walked past him, wishing to offer comfort, but not knowing what she could possibly say or do that would ease the situation.

Feeling like she was walking to her doom, Wynona forced her knees to stop trembling and her shoulders to stay straight. If she was going down, she was going to do it on her terms.

CHAPTER 20

"Have a seat, Ms. Le Doux." Chief Ligurio didn't even look at her as she entered his office, simply waved toward a hard metal chair across the desk from him.

Wynona glanced at Rascal, then moved forward.

He gave her a small smile, but both of them knew they needed to keep their distance at the moment. She had no desire to get the Deputy Chief in trouble and he was tied by the law.

While Rascal stood guard at the door, Wynona gingerly sat down. "How can I help you, Chief Ligurio?"

The vampire snorted. "How can you help me?" He set down the pen he'd been writing with and folded his hands across his desk. "I think the answer is you can *stop* trying to help me."

Wynona pasted a pleasant smile on her face. It was the same one she gave her family when they treated her horribly, but she didn't want them to know she was hurting. This case was bigger than just the police department. While it might be routine for them to solve cases similar to this, this was Wynona's life. Everything she and her granny had worked for. No one cared about what was going on more than she did, and she had learned over the years that if she didn't stand up for herself, few others would.

"I'm not trying to interfere," she began, but cut off when the chief snorted again. "Chief Ligurio..." Wynona leaned forward and rested her fingertips on the edge of the desk. "We both want the same thing here. To see a killer brought to justice. Why does it matter where your information comes from?"

His red eyes narrowed. "You look just—" Suddenly the police chief blinked, leaned back and cleared his throat. "It matters, because you're not authorized to do any of the things you're doing." He leaned in. "I know your family doesn't like to take 'no' for an answer, Ms. Le Doux, but in this case...you simply aren't wanted."

The words hurt more than they should have. He had been unwelcoming from the beginning and it shouldn't surprise her that the longer the investigation went on, the more he would protest her presence.

The chief had no way of knowing she had been unwanted her entire life and that those words pricked an old and still unhealed wound.

"Then I'll be sure not to get in your way," Wynona said, doing her best to hide the pain.

"You'll be sure to go home and let us handle this," Chief Ligurio said more forcefully. He pinned her in place with his gaze. "You're not a member of my force, you're not even a private investigator. You have no jurisdiction to do anything."

Wynona bit back a sharp response. His words were true. She didn't have any jurisdiction. All she had was a worry for her future and that wouldn't hold up in court for two seconds. "I understand," she said, careful not to actually promise to stay home.

The chief's eyes narrowed, but his door opened before he could say anything more.

"Chief?"

Wynona didn't recognize the officer standing in the doorway. He hadn't been at her shop or the Droxon office.

Chief Ligurio raised his eyebrows in response.

"The judge is playing golf with the DA and apparently, that can take three or four hours. His secretary said she'll show him the warrant for Ms. Caseis's office when he gets back."

Chief Ligurio scowled but nodded. "Make sure she knows it's top priority."

Wynona kept her eyes on her lap. She was taking in every word, but didn't want the chief to know that. Right now a plan was forming, but the only way she would manage to pull it off was if Chief Ligurio let her go.

"Hang on a minute," the chief said, rising and following the officer out into the hall. Their voices were muted by the door, but Wynona didn't need to hear any more. She knew enough.

"Don't even think about it," Rascal warned.

Wynona turned to him with her innocent face on. "What?"

His dark brows were furrowed. "I can see it in your face, Wynona. Let us handle this."

Wynona shrugged. "I haven't said a thing."

"You don't need to. Your face says it all."

Wynona made sure to wipe any and all emotion from her face. "No, it doesn't."

He leaned over, an amused grin on his face. "You can't hide from me," he said.

Wynona tilted her head to the side. "I beg to differ." Wynona knew full well she'd been hiding her emotions from others for her entire life. It had taken some practice, but she knew she was good at it. She'd have never survived the castle if she wasn't.

"And I don't beg."

Wynona's mouth pulled into a grin. She couldn't help it. "Is it true that wolves hate being compared to dogs?"

A low growl slipped from his lips, but Wynona wasn't afraid. Rascal had shown his hand too many times. She knew he wouldn't hurt her. "It's like calling a unicorn a pony," he explained. "One is vastly superior to the other."

"Maybe so, but which one?" she teased.

The slow, wonderfully boyish smile that crept across his face was almost more than Wynona could handle. "I've got just the way for you to find out."

How was it that she, who had zero experience with men, was now juggling two handsome gentlemen? Ones who were polar opposites of each other?

The door opened before any more flirting could occur, and the chief came back through, his face a thundercloud, accenting the dead, grey undertone to his skin. "It's time for you to go, Ms. Le Doux." He pointed at her, holding the door at his back. "But stay out of our way."

"Like I said," Wynona said quickly, "I understand." She stood and slipped out without looking at Rascal or the chief again. She was afraid of what Rascal's face would say, and she didn't want to give anything away to Chief Ligurio.

Careful to keep her walk casual, Wynona walked out of the office, nodding politely to everyone she made eye contact with. She didn't want any of them to have any reason to pull her aside and claim she was hiding anything.

Once outside, she got on her scooter and headed toward home. About halfway there, she pulled into a side alley and parked. Coming to the edge of the street, she searched, doing her best to ascertain whether or not the chief had put a tail on her.

When she didn't notice anything suspicious, Wynona jumped back on her scooter and went back the way she had come. Taking a side street, she worked her way deeper into the city until she made it to Runes Road.

Evening was here and many of the businesses were starting to close, flooding the streets with people and creatures of all kinds. It made it easy for Wynona to slip into the alley unnoticed since everybody was eager to get home.

Parking her scooter behind a dumpster, Wynona walked cautiously to the front door. Just as before, it was locked when she tried to pull on it.

"Shoot." She put her hands on her hips, glaring at the door be-fore immediately dropping them, and looked around. No one was paying any attention to her. She blew out a breath and walked back around the corner. There had to be an alternate entrance. Just as she left the front sidewalk, she heard a noise that had her turning back.

Peeking around the corner, she saw a minotaur emerging from the door. He raised his head after ducking through the opening. Straightening his work jacket, the half man/half bull created an auto-matic clearing of the sidewalk. He didn't even appear to notice how the crowd parted for his bulk, and the masses of creatures moved seamlessly around him as if they'd done it a thousand times before.

Wynona had to shake her head at the world she lived in. So dif-ferent from her isolated upbringing.

The glass door shut with a soft sucking sound, catching her atten-tion. She grinned. That was her ticket in.

Staying in the shadows, she waited another ten minutes before another employee came out. Wynona had to dive through the masses and almost didn't manage to grab the edge of the door before it closed. The tips of her fingers burned as she held it open. Blowing out a long breath, Wynona made sure the employee didn't notice her actions. The dark head that had come out was nowhere to be seen, so Wynona assumed she was in the clear.

Straightening, she regripped the door, pulled it open as if she be-longed and walked inside. A blast of cool air smacked her in the face and Wynona had to smooth down her mussed hair.

Her eyes immediately went to the elevators, noting they were both on the upper floors. There had to still be other employees com-ing down. Searching, she found a restroom in the corner that would make the perfect hiding place for the building to clear out.

Going inside, Wynona waited for a solid twenty minutes before venturing out again. She had just poked her head out when the ele-vator door dinged, and she pulled back inside with a soft squeak.

"That's it, Curce," a feminine voice called out. "I'm the last one down."

"Thanks, Eaden," a deeper voice replied. "The front door is already locked."

"See you tomorrow."

Wynona put her hand on her pounding heart, trying to slow it down. Apparently she had a night watch guard or custodian to deal with before she could accomplish her mission. She glanced at the clock on her phone. One minute, then two... Finally five more minutes passed and Wynona tried to look out again.

Only silence met her ears as she cautiously searched the lobby. When nothing worrisome occured, she headed to the door in the corner that indicated the stairwell. Walking ten flights didn't sound appealing, but neither did getting caught and having to face Chief Ligurio.

The stairwell was dark and eerily quiet, but it allowed Wynona to feel safe as she worked her way up. By the time she arrived on the tenth landing, her thighs were screaming bloody murder, her neck was drenched in sweat and Wynona knew she was going to be sore for days. "If I keep this up, I'm gonna need to start working out," she panted quietly to herself. It was a good thing she had no intention of solving any other cases. This was a one and done for her.

She slowly pushed open the door, once again straining for any sound that might indicate another person in the building. She relaxed only slightly when the floor appeared empty. Reminding herself that the guard could come do rounds at any moment, she scurried quickly through the darkness until she reached Delila's office and slipped inside to find her desk.

Wynona pulled up the flashlight feature on her phone and began looking through the secretary's papers.

The top of the desk was littered with everything under the sun and it was difficult to check thoroughly while still keeping things where they belonged.

After twenty minutes, Wynona plopped down in the seat and blew out a breath. This seemed hopeless. She wasn't even quite sure what she was looking for. Huffing, she began opening and closing drawers, starting in the top left, working her way down and then going to the right-hand side of the desk.

Nothing.

"Come on, come on," Wynona urged to the empty room. There had to be something here. Something that could prove Delila's innocence or at least hint at what the secretary had been doing the night of the first murder. If Delila was trying to protect someone, there must be proof of it somewhere, and the police had already checked her home.

Wynona was running out of ideas. She *needed* some kind of break in the case or her shop was doomed. Delila was going to be convicted of something she didn't do and the real killer was going to go free.

A manilla envelope caught Wynona's attention and she picked it up, not feeling particularly enthused about going through more receipts. She dumped the contents in her lap and slowed down.

It appeared to be bank transactions, but after looking through them, Wynona could tell the numbers didn't quite make sense.

"KAD," Wynona mused, noting the letters marked in red on the side of the transactions. "What is KAD?"

A few receipts fluttered about and Wynona grabbed one. It was for a month ago, for a cafe on the far side of town. Nothing important there. She grabbed another one. "Whoa..." Wynona's eyes widened at the amount on the receipt. Looking at the top, she nodded. The dinner had been at the fanciest restaurant in Hex Haven. Well, technically it wasn't in the city limits.

The Goddess's Table had been built inside an old Gothic castle up on Spell Summit, the largest mountain in the area. It was a place her family frequented, though Wynona had never been invited. Only the ultra wealthy or those trying to impress ate there, since their prices were closer to that of a small car than a normal dinner.

The receipt showed two entrees and at least two bottles of wine. "Maybe I should have been a secretary," Wynona grumbled. "Or just a siren."

She began to set the receipt to the side, along with her jealousy, when she paused. Down at the bottom, near the credit card information, was another set of numbers. Wynona sucked in a breath as her mind went on a frantic journey.

This was it. This was what she had been looking for.

Now to put the pieces together and figure out what it all meant.

Carefully putting the envelope back together, Wynona made sure the desk was exactly how it had started. Turning off the light from her phone, she slunk to the staircase, bracing herself for the painful walk downstairs.

Her heart began to speed up in anticipation and sweat broke out on her forehead before she'd barely started. Snorting at her own issues, she let out a muttered prayer to the gods that she'd make it to the street without having a heart attack. Delila and the tea shop were depending on her.

CHAPTER 21

The lights of the city were magnificent as Wynona breezed through the streets toward her cottage. Or at least, they would have been if she had noticed them at all. Instead, her mind was on other matters, leaving the bright neon signs and twinkling fairy lights behind.

Her stomach churned slightly and Wynona came back to herself enough to realize that she needed dinner. It was getting late and her early sandwich was long gone.

Finally paying attention to her surroundings, she began watching for somewhere she could get takeout. She really didn't feel like cooking, but she also didn't want to sit in a crowded restaurant when she was trying to piece everything together.

A greek cafe came into sight and Wynona pulled over. A fresh chicken gyro would be perfect right about now. The line was longer than she wanted, but she used the wait to write down everything she knew on the notes app of her phone.

"I can help who's next!" a perky voice broke through Wynona's concentration.

She smiled and walked up to the counter. "Hello," Wynona said. "I'd like a chicken gyro, please."

"Sure!" The young woman began to punch buttons on her register. Her ultra delicate features and the way her hands fluttered led Wynona to assume she was working with a bird shifter. After what seemed like far too many buttons for the amount that was ordered, the young woman looked up. "Would you like a salad or fries with that?"

"Uh...fries," Wynona said. Tonight wasn't a night to cut calories. She had a feeling she would need the energy.

"Would you like feta on your fries?"

"That'd be great, thank you," Wynona responded.

"What would you like to drink?" the girl chirped.

Good heavens, this was turning out to be much more intensive than Wynona had planned on. No wonder the line was so long. "Just water, please."

Another dozen buttons were pushed.

Wynona pulled out her credit card, but before the girl could give her the total, a plate was set in the window behind the front counter. "OPA!" a sprite screamed before turning around and flitting back into the kitchen.

Wynona froze when the entire staff returned the call. "OPA!"

The shifter helping Wynona grabbed the plate and the ticket attached. "Kevlun! Your moussaka with vegan beef and organic eggplant is ready!"

Wynona moved to the side when a gnome shoved his way past her thigh. He grunted as he climbed a set of steps next to the front counter and took the plate from the shifter, then made his way back down. Wynona made sure she was out of the way this time before the small man could push her again. She wanted food, not a stain on her clothes.

"Miss? Miss?"

Wynona spun. "Me?"

The shifter gave her an incredulous look. "You haven't paid yet."

"Sorry," Wynona murmured, handing over her credit card. One of these days, she would get used to the hustle and bustle of city life, but apparently, today was not that day. The more she experienced, the more she seemed to shake her head at what she saw. It was absolutely nothing like the television shows she had managed to sneak when no one was keeping track of her.

Once done paying, Wynona went to the far corner of the cafe, wanting to stay out of the way of the other patrons. She went back to work on her notes app to pass the time, and the twenty-minute wait went quickly.

"Thank you," Wynona said, after grabbing the bag of food.

"OPA!" the sprite screamed again.

"OPA!"

Wynona ducked her head and wound through the waiting crowd to get outside. Once in the night air, she filled her lungs and bent over to stop the claustrophobia pounding on the edge of her mind.

"I see you've experienced the joy of Greek legends during the dinner hour."

Wynona stiffened. Slowly, she stood, getting control of herself as she went. "Hello, Rascal."

He grinned at her. "Long time no see."

Wynona smiled, then sobered. "You didn't get in trouble, did you?" she asked softly. "Oof!" Someone ran into her from behind, knocking Wynona into Rascal's broad chest.

His arms came up to steady her. "Careful," he said, his voice softer than she'd ever heard before.

"Sorry." Pulling back was much harder than it should have been for a guy she was barely getting to know. He felt a little too strong and the feeling to lean in, letting him bear her weight, was enticing. Wynona straightened her shirt and made sure her food bag was still intact.

"What have you been up to this evening?"

Rascal's question could very well have been completely innocent, but it immediately set Wynona on edge. It wasn't like she could tell him that she had been breaking into Droxon's office building and trying to figure out what Delila wouldn't tell them. Her pulse sped up with her guilt and she crossed her fingers that he couldn't smell deceit. "Oh...this and that..." Wynona hedged. "What about you?"

She pushed back the desire to close her eyes and hang her head. He'd been booking an innocent woman all afternoon, that's what he'd been doing. Wynona already knew that. She was such an idiot.

He chuckled, shoving his hands in his front pockets. "Oh, this and that," he teased.

Wynona gave him a reluctant grin. "Sorry. I spoke before thinking."

He shrugged. "No biggie. We all do it." He took in a long breath, his eyes fluttering for just a second.

Wynona watched, fascinated. It had to be a shifter thing. She tried to discreetly take in her own sniff, but all she could smell was the usual mix of bodies and restaurants. It wasn't near as pleasant as he made it out to be.

Rascal rubbed the back of his neck, the moment growing slightly awkward between them. "So..." He nodded down at her bag. "You have dinner?"

Wynona followed his gaze. "Yep. Just picked it up." His words were kind of weird. Was he trying to get an invitation to eat with her? The idea would normally appeal to her, but right now she was too worried about him finding out about her earlier activities. She felt like a guilty child who was trying to hide that they'd been performing magic behind their mother's back.

Rascal had warned her to steer clear and Wynona had gone directly against those orders. There was no way she could admit that to him.

She nodded, shifting her weight from one side to the next. "It's probably getting cold," she said, holding up the bag for evidence. "I'm gonna head home."

"Right." Rascal stepped back a little. "Sorry. I shouldn't have kept you."

"No, no, it's fine," Wynona assured him, but it didn't matter. There was no saving this encounter. It was doomed to be weird.

"Okay, then..." She started walking toward her scooter. "I'll...see you later?"

Rascal's adorable grin broke out on his face. "Yeah. I'll see you later." He gave her a playful glare. "But not in the police station, right?"

Wynona did her best to smile naturally and held up her free hand. "Nope. Not in the police station." Unless she figured out what she thought she was going to figure out. Then she'd be in the police station again and Chief Ligurio would *not* be happy about it.

"Night," he called out as she got herself seated.

Her smile was real this time. "Goodnight." Her words were soft enough that she worried he wouldn't hear her, but the way his eyebrows and lips twitched let her know he'd heard and the gentle tone hadn't been missed either. Strapping on her helmet before her blush could hit her cheeks, she started the scooter and merged into traffic.

As much as she wanted to go home, the food was getting soggy and Wynona hated that. The shop was much closer than home, so she headed there instead. The shop normally felt warm and familiar, but ever since the murder, Wynona had been struggling to put the eeriness behind her.

She turned on every light in the front room and studiously ignored the hallway that still boasted bright yellow police tape.

Wynona had barely set up her dinner before Violet came rushing up her leg, squeaking in indignation.

"Sorry," Wynona said with a short laugh. "Did you want to join me?"

The purple mouse sniffed and gave a curt nod.

Their interactions were getting more and more human-like, but Wynona couldn't say she wasn't amused by it. "Let's open these up and we'll get settled."

She opened the Styrofoam, breathing in the wonderful scent of tzatziki and red onions. "So good." Her stomach rumbled in response. Picking out a few pieces of vegetable and chicken, Wynona made a pile of food for Violet and the two of them gorged until they were stuffed like a taxidermied unicorn.

Wynona patted her stomach. "Done?" she asked Violet.

Her companion chattered lazily and lay down, closing her eyes.

"I'm ready for bed, too," Wynona said. "But first I need to figure this out."

Violet's ears perked and she raised her head.

"I think I found something significant tonight," Wynona said.

Violet was on her feet in a flash, her nose twitching crazily.

"Okay..." Wynona pushed aside their dinner. "Here's what I've got." She folded her hands in front of her and leaned down closer to Violet's level. "The police have arrested Delila."

Violet chattered and shook her head, tiny hands waving wildly through the air.

"I know, I think she's innocent too."

Violet calmed and sat down, waiting.

"Rascal said they found Droxon's black binder in Delila's home." Wynona held up a finger. "But it could have been planted."

Violet's ears twitched.

"So I think that's circumstantial at best." Wynona tapped her lips. "Delila lied about her alibi, and I think tonight I figured out where she was."

Violet chirped.

"I found a restaurant receipt with two dinners on it." Wynona frowned. "Every receipt had two entrees," she said more quietly. "That means every time she went out, Delila had a companion." She focused on Violet again. "But who? She said it wasn't Chef Droxon, and I believe her."

Violet turned in a circle, lying down again.

"And all those bank statements. Something about them was off, and what in the world is KAD?" Wynona slumped in her seat. "Is there a bank named KAD? I've never heard of it."

Violet's tail twitched.

"No...it can't be a bank. The initials were hand written. If that was the name of the bank, it would have been printed on the statement." She paused. "Initials..." Wynona's eyes widened and she scrambled for her phone.

It only took a few moments to find the number for The Goddess's Table. The line rang twice while Wynona drummed her fingers against the table.

"The Goddess's Table, this is Ivaran speaking. How may I help you?"

"Hello," Wynona responded. "My name is Wynona Le Doux." Now was *definitely* the time to throw her name around. "I have a friend who dined at your fine establishment a few nights ago and I think she had a man with her."

"May I ask what this is about, Ms. Le Doux?" the voice responded cautiously.

"You see, my friend is being very secretive about her new boyfriend and I'm trying to win a bet by figuring out who it is." Wynona bit her lip and crossed her fingers. It was too bad she didn't have a four leaf clover at the moment. Luck was sometimes hard to come by.

"I see, and how may I help you?"

"Do you happen to remember a woman by the name of Delila Caseis?"

There was a pause and Wynona began to grow worried.

"She's a siren. Stunning, of course, with long red hair and bright hazel eyes?"

"Yes, Ms. Le Doux. Ms. Caseis was here just a couple of nights ago."

"Oh, good," Wynona said breathlessly. "Do you happen to know if she had a friend with her? A male friend?"

There was another pause.

"Hello, this is Adum Magmis, head manager of The Goddess's Table. How may I help you, Ms. Le Doux?"

Wynona held back a groan and settled with rolling her eyes. She explained her fictitious situation all over again, hoping against hope that they would cooperate.

"I'm not sure I should be giving out names..." the manager said, trailing off indecisively.

"Perhaps you could just describe him for me?" Wynona pressed, feeling like she was losing her chance. "In fact, I have a guess. Would you be willing to simply confirm if I'm right or not?"

"I believe that would be alright," the manager replied.

"Wonderful!" Wynona gushed. "I knew I could count on you."

"Anything for our presidential family," the man responded.

This conversation went against everything Wynona believed in, but she was growing desperate. Not to mention, Delila's freedom was at stake. "Did her companion have long, blond hair, blue eyes and a very regal bearing?" Wynona asked.

"I believe that would be a very accurate description," the manager said.

Wynona's smile was big enough to split her face. "I knew it!" she whispered loudly.

"Excuse me?"

"I said, that'll do it," she scrambled to reply. "Thank you so much for your wonderful help. I'll be sure to pass on how wonderful you all are."

"Any time, Ms Le Doux. We aim to serve."

Shutting off her phone, Wynona let out a barking laugh. "That's it," she said to Violet. "That's the clue we've been missing." Her eyes became unfocused as the pieces slowly fell into place. "Now the question is...how to prove it?"

CHAPTER 22

"**M**s. Le Doux," Officer Nightshade said with a wide smile. "You're becoming a regular around here."

Wynona smiled in return, but inside, her stomach was clenched. "Hello, Officer. And you're right. I've been around way too much lately. Hopefully life will go back to normal soon."

Wynona wasn't exactly sure what normal was, since she hadn't quite settled into a real routine before the murder hit, but she was excited for what she assumed her normal life would be, and it would not involve skulking around, trying to solve murders.

The officer shrugged. "I don't mind you coming." She leaned in as if imparting a secret. "I don't think Deputy Chief Strongclaw does either."

That stupid blush. Wynona tried to act as if the words hadn't made her feel warm all over. He probably was upset at her today anyway, after she brushed him off last night.

"But to be honest, I don't think the chief feels the same."

There was the splash of cold water Wynona needed to rid her cheeks of her flush. "Oh, I can assure you he does not," Wynona said with a sage nod. "Funny enough, he's the one I was coming to see."

Officer Nightshade shook her head. "Good luck. He's in his office and I don't think he's had his blood this morning."

Wynona gave the front desk officer a tight smile. This was not going to go over well. "Thank you. You've been very helpful." Some of Wynona's tension eased when the officer preened at the praise. Even a small compliment could go a long way.

Wynona nodded at a few people and smiled politely as she walked back to the chief's office. Her eyes flitted to Rascal's door, but

Wynona shook her head. She wasn't here to see him today, though she wanted his support. What she had to say needed to go through the chief and using Rascal as a buffer would only put him in an awkward position. That was the last thing Wynona wanted to do.

She knocked on the chief's door a little more timidly than she would like, but her shaking hands didn't allow anything stronger.

"Enter!" that deep voice growled.

"Here goes nothing," Wynona muttered as she turned the knob. "Good morning, Chief Ligurio."

His face contorted through several emotions, none of which were welcoming. "Ms. Le Doux. Just what do you think you're doing here?"

"Can I get you something to drink?" Wynona asked, waiting in the open doorway. "Have you had breakfast yet?" She studied him for a second, that calm feeling coming over her as she assessed his needs and formulated the perfect tea. She tapped her bottom lip while he sputtered in anger. "Passionflower for calm. Feverfew for the headache." She tilted her head and narrowed her eyes. "St. John's wort to help with the grumpiness and O-positive to help with your hunger."

The chief sat with his jaw hanging open, looking a far cry from the slick, predatory vampire he was. "How did you know I have a headache?"

Wynona walked inside and sat down in the chair across from the desk, crossing her legs the way her mother taught her. There were only a few things she had learned from Marcella Le Doux, but how to be ladylike was one of the more useful ones. "My grandmother, Saffron Le Doux, taught me all about herbs. It's why I built and named the tea shop in her honor."

Deep red eyes glared at her. "But how did you *know*?"

Wynona shrugged. "Lucky guess, I suppose. Anyone with a job as stressful as yours is bound to have one most days."

He huffed and leaned back with his arms folded over his chest. "What do you want, Ms. Le Doux?"

"Well, first I'd like to make you that tea if you have the ingredients?"

"An officer will bring my morning coffee in the next few minutes."

Wynona tsked her tongue. "Chief Ligurio, I don't think all that caffeine is going to be helpful."

"Caffeine is a headache reliever," he pointed out.

"And a caffeine addiction causes one," Wynona shot back. She relaxed even further when the edge of his mouth twitched. Maybe this wouldn't be so bad after all.

Clearing his throat, Chief Ligurio's scowl slipped back into place. "I'll ask one more time what you're doing here before I have you forcibly removed," he snapped.

Or not.

Wynona smiled and sat up straighter. "I want to talk about the case. I think I've figured something out."

Chief Ligurio groaned and rubbed his aching forehead. "Ms. Le Doux. What is it going to take to get you to leave this alone? We've found the culprit, and your name is off the suspect list, unfortunately. Now will you just let this go?"

"I can't," Wynona said firmly. "Because you have the wrong woman."

"We found the binder in her apartment!"

"Have you never experienced a case where someone plants evidence?" Wynona challenged. "How hard would it be to put that in her apartment? Don't you think that was just a little too convenient?"

"So you're saying we should let her go because it was easy to pin it on her?"

"Chief Ligurio," Wynona said softly. She leaned forward onto his desk. "Casting Delila as your killer doesn't make sense. Why would she kill the first man? The thief? She didn't even know my shop existed and it would have been easier for her to steal the recipes from the workplace than to kill for them clear across town." Wynona threw her hands in the air. "It just doesn't make sense! Surely you can see that?"

The chief grumbled under his breath and pushed a button on his phone. "Strongclaw! Get in here!"

Wynona bit her lip. What was Rascal going to say to her? Would he even want to talk to her at all?

"Yeah, Chief?" Rascal looked as bright-eyed and as handsome as ever as he stood in the doorway, his hand on the knob. His golden eyes snapped to hers. "Ms. Le Doux." A small grin played on his lips. "What brings you here this morning?"

"I'm trying to get your chief to listen to the information I found last night."

Rascal raised an eyebrow and folded his arms over his chest. "Was that before or after you grabbed dinner?"

Oops. She shouldn't have phrased it quite like that. "I just mean that I figured something out and I need the police to help me prove it."

Rascal looked to his boss. "Whattya say, chief?"

"I say I want you to get this woman out of my office and never let her back in."

Rascal made a face, looking torn. "Is that really necessary, Chief? Shouldn't we hear what she has to say?"

The chief put his palms on his desk and slowly started to rise. "No. I don't want to hear what she has to say. I want her gone and I want you to make sure she *stays* gone. She has no business—"

"Your coffee, Chief." An officer Wynona didn't recognize stepped around Rascal, holding a steaming mug. He carefully set it on the desk and straightened. It took him a moment to realize he'd interrupted something and soon he slowly began to back out. "Uh, anything else you need?"

Red eyes did their best to glare holes in the officer's forehead.

"No? Alrighty, then, I guess I'll just get back to work." The officer jabbed a thumb over his shoulder, then darted into the hallway.

"You really shouldn't scare him like that," Wynona said in a slightly scolding tone. "It's not good for morale and it's not good for that headache."

Chief Ligurio opened his mouth and pointed a finger in her direction before snapping his mouth shut and shaking his head. "Get her out of here, Strongclaw. Or it's your neck on the line."

Rascal sighed and walked over. "I'm sorry, Wynona. But you need to go."

She pursed her lips and clung to the side of her chair. "You have to listen to me," she demanded. "This is important. You've got the wrong killer!"

"Wynona," Rascal urged.

"No." She stuck her chin in the air. "I won't let you take down Delila just because you found some circumstantial evidence."

"Oooh." Chief Ligurio made a face. "Learning the lingo, are you? Planning to make a habit of being a pest?"

"Chief," Rascal groaned.

Wynona leaned forward. "I know where Delila was the night of the first murder."

Chief Ligurio huffed and leaned back in his seat. "And just where do you think she was?"

Wynona gave him a triumphant grin. "She was at The Goddess's Table." A little pause for added drama. "With a date."

Chief Ligurio eyed her while picking up his mug and drinking half of its contents. "And just how do you know this?" he asked.

"I had a hunch and followed it." Wynona waved at his phone. "Feel free to call them. They'll confirm exactly what I just told you."

Still looking like he was drinking rancid blood, Chief Ligurio shoved the phone at Rascal. "Strongclaw!"

Rascal muttered under his breath, but grabbed the receiver and punched a button. "Hey, Amaris? Can you find the number for The Goddess's Table?" He nodded. "Yeah, that one. No, I don't want a reservation, I prefer to stay out of debt, thank you very much." His eyes drifted toward Wynona when she snorted. "Uh-huh...thanks." Rascal kept his eyes on her while holding a button and setting down the ear piece.

"The Goddess's Table. How may I help you?"

"Hello, this is Deputy Chief Strongclaw of the Hex Haven police," Rascal said in an official tone. "We're calling about a suspect who might have visited your establishment a couple nights ago. One Delila Caseis. Can you please see if you can find her on your reservation list?"

"One moment, please."

The same manager who had helped Wynona came on the line. "Hello, Officer Strongclaw. What can I do for you today?"

Rascal repeated his request and then they were on hold, elevator music tinkling through the line while they waited for the manager to come back.

"Yes, sir. I found her four nights ago. She was here for an eight o'clock reservation."

"And was she with a companion?"

"She was," the manager hedged.

"Who was it?" Rascal pressed.

Wynona grinned, pleased with the fact that the police were having trouble as well. At least she had figured out a sneaky way around the man's reticence.

The manager hesitated. "I'm afraid that—"

"Sir, this is an official investigation and could be a matter of life or death. I assure you that anything you tell me will be kept in trust and will not be traced back to you."

"I understand," the manager said in a resigned tone.

Wynona wanted to roll her eyes. What she wouldn't give to have been able to use that authoritative line. It would definitely have made life so much easier.

"She was eating with Mr. Kayne Droxon."

The words landed in the room with all the finesse of a baby dragon. Both Rascal and Chief Ligurio were dumbfounded as they stared wide-eyed at each other and then at Wynona.

She tried to hold back her gloating, she really did, but for just a split second, it felt *really* good to know that she had been one step ahead of the game. "Now do you believe me?" she whispered, noting that the phone line was still open.

"Deputy Chief Strongclaw?" the manager asked. "Was there anything else you needed, sir?"

Rascal quickly said his thanks and goodbyes and hung up the phone. Leaning back against the desk, he folded his arms over his chest. "Mind letting us know just how you figured that out?"

Wynona did her best to shrug nonchalantly. "Just a hunch, but it panned out."

Rascal narrowed his eyes. "A hunch, huh?"

She opened her eyes wide and did her best to look innocent. "Look, Deputy Chief Strongclaw. It really doesn't matter how I came across my information. The point is, she was with someone else. Which means she didn't kill Mr. Skinflayer. And if she didn't kill Mr. Skinflayer in search of the binder, why would she have killed Chef Droxon?"

"It's possible we have two murderers on our hands," Chief Ligurio said with a slight pout in his tone.

Why was it that when men didn't get their way, they often reverted back to little boys? Wynona held back a small laugh. "It is," she said carefully, "but I don't think that's the case."

"Another hunch?" Rascal asked.

She grinned at him. "You could say that."

Rascal's eyes flashed with pride and Wynona wanted to soak it in. She'd had too little of that in her life.

"Alright, Ms. Le Doux," Chief Ligurio said in a tired tone. "Just who do you think did the murders?"

Wynona shook her head. "I'll admit I don't have that one figured out yet. But I do think I can help with the missing will."

"They're two different cases?" Rascal inserted.

Wynona nodded. "I believe they are."

Chief Ligurio took a long swig of his forgotten coffee, then made a face. Obviously, it wasn't hot anymore. "I can't promise to believe you, but I'm willing to listen."

"Good enough," Wynona said eagerly. She leaned forward. "This is what I propose."

CHAPTER 23

Wynona's heart was pounding in her throat as she walked casually across the road to the front entrance of an apartment building. From the outside, it looked like any other highrise. Built with steel and glass, the collection of residences appeared to be for the business class folks. Which immediately gave Wynona a confidence boost. She was almost positive her idea was correct, especially if a secretary could live in a place like this.

"Wynona Le Doux to visit Delila Caseis," Wynona said politely to the doorman.

The man looked at her with startled eyes. "Le Doux?" He looked her up and down and frowned, obviously noting that she didn't appear as lush as the rest of her family.

"Yes, Le Doux," Wynona said more forcefully. "My father is President Le Doux."

The doorman continued to frown. "How come I've never heard of you?"

Wynona decided now was not the time to spill the fact that her family had kept her a secret because of her curse, not when she was on a mission. "Would you care to call my mother, Marcella?" Wynona pulled out her phone. "Or, perhaps, Celia instead?" Wynona's smile was far from warm at this point. "I'd offer to let you call Granny Saffron, but she passed a few months ago. Did you know?"

The man, who looked like a normal human, branding him as a possible warlock, folded his arms over his chest. Wynona couldn't help but swallow hard. If he decided to use powers on her, she was toast. Although, a warlock working as a doorman meant he wasn't very good, but still... "Everyone knows who the Le Doux family is," he said condescendingly. "Doesn't make you related."

Wynona sighed. She didn't want to do this, but needed to get inside. She dialed her sister's phone.

"This is Ms. Celia Le Doux's personal line. How may I help you?"

Wynona wanted to dance a jig. How lucky was she that Celia's personal assistant had answered, rather than having to deal with Celia herself?

"Hello, Airian," Wynona said in a perky tone. "It's Wynona. Is my sister around?"

There was a pause and a shuffling sound on the other end. Wynona held the phone up so the doorman could hear. "Just one moment, Ms. Le Doux. Let me see if she's receiving calls."

The doorman rolled his eyes and pushed a button. "Come on," he said.

"Never mind, Airian, it sounds like she's busy. I'll chat with her another time."

"Is that my sister?" A screech could be heard in the background and Wynona's eyes opened wide as she realized Celia had obviously entered the room. "What does she need? A handout?" she asked with a snicker.

Wynona hung up and stuffed the phone in her purse, ignoring the buzzing that resulted when Celia tried to call her back. "Thank you," she said to the smirking doorman. It had been too much to hope that he hadn't heard that last comment.

Once inside, Wynona realized she didn't know what floor she was going to, but she wasn't about to go back out and ask the doorman. Even magicless witches had pride. Instead, she headed toward the elevator. Hopefully another resident could help her along the way.

The elevator dinged and a well dressed gentleman stepped out, adjusting his cufflinks.

"Excuse me, sir. Could you, oh!" Wynona broke out in a smile, then immediately panicked. This was definitely not according to the plan.

"Wynona," Roderick said warmly. His smile was as bright as ever. "What brings you here?" Stepping closer, he leaned and gave her another cheek kiss. "Are you here to see me?"

Wynona shook her head. "No, actually. I had no idea you lived here."

Roderick looked slightly disappointed, but he hid it fairly well. "I'll pretend that didn't hurt my ego," he teased. "Do you have another friend in the building?"

That was just the opening she needed. "Yes! I was told that Delila Caseis lives here."

Roderick frowned. "The siren arrested for the murders? Yes, but isn't she at the station?"

Wynona shook her head. "They received some new evidence and had to let her go."

Roderick's frown grew and his eyes went toward the ceiling as if he could see her through the floors. "I see..."

"You wouldn't happen to know what apartment she's in, would you?"

Roderick immediately came back to himself and focused his silver eyes on Wynona. "I didn't realize you two were such good friends."

"Oh, we're not, but I have a few questions for her," Wynona said easily. "You know, trying to solve the murder so I can clear my name and open the shop." She scrunched her nose. "I've only got two days left."

Roderick nodded sadly. "If I didn't have to head to work, I would help, but alas..." He held his arms wide. "I'm afraid business waits for no man."

"It's fine," Wynona assured him. "Go do what you need to do." She gave him a grin. "But letting me know Delila's apartment number would be an easy way to prove what you just said."

Roderick chuckled. "Thirteen A, if I remember correctly." He gave her another quick kiss, this time on the top of her head. "Good luck. I must go."

Wynona barely noticed that he left as she rushed to catch the elevator. How grateful she was that this time she would *not* be walking the stairs. She was certain her thighs and tush would never be the same.

Soft music played as she rode up, but it did nothing to soften Wynona's nerves. She had come here today to run a con and it was wreaking havoc with her emotions. After another hour of persuasion, Chief Ligurio and Rascal had reluctantly agreed to her plan. The problem was, Wynona had never done any acting in her life, unless she counted pretending not to care that her family hated her.

She practically jumped out of her skin when the elevator door opened to the thirteenth floor, and Wynona walked on wooden legs out into the hallway. Glancing at the doors, she turned to the left, finding apartment A immediately.

"Send help, Granny," she muttered to herself. Wishing for the millionth time that she had powers to help protect herself beyond the Banshee Scream in her purse, Wynona raised her hand and knocked.

She fidgeted with her shirt hem and straightened her skirt, hoping she looked professional but approachable.

"Who is it?"

Wynona frowned. The voice sounded hesitant and it worried her. "Delila? It's Wynona. Wynona Le Doux?"

More noises came from the apartment for several seconds before the door cracked open. "Oh, Wynona!" Delila gushed. She opened the door all the way and reached out to pull Wynona into a surpris-

ingly tight hug. "I don't know how you did it, but thank you for getting me out!"

Wynona pulled back. "How did you know it was me?"

Delila smirked and walked over to the couch. "Who else could
it have been? I have no family and you're the only person I spoke to
who actually listened to what I said."

Wynona sat across from the beautiful siren. Delila was dressed
casually today, more than likely only having been home for an hour
or two, but it didn't matter. The woman was still gorgeous. "Delila, I
need to ask you some questions."

Delila huffed in disbelief. "More? What in the world could I offer that I haven't already confessed?"

"How about the truth about where you were when the first murder occurred?"

Delila's plush lips pinched and turned white.

Wynona tilted her head. "Was the salmon good?" she pressed.
"Or perhaps you had the filet mignon? I've heard that it's especially
tasty."

Delila's face drained of color and she sunk into her seat. "How
did you know?" she rasped.

Wynona shook her head. "I followed a hunch." Wynona dropped
the other woman's gaze for a moment, struggling to come up with
the courage to say what needed to come next. Taking a deep breath,
she looked up. "Perhaps Kayne would like to join us for this next
part."

Before Delila could respond, Kayne burst from the bedroom.
"Don't say a word, Delila," he snapped. "Having dinner together isn't
a big deal, especially not with Dad dead."

Wynona's heart hurt. She knew exactly what it was like to break
free of a parent's prejudiced expectations. Even if hers were still alive,
they had little say in her life at the moment. "When did you first start
embezzling from him?"

Delila gasped and brought her hands over her mouth. "Kayne," she squeaked.

Kayne's blue eyes were glued to Wynona, as if daring her to say more. "She's just guessing, Dee. Stay quiet."

And here was where it was going to get tricky. Wynona knew she wasn't the world's best liar, but she needed to convince Kayne she was. "You do realize that with Delila cleared, the police will be looking for a new suspect?" she asked coolly. "How do you think it's going to look when they find the bank records in Delila's desk? Or the receipts of your dates that she's been writing off as business expenses?"

Kayne stiffened even further if that were possible. "I didn't kill my father," he said tightly.

"He didn't!" Delila cried. "He's innocent! He was with me!"

"Quiet, Dee!" he shouted. "They can't pin anything on me. We'll get a lawyer before we say any more."

Wynona shook her head. "The police are investigating now," she said, slowly rising to her feet. "If you're innocent, doesn't cooperating look better than fighting?" Wynona fought to keep her knees steady and her voice from breaking. A single drop of sweat trickled down her spine, tickling and distracting her from her mission. "You've been using Delila's position to suck him dry for years." Wynona stepped forward even though she wanted to step back. "When did he first tell you you were cut off? It wasn't when it leaked to the press. The records go back way before then."

Another step.

"With your father out of the way, you were free to be with the woman you loved," Wynona continued, keeping her voice low and steady. "The woman your father thought beneath you. Her powers weren't enough, were they? He wanted someone like your mother. Someone who could bring wealth and prestige to the table instead of just good looks."

Kayne's face was growing a dangerous shade of purple, while Delila muffled her sobs on the couch, curled into herself like a young child.

"Perhaps you killed him in self defense," Wynona argued.

"NO!" Kayne shouted.

"Did you fight at lunch over how he was treating your mother? Or maybe you fought over money, for the thousandth time," Wynona's voice grew quieter with each word. "Is that when you threw the hex on him? Did he say something about Delila you didn't like?"

Delila shot to her feet. "He didn't do it! He couldn't have! I met them for lunch and we were having dinner the night of the first murder!"

"Stop, Dee," Kayne pleaded. "You have to stop. Nobody can know we're dating."

"I won't let you go to jail for murder," Delila said through her tears. "Not when I can stop it. I don't care what the public thinks...or your mother."

Ooohh, Wynona hadn't figured out that Maeve also disapproved. But she supposed it made sense. Elves saw themselves as vastly superior to every creature except a few. A siren wouldn't have been enough for the son and heir of the Droxon empire.

"He didn't do it." Delila turned her attention to Wynona. "I'll swear to it and I can offer witnesses at the restaurants. We took the money, but only because it should have rightfully been his! He was Chef Droxon's heir! The money was his!"

"That won't be necessary," Wynona said, backing up now. "I know he didn't kill his father, or Mr. Skinflayer."

Delila's mouth flopped open. "But you just said..."

Wynona nodded and wiped at her damp forehead. "I know. But I needed you to confess about the embezzlement."

Kayne's lips curled slightly. "Well done, Ms. Le Doux. I can't say I'm happy with the results, but I can't fault your persistence. When we met, you didn't strike me as the type of woman who gave up easily."

"Not when it means gaining justice," Wynona said sadly. She didn't like having to turn these two in, but what they'd done was wrong and it needed to stop. She might not have caught a murderer yet, but at least she'd helped solve one crime. For the moment, it would be enough.

A banging came on the door and Wynona finally allowed herself to breathe deeply.

"Open up! It's the police!"

Wynona kept an eye on the couple while she opened the door, then stood out of the way as the room flooded with blue uniforms.

"Are you okay?" Rascal stopped at her side, his eyes roaming her face.

Wynona nodded. "Fine. My heart just ran a marathon, but the rest of me is okay."

Rascal chuckled. "A burst of adrenaline is good for the system," he teased.

"Speak for yourself," Wynona shot back. "I think I took ten years off my life due to fear."

Rascal's smile grew. "Pity. That's a lot of time to deprive people of your company." Giving her a quick wink, he followed his officers as they cuffed Delila and Kayne and led them out of the apartment.

Tea. Wynona needed tea. And a chance to look through what was left of the clues. With the embezzling out of the way, hopefully what was left would make more sense and they could have this whole case wrapped up sooner rather than later.

CHAPTER 24

"Mint...chamomile...ashwagandha..." Wynona handed the individual teas to her guests. "And one lavender cookie." She grinned when she set the plate down for Violet, who squeaked in delight. "You're welcome," Wynona said with a laugh.

"I didn't know you could bake," Prim said as she tested the temperature of her tea.

Wynona shrugged. "I'll never be Chef Droxon, but I spent a lot of time in the kitchens growing up. Sometimes I was with Granny and sometimes I was with the cooking staff." She smoothed her skirt and sat down. "You pick up things. Plus, I'll probably have to do my own baking at first, until I can find another professional."

Prim crossed one long leg over the other before reaching for a cookie from the middle plate. "Mm...not bad," she said around her mouthful of dessert.

Wynona smiled her thanks, then passed a napkin to her friend.

Prim rolled her eyes, but accepted the suggestion with good grace. She patted her mouth. "So finish telling us the story."

"Yes." Roderick came into the conversation. "How exactly did you figure out that Kayne and Delila were embezzling funds?"

Her blush skittered up her neck. "I may or may not have seen it inside Delila's desk."

"You were looking through her desk?" Prim whispered loudly. "Nona! Did the police know?"

Wynona shook her head, her fingers resting against the warmth of her tea cup. She had retrieved one of Granny Saffron's cups today, needing to feel close to the one family member who loved her. Wynona had gone way outside her comfort zone today. It might have been for a good cause, but that didn't mean it hadn't taken its toll on her. "I didn't tell them," she responded to Prim. "Though it took careful wording to keep from admitting it."

Roderick chuckled as he set his cup down. "I can only imagine." He leaned forward a little. "While I'm proud of what you managed to accomplish, I'm concerned that this is getting too dangerous for you. You've removed a couple of thieves, which leaves only the murderer. Such a creature wouldn't hesitate to hurt someone as delicate as yourself, Wynona."

Prim sighed as stared longingly at Roderick. "You say the sweetest things, Mr Caligari."

He smirked just slightly and took another sip of tea. "It can't be helped when I'm trying to protect such lovely ladies as you two."

Before Prim could melt into a puddle of goo at Roderick's feet, Wynona changed the subject. "Thank you for your concern, Roderick, but I'll be alright." She hoped. "Now...the question is, what to do next?" She took a sip of the slightly floral tea, closing her eyes as the flavors danced on her tongue. Granny had taught her to always take a moment to savor the flavor. She claimed the herbs always did their job better when you gave them a little recognition.

"That's a good question," Prim mused, breaking into Wynona's moment. "With Delila and Kayne out of the running, who are the leftover suspects?"

Wynona slumped. "Me," she muttered. "And Mrs. Droxon, who had an alibi with her butler, if you recall."

Prim pressed her light pink lips together and squished them to the side. "Well, we know you didn't do it and if Mrs. Droxon didn't do it...then it seems like we must be missing something."

"I agree...but what?" Wynona asked, her frustration bleeding into her tone. "Or maybe the question is who? Who have we overlooked?"

Prim shook her head. "I don't know."

Roderick tapped his finger on the table. "The object was to steal the binder, so perhaps we need to turn our attention to Atherton's competitors."

Wynona paused. "That's actually a really good idea," she said, slightly distracted as her mind began to churn. "But wait." She put her palms on the table and leaned in. "That doesn't explain why Mr. Skinflayer was killed in my shop." She shook her head with a frown. "Actually, that doesn't make sense at all. Why was Mr. Skinflayer here? Was he meeting someone? Who? And why my shop? Especially after almost being caught here earlier, why return to the scene of the crime?" She gave Violet another cookie. "He knew Chef Droxon wasn't here, so what did he hope to gain? Ahh!" Wynona pressed her clenched fists to her temples. "It makes no sense! We have to be overlooking something."

Large, cool hands landed on her shoulders and began to work the tight muscles. "Take it easy," Roderick said in a low tone, very close to Wynona's ear.

A shiver ran down her spine from his touch and words. She kept her eyes closed and hung her head, letting him work a little magic on her back. She could practically feel the sparks transferring from his fingers to her body.

After a minute, his massage became a little less helpful and more...carressive. "Better?" he whispered.

Wynona nodded. "Thank you," she said in a slightly hoarse tone. Straightening, she gave him the signal that it was time for him to let go, which he took with his usual aplomb.

Roderick sat down with grace, his silver eyes still fixated on her.

"I'm sorry," she said with a sheepish smile. "I didn't mean to have a breakdown."

Roderick shrugged. "I think it's completely understandable under the circumstances."

"Oh yes," Prim said quickly, nodding her head too fast. "You're supposed to open in only two days and we still haven't found the killer! I can't imagine how you're feeling." She frowned. "Not to mention, you just put two people behind bars this morning."

Wynona wanted to groan again, but she fought the sensation. Prim meant well, but sometimes her rants weren't helpful. Instead, Wynona nodded. "Thanks. I appreciate you two...a lot."

Violet squeaked in outrage and ran up Wynona arm, nuzzling just under her ear.

Wynona laughed softly and gave her new friend a pat. "And you, Vi. I'm grateful for you as well."

A regal nod followed Wynona's recognition and Violet promptly settled into a tight ball, a nap obviously next on the agenda.

"And that's my cue," Prim said, bouncing to her feet.

Sometimes Wynona was jealous of her friend's energy. It had to be a fairy thing.

"I'll check in with you soon," Prim said, giving her usual kiss goodbye before hurrying out the door.

Roderick watched Wynona for a moment longer before sighing. "You sure you won't let this go?" He leaned forward, taking her hand in his. "I'm worried about you."

Wynona let the warm feeling of his concern wash over her. "I'll be fine," she said. "But I need to see this through."

Roderick nodded reluctantly. "I suppose I understand, but it doesn't mean I won't keep checking in."

"I'll look forward to it," Wynona replied.

He stood, took her hand and gave it a squeeze before leaving.

Wynona sat, watching the room entrance as if he was going to come back and help solve all her problems. What would that be like? Her friends were wonderful, but they all had their own lives and she was mostly on her own as she worked on this case.

Flashing golden eyes of a man who had helped her more than once came to mind and Wynona had a flash of shame. She felt like some kind of floozy for the fact that she enjoyed both men's attention. While she hadn't done much to encourage either of them, she also hadn't done anything to dissuade them.

Wynona shook her head. "So ridiculous," she scolded herself, gathering all the tea cups and saucers together. "Neither of them has done anything but flirt. There's nothing wrong with enjoying that." She huffed. "If only I could get a little more information rather than attention. Maybe it would help me break this mystery." What she wouldn't give for just a small portion of Granny's powers right about now.

Carefully, she stood and prepared to take the dishes to the kitchen when the cups began to rattle.

"What?" Wynona blinked rapidly and stepped back slightly. A tiny pressure on her neck had Wynona glancing down to see Violet standing on her hind legs, eyes focused on the table. "Are you doing this?" Wynona whispered, noting that the cups were all starting to rise into the air.

Violet blinked black eyes up at Wynona and shook her head.

"Whoa!" Wynona stepped back, her heart starting to race. The three cups stayed in the air and then began to spin. "What is this?" She searched the room, wondering if someone was playing a prank on her, but Wynona didn't see anyone or anything.

One cup broke free from the spinning group and slowly floated her way.

Wynona leaned back, afraid someone had hexed her dishes and touching them would spread it to her. The cup, itself, waited patiently in the air, as if understanding her reticence. "Lusgu?" she called out over her shoulder, keeping her eyes on the cup. "Lusgu, are you here?"

The brownie didn't respond to her call, but Wynona knew that didn't mean he wasn't around. He had magic. Could he be doing this? But why? Was it some bizarre way of trying to clean up?

The cup shook slightly, as if urging her to take it.

"Lusgu?" Wynona called out one more time. Still nothing. She glanced down at Violet. "What do you think?"

Violet chattered and waved at the cup.

"You think I should take it?"

Violet nodded quickly, clasping her paws together.

Wynona pinched her lips together. "Okay, but if I end up in the hospital, I'm blaming you."

If a mouse could roll their eyes, Wynona was fairly certain Violet had just done so.

Taking a deep breath, Wynona reached out and gingerly grasped the cup. She squeezed her eyes shut, waiting for the spell to hit her, but nothing happened. Well, nothing except that the other cups lowered themselves to the table and the one Wynona was touching stopped holding itself up.

She cautiously brought the cup closer, studying it for clues as to its weird behavior. "What in the world just—" Her eyes became glued to the tea dregs and Wynona found herself transported back to Granny's greenhouse.

Remember, Wynona...the tea always knows.

Granny would tap the end of her nose and smile.

The longer Wynona stared at the dregs, the less she became aware of her surroundings. The room disappeared and every worry that had been running through her head dissolved as if they had never existed to begin with. She felt as if she had been sucked into space and that nothing else was real.

Hidden.

The word boomed in her mind, after Wynona recognized the shape in the bottom left corner.

Dark.

Underground.

Murder.

After the last word rang through her head, Wynona stumbled backward and blinked until she came back to the present. Her chest was heaving and she struggled to catch her breath. The cup was quickly set down on the table and Wynona stepped backward several feet. "What was that?" she gasped, looking at Violet.

Violet looked unperturbed as she stared at Wynona with her nose twitching in anticipation.

The words that she had heard came back to Wynona and she sat down in the closest seat, her legs feeling weak. "Hidden. Dark..." Wynona struggled to remember the other two. "Underground, I think." She paused before saying the last one. It wasn't like saying a word was bad, but the feeling behind the voice when it said the last word had made Wynona feel dirty. "Murder," she whispered. "What could it mean, Vi? Hidden and dark and underground. That makes it sound like it's beneath the city."

She stiffened.

No. It couldn't be. Could it?

Her heart rate, which had been starting to slow down, sped right back up. "Vi...do you think it was talking about the paranormal underworld? Do you think the tea reading was literal?"

Wynona shook her head and rubbed her aching forehead. "What am I talking about? I can't read tea leaves. I have no magic."

Violet chittered viciously until Wynona held up her hand.

"Okay, I get it. Whether I have magic or not, something just happened and I was able to read those leaves." She slumped, feeling like she had been hit by a rock troll. "Do you think it had to do with the case?"

Violet sniffed.

"And the words were literal?"

Violet sneezed.

Wynona cursed, then immediately apologized. "Sorry, Vi. I shouldn't have said that."

Violet nuzzled her neck.

"Thanks," Wynona said softly. "But if the underground has something to do with these murders, I'm not sure even your kisses are going to fix it." Wynona swallowed hard. "I'm not sure anything is going to fix it. Because this situation just went from dangerous to deadly."

CHAPTER 25

Coming back to Rascal's apartment was more than likely a little reckless, but Wynona needed to speak to someone about what she had learned. She couldn't tell anyone about the tea reading. First of all...who would believe her? She had no magic, everyone knew that. But also, the experience had been more than bizarre, even for a tea reading. It had almost been like a vision or premonition.

It had left Wynona with a lot of questions, but it had also left her a little frightened. She had been nervous about stepping outside her comfort zone for a lot of this investigation, but this...this was something different.

If the mob was involved in this case, then Wynona wasn't just in over her head, she was as good as dead.

Even in her tiny bubble in the castle, Wynona had heard whispers about the underground. Like all black markets, there were a couple of bigwigs who ruled particular sections and fought for more power within their world. Like bickering gangs, only much more violent.

At times their world would infiltrate the normal side of Hex Haven, but always in hushed whispers. Most people turned a blind eye to the goings-on in the underground, afraid that if they voiced an opinion, the boogie man would come for them...literally.

Wynona knocked on Rascal's door, even though she wanted to pound and demand that he let her in. She was frightened and desperate for safety, but this wasn't how she was going to get it.

She hadn't escaped thirty years of abuse just to bury her head in the sand and look for someone to take care of her. No. She pushed back her shoulders and forced a confidence she didn't feel. She hadn't come for protection. She'd come for advice. Surely as a police officer, Rascal would have more knowledge into what Wynona was looking at.

The door cracked open, then immediately swung wide. "Wynona!" he hissed. Grabbing her hand, he pulled her inside.

Wynona frowned and looked down at the paw that was holding onto her. Within a few seconds the fur and claws had retracted and only his large, warm hand remained.

Rascal pulled back, looking slightly sheepish. "Sorry. Never startle a wolf late at night."

She made a face. "Is it really that late?" Wynona hadn't paid any attention to the time when she'd headed over. Yes, it had been dark, but her mind had been on what she'd just learned and how that affected the case. Her time was running out and if she needed to work all night, she would. Problem was, she forgot she couldn't expect the same of everyone else.

Rascal ran a hand through his hair, which was messier than normal, and glanced at the wall clock.

Wynona winced when she noticed the time. "Sorry. I was caught up in my thoughts and didn't realize how late it was."

Rascal sighed. "It's fine. You're just lucky Mrs. Reyna down the hall didn't see you first." He began walking toward the kitchen. "Coffee?"

"No, thank you," Wynona said softly. She gripped her purse with both hands. "Was that the woman who glared at me when I visited the other day?"

Rascal chuckled. "If that's all she did, then she must like you."

Wynona settled herself on a barstool while Rascal brewed himself a cup of joe. "Actually, I think it was you she liked. I saw her smiling at you like you'd hung the moon."

Rascal snorted. "I unclogged her sink. That only bought me about ten minutes of good will." He turned his head and grinned at Wynona. "I was back to being Rascal by the end of the day."

Wynona laughed softly. "Nice to know cranky old ladies are the same no matter which species we're talking about."

"That they are." He turned, resting his hips against the counter, and sipped his coffee. "So...what did you figure out now?"

Wynona sighed. "I didn't exactly figure something out, but I have some questions for you." She pinched her lips. "I really am sorry about the time. I've been so worried about how little time I have left that I just keep going, but it wasn't fair to ask the same of you."

Rascal shrugged. "It's all part of the job. I've pulled more all-nighters than a group of college kids studying for finals. Go ahead."

Wynona took a deep breath. She needed to handle this carefully. Rascal had the power to stop her from investigating any more and she couldn't take that. Not when the grand opening was so close. "Have you ever dealt with...the unsavory side of Hex Haven?"

His eyebrows shot up. "Doesn't every cop?"

"Yes, I suppose so," Wynona murmured. This was a bad idea. She shouldn't have come. How was she supposed to get him to tell her more without tipping him off to her suspicions?

"Wynona," Rascal said in a tender tone.

"Hm?" She looked up and jolted a little when she realized how close he was. Maybe it was his bigger than life personality, or his thick muscles, but the distance of the countertop seemed awfully small at the moment.

"What is it?" he asked in a low tone.

She hesitated, then blurted out, "What can you tell me about the underground mobs?"

Rascal stilled, his mug halfway to his mouth. "Have you been threatened?" he asked. This time his tone was menacing, with a slight growl on the edges.

Wynona held back a shiver. She definitely didn't want to get on his bad side. "No, no threats."

"But?"

"But what if the murders have something to do with...them?"

Rascal set down his mug and leaned onto the counter. "Explain."

She dropped his gaze, unable to keep staring at those bright golden orbs without feeling things she shouldn't. This wasn't a social call and they didn't have that kind of relationship. "I was going over suspects this afternoon after you took in Delila and Kayne." Wynona peeked up from under her lashes. "And the list is short."

He nodded. "You and Mrs. Droxon, essentially."

Wynona huffed. "Yes. Neither of which are good suspects."

Rascal grinned. "Because...?"

Wynona tilted her head and gave him a stern look. "Because I know I didn't do it, and Maeve doesn't have a good motive. She literally gains nothing by her husband's death."

Rascal scratched his chin. "Good points. But what made you think of the mob?"

Wynona spread her hands sideways. "Who else? I keep going back to the fact that Mr. Skinflayer was trying to steal Chef Droxon's binder. He managed to get away, but why come back to my office for it? There was no practical purpose for it. Unless..."

"Unless what?" Rascal pressed.

"Unless he was meeting someone," Wynona said softly. "And my shop just happened to be neutral territory."

"So you don't think he was killed because he was mistaken for Droxon?" Rascal frowned.

Wynona shook her head. "No, I don't." She leaned forward. "I think the killer knew exactly who they were killing."

"But why the chef's clothes?" Rascal asked. "Why be dressed like Droxon if he wasn't pretending to be him?"

Wynona tapped the countertop. "I'm not quite sure yet. But what if it was simply to throw us off? Perhaps the killer was trying to build a false lead."

Rascal shook his head and straightened, then whistled low under his breath. "This is quite the conspiracy theory, Wy."

She raised her eyebrows. "Wy?"

He grinned unapologetically. "I like nicknames."

"Prim calls me Nona. You could call me that."

He shook his head. "No thanks. I like Wy."

Wynona rolled her eyes. "Whatever. But still. Maybe we've been looking at this all wrong."

"It's possible." Rascal yawned, his incisors flashing in the light as just a little sharper than a normal person's. He scratched the back of his head. "But I'm not sure how that works in the long run. Why lead us directly to Droxon, only to kill Droxon? A killer wouldn't want the police roaming around their next hit."

Wynona slumped in her seat. "I can't answer that one."

Rascal tapped the counter with his palm a few times. "I think maybe we need to sleep on this. You've brought up some good points, but it'll take some time to figure it all out."

Wynona rose to her feet, understanding the dismissal, but she was frustrated she hadn't really learned anything. "Can't you tell me anything about the underground?" she asked as she walked toward the door.

"Stay away from them," Rascal said in an unusually serious tone. "That's all you need to know."

She huffed. "That's not very helpful. If they killed someone in my shop, how am I supposed to stay away?"

"Are you worried we can't keep you safe?" Rascal teased.

"Your chief wants me behind bars," Wynona said wryly. "It probably doesn't get much safer than that."

"Actually, I think you surprised him today," Rascal mused.

Wynona beamed. "Really?"

The wolf put his hands in the air. "Don't get me wrong. I'm pretty sure he's not ready to sing songs by the campfire, but when your name was mentioned today, he didn't break into his usual tirade of how horrible witches are."

Wynona dramatically wiped her forehead. "Good to know I'm making headway."

"You planning to become besties with him?" Rascal chuckled.

"Oh no," Wynona sang out. "I'm just hoping to survive this without him biting me."

One eyebrow rose ever so slowly. "Biting isn't all bad, you know..."

Aaaaand, there was that dang flush again. So she wouldn't embarrass herself further, Wynona squeaked out a goodbye and practically dove into the hallway. She could still hear Rascal's soft laughter behind her as she walked out to the street and her scooter.

She secured her purse and sat down, strapping on her helmet before glancing up at the area Rascal's apartment should have been. When she didn't see him looking through the window, she took a second to fan the heat on her cheeks. "Good heavens," she whispered to the night. "If the mob doesn't kill me, dealing with flirty men just might."

CHAPTER 26

Normally Wynona hated to make a single pot of tea and share it with everyone. It felt so impersonal and didn't allow her to cater to individual needs. This morning, however, it was all she could bring herself to do.

Every time she poured a cup for her friends from the pot, she wanted to apologize, but the grumpy, sleep-deprived side of her grumbled internally that she didn't owe anyone an apology. Trying to come to a happy medium between the two voices, Wynona smiled pleasantly and distributed the cups. "Hope you like ginger lemon," she said.

"Nothing like a little citrus in the morning," Prim said.

"This is wonderful, thank you," Roderick replied with a sly smile in her direction.

Wynona relaxed a little. After waking up this morning, she had automatically called her friends and asked them to come over. She had learned very little from Rascal last night, but the more Wynona thought about it, the more she was sure she was on the right track. "As much as I'd like to say this is supposed to be a social visit, I'm afraid I have an ulterior motive."

Prim giggled. "I think we both knew that, Nona."

Wynona gave her friend a sheepish grin. "When this is all over, I promise I'll host a tea party just for your sweet company."

Prim pointed a purple nail at Wynona. "I'll hold you to that." She set her cup down. "Now. What's going on?" Her brows furrowed. "You're supposed to open tomorrow. Is there no chance of it happening?"

Wynona immediately felt a migraine begin to build in the back of her head. Twenty-four hours. She had twenty-four hours to figure this out or the label *murderer* would continue to hang over her head and her opening would be ruined. "I haven't given up yet," she assured Prim.

"What can I do?" Roderick asked. He glanced over his shoulder. "Have the police cleared the crime scene?"

Wynona nodded. "Yes. My concern no longer lies with that, but the fact that customers are going to be terrified to show up. I'm down to about fifty percent of the bookings I had."

"Aw, sweetie," Prim cooed. "This is so ridiculous! Anyone who knows you knows you couldn't hurt a sprite!"

Wynona nodded wearily. "Thanks, Prim. But right now I just need this case over and done. Then hopefully word will get out I'm innocent and the opening can continue as planned."

"Right." Prim straightened in her seat. "What's new with the case?"

"A theory."

Roderick slowly set his cup down. "A theory? Nothing more concrete?"

Wynona debated telling them about the tea reading, but just like with Rascal, she couldn't quite bring herself to do it. If the impossible had happened and Wynona had actually performed magic, the worst thing in the world would be for her family to catch wind of it, and if others besides her knew, they would definitely hear about it.

Instead, she shook her head. "No, sorry. Just a theory."

"Well...go ahead." Prim's eyes were wide in anticipation while she sipped her steaming brew.

Violet's squeak broke the silence and she scrambled up Wynona's leg. "Sorry," Wynona said softly. "I wasn't trying to exclude you."

Violet's eyes seemed to narrow and she chattered in an angry tone.

"If I didn't know any better, I'd think you're getting scolded from a mouse," Prim said between laughter.

"I think you're right," Wynona responded with a chuckle of her own. "Here." She picked up a strawberry from the fruit tray and handed it to Violet. "Better?"

Violet sniffed and took her bounty a little farther down the table, much to Wynona's amusement.

"Now that the mouse is settled..." Roderick urged.

Wynona's demeanor grew serious. "I think it's possible that we've been looking at the first murder all wrong," she said solemnly. "And I think it's possible our would-be thief, Mr. Skinflayer, had ties to the paranormal underground."

Prim choked and began coughing harshly, while Roderick's blond brows shot up so high, Wynona was sure they would reach his hairline. "The mob?" he asked carefully. "Are you sure, Wynona?"

After making sure Prim was breathing and well, Wynona responded with a nod. "I do."

"And how did you come to that conclusion?" Roderick leaned casually back in his seat, but Wynona could see that every muscle in his body was wound tighter than a sprite on a sugar high. He was reacting just like Rascal had, and the protective demeanors of both men were incredibly flattering to her.

"Hear me out," Wynona said, leaning forward. "What if the killer wasn't after Chef Droxon at all? What if they knew they were killing Joksac Skinflayer?"

Prim squeaked. "What would that mean for the case?"

"It would mean that someone was upset with Mr. Skinflayer," Roderick said with a narrowed gaze. His fingers strummed rhythmically on the table. "But who? And why?"

"Mr. Skinflayer had been attempting to steal Chef Droxon's binder of recipes," Wynona continued. "Perhaps he wasn't stealing them for himself, but for someone else."

"Someone who killed him when his mission failed," Roderick finished for her. He nodded slowly. "That is an excellent deduction, Wynona."

"But then why kill Chef Droxon?" Prim inserted. Her lips were pursed. "If all they wanted was the binder, why did they kill the chef?"

"Perhaps they were caught in the act?" Roderick proposed. "The thief ended up killing out of self preservation?"

Wynona shook her head. "No...there had to be more to it than that. Chef Droxon was killed in the middle of the day. Why would a thief, more than likely a seasoned one, kill a person in broad daylight?"

"And wasn't the doppleganger dressed like Chef Droxon?" Prim offered. "Why would he be in the chef's clothes?"

Wynona scrunched up her nose. "I have to admit that I haven't figured it all out yet. But I feel like I'm closer." She rubbed her temples. "But there's something I'm still missing. I'm positive that if I can find that one little clue, it'll all fall into place."

"Wynona," Roderick said in a firm tone, catching her attention. "I don't think you should continue this pursuit." He held up a hand to stop her rebuttal. "I know you want to open tomorrow. I know how much work you've put into this shop and how much it means to you. I do. I understand, but just yesterday we were talking about the possibility of you chasing a clumsy, blind thief. Now we're looking at the possibility of Hex Haven's most notorious and evil criminals." He shook his head slowly. "I cannot in good conscience allow you to continue. Not when it's so dangerous." He reached out and put his hand over hers.

The coolness of his skin was so different from Rascal's heat, yet both were soothing in their own way. Wynona gave him an understanding smile. "Thank you for your concern," she said softly. "As someone who has never had much in the way of friends, I can't tell

you how much it means to me. But I just don't think I can let this go."
She pulled away from his touch and splayed her hands to the side.
"I can't open with the word *killer* hanging over me. I know I didn't
murder anyone. You two—" Wynona glanced at Violet, "three know
I didn't kill anyone. Even Deputy Chief Strongclaw knows I didn't
kill anyone, but my customers don't. They were putting their trust in
me before they ever met me, and now it's coming back to bite them
on the ankle."

She sighed and pinched the bridge of her nose. "They deserve to
come in here and relax, not worry for their lives." She snorted. "If
anyone even has the courage to come." She actually had an appointment later that afternoon with a celebrity who was planning a private
tea party. So far, the cat shifter hadn't cancelled, but Wynona was on
edge with the possibility that every text she received would be exactly that.

With so many people backing out, a good review from Ms. Akina Kimoko would go a long way in restoring Saffron's Tea House reputation in the media.

Roderick sighed. "It isn't safe," he argued.

"It wasn't safe before," Wynona responded, though she understood his concern. They were talking about a whole new level of danger with her recent evidence.

"Promise me you'll be careful," Prim whispered, her white hands
clasped tightly. "I know we haven't been friends that long, but I don't
know what I'd do without you."

If Wynona's eyes grew a little misty, no one could blame her. She
had so few people she counted as friends. It was a new experience to
have people worried about her, and Wynona hoped she never took it
for granted. She stood and walked over to Prim with her arms out.

Prim jumped to her feet and wrapped Wynona in a tight hug.
For as thin as the fairy was, she sure had a tight grip. "Please be careful," Prim whispered thickly.

Wynona nodded against her friend's shoulder. "I will."

Prim pulled back, stared into Wynona's eyes, then added, "Okay. I believe you." She glanced at the wall clock. "But if I'm going to have all your arrangements ready for tomorrow, I have to flit."

Wynona smiled and wiped at the corner of her eye. "Thanks for coming this morning."

"I know I've been useless in this case," Prim said. "But I really am willing to help if possible."

"There isn't anything you can do," Wynona reassured Prim. "I've mostly been chasing shadows."

"Sometimes what's lurking in the shadows is hidden for a reason." The stoic words came from Roderick, who still looked less than pleased with Wynona's decision.

Knowing she would need to face him directly, Wynona saw Prim to the door first. This was a talk that more than likely required privacy.

He was still brooding in his seat when Wynona came back into the room. She sat down across from him and put her chin high. "Just say it, Roderick."

At her declaration, the stiffness of his shoulders relaxed. "What *can* I say?" he said, his tone softer than she'd expected. "You seem to have made up your mind."

Wynona relaxed a little, grateful this wasn't going to be a shouting match. "I have," she said carefully. "But I always want to hear what my friends have to say."

One side of his mouth pulled up. "Friends? Is that all we are?"

Well, that came out of nowhere. Wynona had no idea how to answer. She clasped her suddenly trembling hands in front of her. Yes, she found him attractive. Yes, she was drawn in by his confidence and suave manner, but she hadn't been willing to let herself entertain the thought of anything more with the case and the opening of her business hanging over her head.

Plus, none of that took into account that she felt all those same things for Rascal.

Roderick's chuckle sounded anything but amused and he started to stand from his chair. "I suppose that answers that question."

Wynona jumped to her feet. "Please understand," she begged. "It's not that...I mean, I'm..." Each time she tried to confess her thoughts and feelings, the words failed her. What could she say? She just wasn't ready, yet at the same time, she didn't want to lose him completely.

Tilting his head, Roderick gave her a considering look. When he moved, it was with the sleekness of a lion. He exuded power and strength, a man who knew exactly what he wanted and planned to take it.

His touch, however, was much gentler than his aura as he stopped just shy of her and cradled her cheek in his hand. Slowly, as if asking permission, he leaned forward and left the lightest of kisses at the edge of her mouth.

Wynona's heart fluttered so wildly, she was sure it would leave her chest completely. How could such a small touch elicit such strong emotions? Wynona locked her knees to keep them from giving out and wished for yet the millionth time that she had the power to control the temperature in the room. Apparently her thermostat was in severe need of work.

"I can be patient," he said, staying so close to her mouth that the breath of his words washed over her skin, leaving goosebumps in its wake.

She had no words for him. All she could do at the moment was *feel*.

Several seconds later, she fluttered open her eyes, only to discover he was gone. The sound of the door clicking shut let her know he had left the building, leaving Wynona a mess of tingles and anticipation.

Slowly, she sank to her seat and put a trembling hand to her throat.

Violet caught Wynona's attention when the tiny creature huffed and chittered angrily.

"What am I going to do, Vi?" Wynona asked, her eyes stuck on the room entrance. "How do I choose?"

Violet grumbled and smoothed down her fur.

Wynona had no idea what the mouse was saying, but she was definitely upset. "No ideas?"

Violet snorted.

Wynona shrugged. "I suppose that makes two of us." She shook her head. "But again, I can't do this now. The case needs to come first." She glanced at the clock. "Oh my gosh! Ms. Kimoko is going to be here in just a few minutes. I have to hurry."

Gathering up the tea set, Wynona began to haul everything back to the kitchen area. She nearly ran over Lusgu as she went through the swinging door.

"Run me over," Lusgu grumbled, waving his hand at a sink of sudsy dishes. "Snake in the grass."

Wynona paused and frowned. "Is something wrong, Lusgu?"

The brownie shook his head. "Can't see it. Can't see it at all. Dirty, dirty, dirty."

Wynona glanced at the tray of dishes. "I'm sorry to keep making such a mess. I can wash these if you want."

The tray lifted from her hands and floated smoothly to the sink area.

Sighing, Wynona went to the cupboard in order to prepare another pot for her coming guest. Lusgu was always muttering about one thing or another, though his favorite line seemed to be about wolves. Most of the time, Wynona had no idea what he was talking about. Perhaps when things settled down, she would be able to take the time to really get to know her employee.

If she even had need of an employee after this.

CHAPTER 27

"Welcome, Ms. Kimoko," Wynona said with a broad smile. "Please, come in."

The star wore a headwrap and large sunglasses, as if that could hide her glamorous looks and the svelt way she walked. The limo that pulled away from the curb was another dead giveaway that this was no ordinary client.

The cat shifter walked in and took off her glasses. "It's so quaint in here," she purred. "Just right for curling up with a hot tea and a good book."

"That's exactly what I was going for," Wynona responded, clasping her hands in front of her. "Please. Come to the dining area and we'll discuss your upcoming tea party."

Wynona tried to ignore the bodyguard that followed them through the shop, but it was difficult. Trolls weren't known for being small and Wynona was positive that he could snap her in half without breaking a sweat.

She settled Ms. Kimoko at the table closest to the back window where the sunlight could filter in. "I have several teas for you to try," Wynona said, settling the mugs in front of her guest. "Or, if you wish, I can customize something for you and each of your guests."

"How long does it take for a custom brew?" Ms. Kimoko said in the alto tone she was known for, her eyes flitting across the mugs.

"It takes me just a few seconds for each person," Wynona said, sitting down across from the star. "I then have to mix the herbs and brew it, so depending on the amount of guests, it can take up to a half hour."

Ms. Kimoko pursed her bright red lips. "That might be acceptable if we had other things to occupy our time. Such as appetizers or finger foods?"

Wynona nodded. "Yes. We have a variety of pastries and sandwiches that can be ready for any number of guests." Oh, how she lamented the loss of Chef Droxon in that moment. Being able to add his name to the mix would have been so helpful and certainly clench the deal, but Wynona would have to settle for another baker.

Truth be told, she wasn't quite sure who that would be yet, since she'd been too busy running around after killers and thieves. But she was confident she could find someone quickly. She would have to begin by doing it herself, then hire a baker as soon as she could find the time.

"Excellent," Ms. Kimono said silkily. She reached for the first cup and took a deep sniff. Her eyes flared. "Is that cat thyme?"

Wynona nodded, pleased her concoction had worked. "Yes. Each tea in front of you has an herb that should appeal to your feline side. It all just depends on what type of stimulant you are looking for." She hoped her idea would pay off. Each of the herbs had been difficult to come by and the cat thyme in particular smelled like rancid gym socks. Working with the leaves of it nearly had Wynona passing out, so she crossed her fingers under the table that Ms. Kimoko didn't feel the same.

After taking a tentative sip, the shifter purred. "Oooh...what is that other flavor?"

"Mint," Wynona supplied. "I tempered each stimulant with something soothing so you didn't come away feeling drugged at the end of our meeting."

"Puurrrrfect." The actress quickly tested all the other teas, her pleased rumbling growing with each sip. After the last one, which was laced with cat mint and chamomile, she closed her eyes and hung her head back in apparent euphoria. "Ms. Le Doux..." Yellow eyes met Wynona. "I do believe you and I have a contract."

Wynona held in the sigh of relief. "I'm thrilled to hear that, Ms Kimoko."

"Please, call me Akina." Small, delicate fingers came across the table to tap Wynona's hand. "I feel that you and I will be seeing much of each other as long as you offer teas such as these."

Wynona could only smile. After so much trouble with the case and the subsequent cancellations, she was finally seeing a glimmer of hope. She pulled the binder with her calendar in it in front of her and opened it up. "I still have the questionnaire you filled out," Wynona said. "Is there anything on here that you would like to change?"

She turned the paperwork to face her guest and Akina looked it over. A gentle blush came over the woman's cheeks and Wynona grew jealous. Why did she get to have such a beautiful blush when Wynona felt like she looked sunburnt at every turn?

"All of it is correct," Akina said, leaning in and dropping her voice. "But I need to speak to you about my... allergy."

"Ah, yes." Wynona leaned in as well. "You mentioned in the comments section that you wished for this to be a secret. I promise anything you tell me is strictly confidential. How can I set this up so you can feel safe and comfortable?"

Akina preened slightly and pushed her satiny hair behind her shoulder. "I assume your tea service includes the usual add-ins, such as sugar and cream?"

Wynona nodded. "Of course. Just as with anything, I can also do a customization, if necessary."

"I am...lactose intolerant," Akina said carefully. "As a cat shifter, and someone who spends much of their life in the public eye, I assume you can see why I would wish to keep such a thing quiet."

Wynona nodded again. As one of the paranormal world's most famous actresses, Akina would need to appear perfect, especially since she was sponsored by companies who sold products that she would be allergic to. If word got out, it would put a big dent in the star's career. "How about this?" Wynona scribbled on the page, her mind churning quickly. "I can have a separate tea caddy for you with your own miniature pitcher of milk." She raised her eyebrows. "Do you prefer almond or coconut milk?"

"Mmm...coconut," Akina cooed. "I believe it would go well with the cat mint."

Wynona grinned. "I think you're correct. So, we keep your set separate, but I can have multiple other small sets around that look similar, but contain the normal cream. As the hostess, we'll set it all up so you don't have to share and I doubt anyone will even notice. Your secret will stay safe."

Akina leaned back casually in her chair. "You do your family credit, Ms. Le Doux. Your sister Celia and I don't always see eye to eye, so I'm pleased to see that we understand each other."

Wynona wanted to cringe. In other words, Celia wasn't willing to cater to the actress's wants. Both women were in the headlines enough to be famous in their own right, which meant they more than likely clashed when together. Since Wynona didn't want to be in the limelight, she was definitely not a threat.

"Despite all that," Akina waved her perfectly manicured hand through the air, "I knew with the president's daughter opening a tea shop, I needed to be a part of it. Your name can only bring publicity, Ms. Le Doux." Her smile was purely calculated. "And I do love publicity."

Wynona acknowledged her guest's words without giving into the desire to walk out of the room. She couldn't admit it right now. She needed Akina more than Akina needed her. This contract just might be Wynona's saving grace.

"I'm glad we got this all figured out." Wynona made a few notes on the contract, then turned it around for her guest to sign. "I'll send you a list of the menu as soon as I have your guest list and you can tweak it as necessary."

"Good." Akina snapped her finger at the troll bodyguard, who rushed over to pull out her chair, allowing her to rise like a selkie emerging from the sea.

"Allow me to walk you out," Wynona said, forcing her eyes away from the spectacle. Her jealousy was growing stronger and stronger with each moment she spent with the woman. Maybe one of these days, Wynona would learn to be as feminine and in touch with her witchy side, the way this shifter was with her cat side. One could only hope.

"Thank you so much for coming," Wynona said as she opened the door. Flashes practically blinded her and Wynona stepped back, knowing she was not the person they were there for.

The ghost media were back, only this time they wanted a peek at Ms. Kimoko. The shifter clung to her bodyguard's arm as she walked, looking as delicate and soft as a cream puff. But after her little speech about using Wynona for her own gain, Wynona knew behind the soft smile lay a mind as sharp as a werewolf's claws.

It took several minutes for Ms. Kimoko to walk out the door enough that Wynona could shut and lock it. She rested her forehead against the wood and let out a long breath. "I hope I don't have to do that very often," she muttered.

A squeak caught her attention and Wynona straightened, then turned around to find Violet in the doorway. "Hey," she said softly. She walked over and squatted down carefully in her heels before holding out her hand. Violet ran over and climbed on.

Standing, Wynona put the creature on her shoulder as she headed back to the table. "Let's hope all our clients aren't so unique, hm?"

Violet chittered in agreement.

Wynona began to gather the cups from the table when her eyes were caught on the binder. She frowned. "I had forgotten about the allergy," she murmured. But there it was, plain as day in her binder. "Next time I need to be sure to look through a client's information before the meeting." She shook her head and glanced at Violet. "Being unprepared was definitely not professional. Good thing this one was an easy fix."

Violet chittered and began to skitter down Wynona's arm.

"Whoa," Wynona gasped, moving her hand so the mouse landed on the table. "Warn me next time and I'll set you down." She smiled. "I don't want you to get hurt. Are you hungry?"

Violet raced to the binder and sat on the open page.

Wynona frowned. "What are you doing?"

The purple mouse ran circles, squeaking the whole time.

Wynona set down the cups she'd been collecting and watched. "I don't understand. You want me to look at the paper?"

Violet stood on her hind legs, finally stopping her frantic race.

Wynona stepped over so she could better read over the questionnaire. She studied it thoroughly, but nothing looked out of place, other than the allergy note she had forgotten.

Wait.

Wynona gasped. "It can't be," she whispered hoarsely.

Violet laid down and covered her face with her hands.

Shaking knees caused Wynona to fall into the chair and she grasped the table for support. "It can't. Can it?"

Sounding apologetic, Violet cautiously worked her way up Wynona's arm and nuzzled her neck.

A sharp pain hit Wynona in the sternum and she put her hand over the spot, tears springing to her eyes. It wasn't fair. It just wasn't fair.

One by one, all the pieces were starting to come together and now, after all this time, Wynona didn't want the answer. The responsibility of her revelation felt like more than she could bear.

Her eyes went to her cell phone. Should she call Rascal? Chief Ligurio?

"No," Wynona said firmly. She straightened in her seat. "Everyone is innocent until proven guilty," she said to Violet. "I'm sure there's a perfectly natural explanation for all of this." She stood and hurriedly gathered the cups. Even in her hurry, she didn't want to leave Lusgu with a mess. The brownie would complain about it for weeks.

"I'm going out," she told her janitor after setting the cups in the sink. "Do you want any help before I go?"

"Can't leave well enough alone," Lusgu grumbled, shooing her away. With a sweep of his hands, the sink turned on and began to fill with suds, tea cups dancing through the water.

"Thank you," Wynona sang out, doing her best not to let Lusgu know of her distress. The more she walked, the more determined she became. She had to be wrong. She just had to be.

Wynona stopped by the bookcase and tried to drop off Violet, but the mouse refused. Instead, she tucked herself in under Wynona's hair and hung on.

"Are you sure you want to come?" Wynona asked softly. "I don't know what I'm going to find."

Violet's response was decisive.

"Okay." Wynona took a deep breath. "Then we'll do this together."

CHAPTER 28

Wynona shivered as the temperature continued to decline for the day. She had been in such a hurry to leave her shop that she had forgotten a jacket and now was regretting it.

Violet poked her head out of Wynona's hair and chittered.

"As soon as I see him leave, we'll go in," Wynona reminded her.

Violet ducked away again. Apparently she had found a way to stay warm just fine. Too bad it included stealing some of Wynona's precious body heat.

She rubbed her upper arms, trying to use friction to get rid of her goosebumps, cursing her own cursed state when a man in a power suit caught her attention.

Immediately, Wynona's heart began to hurt. Betrayal was sharper than any vampire bite and it cut deep. "It can't be him," she whispered for the thousandth time. "I have to be remembering it wrong."

Violet shifted, but didn't speak.

Roderick stood at the edge of the sidewalk until a limo pulled up and parked. The chauffeur stepped out and opened the door for his employer. Before ducking inside, Roderick glanced casually around the street and Wynona ducked back into the shadows, hoping he wouldn't notice her or use any magic that told him of her whereabouts. He had never used magic around her before and at first Wynona had thought the gesture sweet. That he was thinking of her feelings and didn't want to show off.

Now, however, she was beginning to wonder if he had simply been hiding his abilities. She had no idea what level of power he held. His wealth and powerful aura were all she had to go on.

The limo pulled away from the curb and Wynona stepped away from the alley wall. "Here we go," she told Violet.

A soft squeak was her only response.

Taking a deep breath for courage, Wynona walked out of her hiding place and made her way to the office building. It seemed far more intimidating in the disappearing light than it had the other day when she'd stopped by. But there was no time for her to stand around gawking.

The front door was still unlocked and Wynona let out a sigh of relief when she got inside without effort. Roderick's office wouldn't be so easy, but at least she wasn't going to have to break in twice.

Walking to the corner, she began to climb the utility stairs, a feeling of deja vu overcoming her as her thighs began to burn with the effort.

"If we make it out of this alive," Wynona whispered to Violet, "I'm going to start doing cardio. You with me?"

Violet just snuggled against Wynona's neck a little more firmly.

"Some help you are," Wynona puffed. She finally reached Roderick's floor and cautiously poked her head out of the door. The floor was silent and she made her way to his office.

Carefully, as if the knob was booby trapped, Wynona tried to turn it. "Shoot," she grumbled. It would have been too easy for it to be unlocked as well. She had figured she would need to break in, but Wynona had never actually picked a lock before. That definitely wasn't a skill her granny had taught her and without any magic, she was a little stumped.

Violet scrambled down Wynona's arm and Wynona froze as she watched the purple rodent disappear under the door. Tiny scratches could be heard climbing higher and higher until there was a soft click.

Trying again, Wynona slowly pulled the knob and the door swung open, Violet dangling from the knob like an acrobat.

Wynona quickly held out her hand and caught the mouse. "Why, you clever little creature." With a grin, Wynona tucked Violet back into her hair. "That's an extra cookie for you tonight."

Violet chittered happily and settled down.

Wynona was sure to close the door behind her, and she stayed bent over so people wouldn't be able to see her silhouette through the windows. One thing she couldn't avoid, however, was using her flashlight in order to read the words on Roderick's documents.

She began to shuffle through the papers on his desk, but even without saying so, Wynona was fairly certain that Roderick was too smart to have left something incriminating out in the open. She moved around to the back of the desk and methodically went through his drawers.

She wasn't even sure what she was looking for. Just something to confirm her suspicions. While waiting in the alley, Wynona had done a little more investigating and despite her hurt, she felt like she was finally on the right track.

When a search of the drawers brought nothing unusual to light, she began to flitter her hands around the edges of the desk. She had once seen in a movie that desks could have hidden drawers. Perhaps...

Wynona gasped when she found what felt like a button. Anticipation had her pushing it before she could think better of it and a click sounded before a small part of the wall swung open.

"Did you see that?" Wynona asked Violet.

Violet was clinging to Wynona's neck, but gave a tiny squeak.

Wynona walked over and pulled open the safe. A single manilla envelope lay inside. Sweat beaded on Wynona's forehead and bile churned in her stomach as she pulled it out. Reaching inside, she pulled out a bundle of pages.

It didn't take her long to figure out that what she held was more than enough to put Roderick in jail for a very long time.

That same sense of betrayal flooded her and Wynona found it hard to breathe. How could this be happening? He had been by her side this entire time. He'd encouraged her, supported her, made her feel beautiful and worthwhile despite her cursed state.

It seemed unreal.

"I see you found it."

Wynona jerked her head up just in time to be blinded by the overhead light. Blinking rapidly, she stumbled backward a few steps. When her vision finally cleared, her heart sank like a petrified gnome. "Roderick," she said tightly. "How could you?"

His eyes fell to the floor, but a soft smile spread across his face. "Doesn't quite seem right, does it?" Slowly, he began walking around the room.

Wynona matched his steps, not wanting to be any closer to him than she had to be. "You were going to let me be a sacrifice to your crime? All for what? Some recipes?" Anger joined her hurt. This man had no right to treat her this way. As nothing more than a scapegoat, worthless.

Roderick stopped walking and shook his head. "It wasn't that way at all," he insisted. "I knew you wouldn't be convicted. No one who knows you would ever think you could kill a person." He shrugged. "If Chief Ligurio hadn't been so caught up in trying to exact revenge on your sister by using you, he would have seen that as well."

Wynona's mouth dropped open. "What?"

Roderick began walking again. Even in slow motion, he was difficult to look away from. His gait was strong and assured. He oozed power from every pore, but instead of being impressed, Wynona felt choked by it.

Since he was headed for his desk, she began to inch her way to the door. Perhaps she could slip out and reach the police before he could catch her.

"I don't think you should go any farther," he said coolly. His lips turned down in a frown. "I really did like you, you know. I had great plans for us once this was all over."

"You really think I would welcome the attention of a killer?" Wynona said incredulously. "That goes against everything I stand for!"

"You weren't supposed to find out." He tilted his head, and his silver eyes practically glowed as he studied her. "I suppose I didn't give you enough credit. If the spell on my safe hadn't let me know someone had broken in, I might have missed the chance to stop you."

Wynona's jaw clenched tighter. She'd looked everywhere for traps, except for the magic ones. She was a fool.

"Even with your curse, genetically speaking you should hold great power from your family line. Plus, it's not as if you're bad to look at. You might need a little help in the fashion department, but you're still a very beautiful woman. Marrying you would give my children more than just power. Looks, magic and intelligence...what an intoxicating combination."

Wynona wanted to gag. He had never liked her for her. All he had wanted was her genes. If she threw up, she hoped it left a stain on his carpet. Why were witches and warlocks so obsessed with building powerful family lines? What happened to marrying for happiness and love?

"Tell me," he said in that annoyingly calm tone. "Just how did you figure it out?"

Wynona pinched her lips together. She shifted her weight, ready to run for the door as soon as the opportunity arose. "There were several things, but it wasn't until I had my meeting with Ms. Kimoko this afternoon that I remembered about the allergy." She glared at him. "No one knows about that. You shouldn't have known about that."

He raised his eyebrows. "Perhaps it was simply a word that slipped into an impassioned speech from an ardent suitor."

Wynona shook her head. "It was too much of a coincidence. The only way you could have known about that was if you were in my office, snooping through my books." Her nostrils flared in indignation. "My guess is you looked around the night that you killed Mr. Skinflayer."

"Ah." Roderick trailed his finger along the edge of his desk. "Mr. Skinflayer. He had one simple job, and yet..." Roderick shrugged.

"So you killed him. All because of some recipes," Wynona accused.

"Not just some recipes," Roderick said as if scolding a recalcitrant child. "*The* recipes. You tasted Atherton's pastries. Surely you didn't miss how much they kept pulling you back for more."

"So...what? You wanted to be able to open a competing business with them?"

Roderick tsked his tongue. "Have you no imagination, Wynona?" His grin was nothing short of malicious. "I was going to sell them to the highest bidder. My legacy would have been assured."

"Money," Wynona spat, moving a couple more inches toward the door. "Two dead men because of money." She shook her head. "You make me sick." She could feel Violet moving down the back of her shirt and Wynona fought panic at the thought of the mouse coming out where Roderick could see her. She tried to shift and stop her, but Violet soon was out of reach.

"You said there were several things," Roderick continued and Wynona found herself grateful for the distraction. Maybe if she kept him talking, he wouldn't notice a purple mouse. "Tell me...where else did I slip up?"

"After I figured out that you had been in my office, other things started popping up." She took another step. "I hadn't realized it at the time, when I walked in on you talking about delivering the package. The story about your sister was completely believable," she said, trying to stroke his ego a little.

His smirk let her know it worked. She took another step toward the door.

"But knowing you'd been in my office made me question it." She bit back a smart remark. "You don't have a sister, do you?"

Roderick's chuckle was low and eerie. "Very good, Wynona." He scratched his chin. "I suppose in our courtship that lie would have eventually come out anyway, but sometimes we have to improvise."

She tried to move again.

"Not another step, dear." Roderick tilted his head in a way that made her feel like a mouse being watched by a cat. He gave her a fake frown. "As much as I would love to continue hearing about my mistakes, I believe that if we draw this out any longer, you're going to hold onto the hope that you'll escape, and that would just be cruel."

His hand rose in the air, palm toward her.

Wynona knew she was about to see just how powerful his magic was. "Why kill Chef Droxon?" she blurted out, knowing she was only delaying the inevitable. "I still haven't put that together. Surely you could have stolen the recipes without killing him."

His hand dropped a couple of inches and she let out a tentative breath. "Not quite as smart as you thought, then?" He grinned. He looked too happy for the situation, as if it were normal to go around eliminating people. "Chef Droxon was nothing but a decoy."

Wynona's brain sped through his words, putting it in place with the rest of her facts. "You needed to throw us off," she accused. "You needed us to believe Droxon had been the original target. The chef's apron wasn't enough."

He clapped in a derogatory manner and gave Wynona a bow. "Very good. Any other questions?"

Wynona couldn't think of anything else to keep him talking and his hand came up again.

"Like I said, it's a pity. I really did have plans for the two of us." He sighed. "But I can't have any loose ends." He grinned. "At least we know the chief won't miss you." Sparks began to drip from his hand and Wynona's panic became all consuming.

Light shot toward her and Wynona screamed as an automatic response. Her hands came up as if they could stop the spell, her head turning to the side with her eyes squeezed shut.

Cursing filled the room and Wynona chanced opening her eyes in time to see purple sparks dissipating throughout the room.

"You said you didn't have any magic," he snarled. Gone was cool, collected Roderick, and in his place was an angry warlock who had just been thwarted. The problem was, Wynona had no idea how.

"I don't," she whispered in a hoarse tone. She looked at her hands, but they weren't lit up or showing any signs of a spell. How in the world had that just happened?

"No matter," Roderick muttered to himself. He hunted through his top drawer. "Luckily, I come prepared for just such an occasion." His hand came out again, but this time instead of light, it was filled with silver that flashed in the light. "Goodbye, Wynona."

CHAPTER 29

This was it. Wynona had no idea what had happened with the hex, but she had no way of stopping a gun. It felt as if everything blurred into slow motion as she watched his finger begin to squeeze the trigger.

"AH!"

Wynona flinched as his voice mixed with the sound of the shot, and just like before, she waited for the world to disappear, but once again, she was still standing.

Roderick swung his gun toward the ground. "Stupid mouse," he ground out.

"NO!" Wynona screamed, realizing that Violet had saved the day. She rushed forward, only to scream again and drop to the floor when the door behind her smashed in and a snarling, giant wolf landed in the middle of the room. Wynona looked over her shoulder. "Rascal," she breathed.

The wolf's shoulder would have been in line with Wynona's, making him much larger than a biological wolf. His fur was multiple shades of brown, ranging from light caramel to the deepest chocolate. But his golden eyes were unmistakable.

His hackles were raised and a deep growl shook the room, causing Wynona to cover her head, half afraid the ceiling would come down on them.

"Well, if it isn't the little Rascal," Roderick drawled. The curled lip and line of drool hanging from the wolf's mouth apparently wasn't nearly as intimidating to him as it was to Wynona.

Even though she knew Rascal wasn't going to hurt her, his appearance was terrifying.

The wolf howled, his head raised to the ceiling.

The sound was eerie and Wynona whimpered slightly as she covered her ears. Never had she felt more helpless with her lack of magic. One of these days her inability to protect herself was going to get her killed. Her mind went to the Banshee Scream Rascal had given her and she lamented the fact that in her hurry, she had left it at the shop. If she survived this, she would never leave the house without it again.

"Impressive," Roderick said sarcastically. He waved the gun around. "But not even you can withstand a couple of bullets."

Rascal growled again and took a couple steps forward.

"Careful," Roderick warned. He turned the gun to face Wynona. "Another step and she's gone."

Rascal backed up, whimpering slightly.

"Don't listen," Wynona whispered, knowing his wolf hearing would allow him to hear. "Just worry about stopping him."

Another whimper and those golden eyes met hers for a split second before going back to watch Roderick.

"Cursed mouse." Roderick once again turned his head toward the ground and Rascal took full advantage. He leapt forward, landing on Roderick, the gun going off before it flew through the air.

Wynona automatically covered her head once more, then looked up as she heard Roderick cursing rapidly. Magic flew through the room and she began to worry that Rascal could be hit by a spell.

Gathering all her courage, Wynona climbed up on her knees, looking for something in the room she could use to help Rascal, but there was nothing within view. A table full of paperwork was going to do very little against an angry wolf and an evil warlock.

A brush of fur against her arm caught Wynona's attention and she jerked toward it. "Violet!" Wynona grasped the mouse and brought her close to her chest. "Oh my goodness, never scare me like that again." The tiny body was shivering, but Violet snuggled in, relaxing in Wynona's hold.

"Okay, we need to help," Wynona whispered. She ducked as an errant spell shot over her head. "Go on up." Wynona handed Violet up to her neck and the creature immediately nestled back in her hair.

Wynona rose up just enough to see man and wolf rolling around on the floor. Roderick was holding Rascal's snout away from him. Sharp teeth flashed as Rascal strained against the warlock's hold. Roderick had to be using some kind of strength spell in order to keep Rascal at bay.

Scurrying to the side of the desk, Wynona popped her head up just enough to see what was on top. "Please, please, please," she chanted. Her eyes widened. "Bingo." Keeping one eye on the men, she reached out and grabbed a heavy paperweight. The shape was square, which was going to make it awkward to throw, but all Wynona needed was a small distraction.

Another set of sparks hit the ceiling and Wynona ducked down, covering her head when dust and debris began to fall.

Roderick laughed in a dark tone. "You can't win, Strongclaw. Might as well let me go."

Wynona peeked around the corner of the desk to see Roderick and Rascal facing off. Roderick had never looked so disheveled, with tears in his suit and bruises forming around one of his eyes. A quick glance at Rascal told her nothing. She couldn't see if he was injured with all that fur.

Closing her eyes, she whispered a quick prayer and spun, throwing the paperweight at the back of Roderick's leg. Magic or no, Wynona knew a miracle had occurred when it landed on his knee, causing it to buckle.

Rascal had obviously been waiting for just such an opportunity, since he leapt almost as Roderick fell. Slamming to the ground, his forepaws on Roderick's chest, pinning not only the warlock's body, but his arms as well, without his hands, Roderick wouldn't be able to cast any more spells. The wolf snarled directly in Roderick's face.

"Oh, thank goodness," Wynona said as she panted for breath. She pushed a hand through her hair, which had become a wild tangle with all of the fighting. Looking up, she met Rascal's golden eyes.

He tilted his head at the desk and Wynona sat up to see what he was talking about. "Oh, the phone! Of course." Despite the giant wolf holding him down, Wynona couldn't help but keep one eye on their prisoner. She wasn't about to underestimate him again.

"Para-one-one," a bored voice said on the other end of the line. "What is your emergency?"

"Hello. My name is Wynona Le Doux. I'm with Deputy Chief Officer Strongclaw at the Creatures Park Business Plaza. We have a criminal in custody. Please send help." Wynona listened and nodded, answering all the other questions that the woman asked before hanging up. "They're on their way," she said softly to Rascal.

A string of curses broke free from Roderick for the thousandth time and Wynona wondered what she'd ever seen in the man. His slick persona was an act. Underneath, he was crude and horrible, and she hoped after today she never laid eyes on him again.

Rascal snapped in Roderick's face, barking loud enough to wake the dead, and Roderick clenched his teeth. His face was red and his nostrils flared, but he didn't speak.

The next five minutes were the longest of Wynona's life as she waited on pins and needles for the police to arrive. Rascal stayed at steady attention the whole time, but when his ears twitched toward the window, Wynona knew help was on the way.

Thundering footsteps came through the main foyer and soon the office was too full of people to move.

"Ms. Le Doux." Officer Nightshade came up beside Wynona.

"Amaris," Wynona stammered. "I'm so glad you're here."

The vampire officer put her arm around Wynona. "Let's go out in the lobby and have a seat, hm? It'll be a few minutes before the chief can get to you."

Wynona nodded wearily. It seemed as if every bit of energy in her body had suddenly been drained. Stumbling slightly, she walked with the officer to a couch away from the chaos. Wynona slumped down and leaned her head back. Violet chirped a few soothing sounds and nuzzled into the crook of her neck, leading Wynona to automatically reach up and pet her creature's fur. She had to admit that the silky texture was calming.

"Is that a purple mouse?" Officer Nightshade's voice rose high at the end.

Wynona cracked open an eye. "Yep."

"How did it get purple?"

Wynona shrugged and yawned. "I don't know. I found her this way."

"Huh." Officer Nightshade put her hands on her hips.

"Wynona." Rascal's voice was tinged with the lightest touch of panic as he rushed toward them. He sat down on his hip, angled toward her on the couch. "Are you alright? Did I get there in time?"

Wynona gave him a tired smile. "I'm fine. You burst in just in time to save me." Frowning, Wynona sat up. "How did you know where I was? Or that I needed your help?"

Rascal's skin was fairly tan, but the red that tinged his ears was easily visible. "I, uh... " He rubbed the back of his neck.

Laughing softly, Office Nightshade started to walk away. "Perhaps you would like to get her statement, Deputy Chief?" Her grin was nothing short of mischievous.

He tilted his chin at his officer. "I'll take it from here. Thanks." He turned back to Wynona and opened his mouth, but another voice took over.

"I think I'd like to be a part of that." Chief Ligurio sauntered over, one eyebrow raised high in challenge at his Deputy Chief.

"Yes, sir," Rascal said quickly. He glanced sideways and winked at Wynona.

She held back a grin and gave the chief her attention.

"Care to explain exactly what happened tonight?" the chief asked in a tone that said he wasn't willing to take no for an answer.

Wynona didn't mind. She wanted all this behind her. Her shop was set to open in just a few hours, and though she was going to be massively sleep-deprived, at least it would open free and clear of any suspicion. The next twenty minutes were spent going over the events of the evening, she and Rascal taking turns explaining things from their point of view.

"Your...mouse?" The chief's eyebrows rose. "Attacked Mr. Caligari?"

Wynona shifted her hair so the vampire could see Violet.

He huffed, shook his head and wrote something down in his notebook. "Don't know what kind of spells you kids are doing these days, but a purple mouse is ridiculous."

"That *ridiculous* mouse saved my life," Wynona said defensively. "And as far as I know, there was no magic involved. I found Violet this way and when I started feeding her, we just became...friends."

Violet snorted and snuggled in deeper.

"May we go home?" she asked. "It's been a really long night and I have an equally long day ahead. You've got your killer, and recovered the recipes. Perhaps I could be set free?" She hoped he understood that she was asking for freedom from more than going home. She wanted freedom from suspicion and his neverending disdain as well. The shrewd look he gave her said she was no longer a suspect, but she wouldn't be invited to dinner at his house anytime soon.

Chief Ligurio stuffed his notebook in the front pocket of his shirt. "Excuse me for taking up your precious time," he said with more than a hint of sarcasm. "But there are a few loose ends I'd like to tie up." His red eyes narrowed. "Starting with why you were here at a closed office building to begin with."

Wynona pinched her lips between her teeth. How was she going to get out of this one? When she'd snuck in to look through Delila's desk, no one had been any wiser. But this time, Wynona had been caught at the scene of the crime...literally.

"Mr. Caligari and I are...*were*...friends," Wynona said. "Does it really matter why I was here?"

Chief Ligurio folded his arms over his chest. "Then it shouldn't be a big deal to tell me why."

Wynona wrung her hands together, then paused to stare at them. Something funny had happened tonight. In fact, several funny things had been happening to her lately. Magical things she couldn't quite explain. She knew she didn't have any powers, so why did odd magic keep showing up? "You know...I think my granny might have been with me tonight." The words were quiet and she hadn't really meant to say them out loud, not having truly thought them through, but it was too late now.

"You think your dead grandmother was here?" The chief's eyebrows shot up. "And she what? Helped you?"

It wasn't like ghosts were unheard of in the paranormal world, but they rarely took an interest in anything but themselves. Some even going so far as to create an entirely new afterlife for themselves, as seen in the ghost media. But a spectre who hung around the living as some sort of guardian angel? That was rare. As in...it had never happened before.

Wynona stuck her chin in the air, projecting a confidence she didn't feel. "Yes. I think that's exactly what happened."

CHAPTER 30

"**E**xplain," Chief Ligurio demanded.

Rascal shifted next to Wynona and she found herself wanting to lean into his warmth and strength. She was so grateful he was next to her, rather than standing across with the chief, who looked like he wanted to throw her out the window.

"When Roderick walked into the office, I didn't hear him at first. He surprised me and as we spoke, he worked his way around to his desk."

"Where he kept the gun," Rascal inserted.

Wynona nodded. "Yes. First he tried throwing a hex at me." She felt the blood drain from her face as she remembered how close she had come to dying tonight. "I'm pretty sure it was the same one he used on Mr. Skinflayer and Chef Droxon."

Chief Ligurio huffed. "And you know this how? I thought you had no magic."

"My magic is bound," Wynona pointed out. After Roderick's little rant, she was beginning to realize there was a difference. She had magic. She just had no access to it, which to be fair, made her feel magicless. "I can still see magic and sometimes, if the spell is strong enough, I can feel it."

He made a noncommittal sound, then waved her on.

"Roderick sent the spell at me and I had no way of fighting him off." Violet stirred on her shoulder and Wynona reached up to pet her again. "I remember screaming and putting my hands up, but then...nothing." She tucked some hair behind her ear. "When I looked up again, there were purple sparks, but I was still alive."

Chief Ligurio stared at her, looking surprised for the first time since she'd known him. "The hex just...didn't work?"

"See, this is where I think my granny had to have been there!" Wynona said, her conviction and eagerness growing the more she thought about it. She scooched forward to the edge of the couch. "I think she protected me. Granny Saffron, if you recall, was one of the most powerful witches in history."

"I remember," the chief grumbled. "I'm fairly certain no one has ever forgotten your family, Ms. Le Doux."

Wynona sighed. "I was simply pointing out that her interference is entirely possible. She would be more than strong enough to come back if she wanted to, not to mention Granny is the only one..." She trailed off. Suddenly they were getting into personal territory and Wynona wasn't sure she wanted to share.

"Don't stop now, Ms. Le Doux." Chief Ligurio sneered. "Things were just getting interesting."

"Does it really matter if the ghost of her grandmother helped?" Rascal asked in a soothing tone. Obviously, the wolf had had to tame the vampire on more than one occasion. "The point is, something went wrong with the hex and Wynona, Ms. Le Doux, is still here to tell us about it."

"It matters if knowing everything means she's lying to us," the chief argued. "Something fishy is going on with your claim to be cursed. No one knew who you were before you suddenly arrived in the city a few months ago. No one had ever heard your name before. Now you claim to be related to the most powerful family in Hex Haven, and if you didn't look like an exact replica of your mother and sister, I'm not sure I'd believe your story." His brows furrowed menacingly and Wynona was reminded of a comment Roderick made about Chief Ligurio wanting revenge on her sister.

There was obviously some history there, but what? And when would be a safe time to ask about it? Right now was definitely not the time.

"When I was born, I was cursed immediately. My family didn't even have a chance to test my powers before they were gone," Wynona said through gritted teeth. Somehow, she was going to get through to this police chief. She was innocent and he needed to recognize that. "I don't know how much you've dealt with my family, Chief, but they aren't exactly the warm and fuzzy type. In fact, they're the "if you aren't useful to me, I want nothing to do with you" type."

Her eyes were tired and began to sting a little, but Wynona pushed the tears back. She would have her pity party later.

"I was useless in their eyes. So, I spent my childhood and a chunk of my adulthood being kept out of the spotlight and treated like a dirty little secret. They were afraid if the media knew I existed, it would weaken their reign. I would be seen as a liability."

"How did you escape?" The softly spoken question came from Rascal. His golden eyes were glowing with compassion, but his fists were forming claws. Wynona couldn't tell if he was angry at her or her family.

"Granny," she answered just as quietly. "She gave me instructions on what to do and promised to provide a distraction. On the night of the summer solstice, when an earth witch's magic is most powerful, I managed to get out." She took in a shaky breath. "I didn't know until later that Granny's distraction was her own demise." Wynona's eyes fell to her lap. "She was a great reader of tea leaves. My guess is she read about her impending death through a cup and set everything up with that in mind."

Chief Ligurio sighed. "If your family is so against people knowing you, why haven't they come after you?"

Wynona glanced back up. "Because it would cause too much of a scene. Right now they can spin it that they're being magnanimous at letting me have my shop and do something useful for society. If they came dragging me back to the palace, it would reflect badly on them."

The chief nodded, but the scowl on his face didn't move. Wynona had no idea how he felt about her story. In the end, it didn't truly matter, but she was tired of being treated badly because of who gave birth to her.

"Why don't you tell me how you figured out it was Mr. Caligari," Chief Ligurio said. "None of the evidence I had pointed in his direction at all."

Wynona relaxed a little, grateful for the change in topic. "I'll be honest, most of it was hindsight," she explained. "Roderick was always *very* adamant that I wouldn't be convicted of the murders, even though I was at the top of your list." She scrunched her nose. "I think that's part of why he chose my shop for the first one. It was basically neutral ground. I was untouchable, or so he thought, and so it made a great way to throw you off his own trail."

Rascal growled low and shook his head.

"Secondly, I came to visit him once, here at his office, and accidently disturbed him during a phone call where he was talking about a package." She shook her head. "I didn't realize it at the time, but that *package* was the binder of recipes. He told me it was about a gift for his sister, but just tonight, I figured out he doesn't have a sister."

"So his lie wasn't what tipped you off?"

Wynona slumped back on the couch, exhaustion creeping in once more. "No. It was..." She paused. How could she say this without telling Ms. Kimoko's secret? "Roderick once mentioned in passing something that seemed innocuous at the time, but later I realized it was information he shouldn't have known."

"Such as?"

"I can't tell you," Wynona said carefully. "It's confidential information about a client of mine, who wishes to keep it a secret. I only know because it's pertinent to my business with them."

"And it's not pertinent to a murder investigation?" he snapped.

"No. The information itself isn't," Wynona argued. "Just that Roderick knew it." She clasped her hands in her lap. "The only way for him to know that particular piece of information was if he'd been in my office and been snooping through my books."

"Ah." Chief Ligurio regarded her studiously. "And you put together that he had been in your office when he'd killed the doppleganger?"

"Yes." Wynona nodded. "He killed Mr. Skinflayer because he failed to steal the binder earlier in the day, using the chef's clothes and my office to throw everyone off. But as we started gathering evidence, Roderick became concerned when I suggested that Chef Droxon wasn't the actual target. Since he couldn't get me to stop investigating, he went ahead and killed the chef, leading us farther and farther away from the truth."

"But he wanted the binder," Chief Ligurio pointed out. "So wasn't he after Droxon the whole time?"

"No. He wanted the binder. Chef Droxon's death helped cover up the fact that Roderick has ties to the paranormal underground. He was planning to sell the recipes to the highest bidder. The mess with the Droxon family only helped make things more complicated and keep suspicion away from him." Wynona frowned. "I wonder if he didn't already know about the embezzling. That was something I didn't clarify when he and I were talking. But Roderick and Delila live in the same apartment building. It wouldn't have been difficult for a warlock with his power to sneak something into her room." She rubbed her forehead. "The more I think about it, the more my head hurts. He basically ran us in circles so we wouldn't ever think to look deeper."

"So, that's why you came over asking questions about the mobs," Rascal said. He huffed in surprise and pushed a hand through his hair. "I'm just glad it didn't go any farther underground. If Roderick was planning to sell the binder himself, then he wasn't working under a bigger boss. This should be the end of it."

"We can only hope," Chief Ligurio said. He sounded tired. "You." He pointed at Wynona. "Don't leave town. If I have questions later, I want to know where to find you."

Wynona let out a long breath, but nodded. "I wasn't planning on it."

"And you, Strongclaw," Chief Ligurio continued. "Take this woman home and don't let her out of your sight until she's inside." He straightened and shook his head. "Every time I turn around, she's somewhere she's not supposed to be."

Wynona watched him walk away. "You're welcome," she muttered under her breath.

The chief didn't hear her, but apparently Rascal did, since he snorted and then quickly hid his smile. "Come on, Wy. Let's get you to bed." He glanced at his watch. "The ghost media will have this all over the headlines in a couple hours and then your little party this afternoon will be overflowing with curious patrons."

"Well, at this point, I don't care why they come," Wynona said, welcoming his hand as he helped her to her feet. "The more people come through the door, the more I have a chance of convincing them to come back."

"That's a good way to look at it," Rascal said, opening the door for her. "But by the end of the party, you might feel differently when the gawkers just won't leave you alone."

"Wow. You're a cauldron-half-empty kind of guy, huh?" Wynona teased. The cool night air hit her face and she felt her muscles begin to unwind. She was so glad to be out of that building and away from all that had occurred in the last few hours.

Rascal chuckled, that deliciously dark sound that Wynona enjoyed. "Not really. I've just had experience with the masses and I never come out of it feeling like I won."

She pulled her scooter out of the shadows. "Thank you, Rascal," she said sincerely as she straddled the vehicle. "For everything."

Stepping a little closer, he tapped the end of her nose and gave her a wink. "Anytime." He didn't try to hide the fact that he meant it in more ways than one and Wynona was grateful for the cool evening that helped keep her blush at bay.

Wynona's heart fluttered a little and she wondered if she would ever get to see this handsome Deputy Chief again.

"I'll see you soon," Rascal said as he backed away, as if he could read her mind.

Her heart began to beat harder and she couldn't look away from his eyes.

Rascal tilted his head to the side. "I'll follow you in the patrol car to make sure you make it home safely. Give me a minute." Like the predator he was, Rascal disappeared without another word, blending in like he belonged to the night.

Wynona sucked in a large breath after he moved, the evening air suddenly feeling thick and slow. She put a hand to her heart to try and calm it down. It was too soon to be turning all her attention to Rascal. Roderick had barely been taken away and Wynona was still faced with the difficult task of getting her business going.

She shook her head and turned the key to the scooter. She liked Rascal and she was definitely attracted to him, but just like before, she wasn't in a position for anything more. If he was as interested as he seemed to be, she hoped he was a patient man, because she had no idea when the ideal time for a relationship would finally come her way.

She just knew it wasn't now.

CHAPTER 31

If Wynona thought her nerves were on full alert last night, they were nothing compared to what she was feeling at the moment. She glanced at the clock before shifting the vase of flowers just so. She was sure the quarter of an inch she moved it helped the sunlight better reflect the soft colors of the daisies Prim had put together for the occasion. Wynona's fairy friend had assured her that daisies stood for new beginnings and rebirth, the perfect complement to Wynona's grand opening.

Lean arms grabbed her from behind, causing Wynona to jump. "It's going to be so perfect," Prim gushed. She squeezed extra tight before releasing Wynona. Purple eyes surveyed the room with a content sigh. "The shabby chic thing is wonderful. Cozy, yet elegant. Beautiful, yet touchable. No one will want to leave!" Prim squealed.

Wynona gave her friend a grateful smile. "Let's hope so. I'm a little worried no one is going to show up."

"Oh, they'll show up," Prim said knowingly. She glanced slyly at Wynona. "Did you see the full page spread the ghosties put out this morning? Someone at the police station is claiming you solved the whole case single-handedly." Prim put a hand to the side of her mouth in a mock whisper. "And it wasn't the grumpy chief."

Wynona laughed a little, her cheeks heating as she thought of just who might have worked so hard to give her a boost. "I did," she admitted. "But I definitely didn't deserve all that credit. The police did much more than I did. I basically stumbled into trouble and they saved my tush." She blew a hair out of her face. "More than once, I hate to say."

"At least it's a cute tush to save," Prim said with a laugh.

Wynona joined her. "Should I count that as a compliment?"

"Of course!" Prim nudged Wynona's shoulder then tilted her head toward the door. "I think it's time."

Wynona gasped and looked up at the clock. Ten seconds until the official time. Tiny paws scrambled across the floor and Wynona barely noticed when Violet began pushing on her shoe. With a skirt on, the mouse had nothing to climb. Reaching down, Wynona held out her hand and Violet automatically jumped on.

"Wouldn't be a grand opening without a rodent in the house," Prim grumbled, still frustrated that Violet wouldn't let the fairy hold her.

"Violet bathed this morning," Wynona protested. "But she's as much a part of the shop as I am. And you." She wrapped an arm around Prim's shoulders. "We're all in this together."

The clock dinged the hour and Wynona felt sick to her stomach. "This is it," she whispered.

"Go let them in," Prim urged, giving Wynona a little push.

"What if there's no one there?" Wynona asked, her panic clearly audible.

Prim just smirked and pointed to the door.

Sighing in resignation, Wynona reached a shaking hand to the knob and unlocked the door. Knowing procrastination wouldn't help anyone, she pulled the door open and nearly collapsed to her knees.

There must have been fifty people waiting outside her shop door. Flashes of light went off from unseen sources, letting her know the ghost media was there. A limo waited on the curb with three body-guards standing nearby, glaring at anyone who got too close. Dozens of other smiling faces were beaming up at Wynona as they all waited for their chance to come inside.

Gasps rang through the crowd and Wynona noticed the door of the limo opening. Ms. Kimoko slid out in perfect movements, as usual. She had on a cocktail dress and large sunglasses. Waving to the crowd, she smiled brilliantly and sashayed up the suddenly empty sidewalk.

Her bodyguards were apparently very good at their jobs because the mass of people simply parted without any kind of command.

"Ms. Le Doux," Akina purred as she got closer. She held out both hands as if she and Wynona were long time friends. Grabbing Wynona's clammy ones, the actress air-kissed Wynona's cheeks. "I came for another sip of that *marvelous* cat mint tea." She turned and smiled at the adoring crowd, utilizing the free publicity to its best advantage.

The custom tea blend wasn't one of the ones Wynona had prepared for the opening, but luckily, she still had the ingredients on hand. "Of course," Wynona said, forcing herself into action. "If you'll come in, I'll show you to your favorite table." If Akina could live it up, so could Wynona.

The small smirk on Akina's face said she didn't miss Wynona's choice of verbiage. "Lead the way."

After getting her celebrity guest settled, Wynona began to let in other small groups, setting them up with a full tea service until the small shop was full to the brim. Since there were others still outside, she began to run trays of pastries and sandwiches around to those waiting, hoping none of them would grow tired and go home before she could show off what her shop would really offer.

"Thank you so much for coming," Wynona said as she handed out the food. "I'll be delighted to have you inside very soon."

"Have room for a tea drinking wolf?" The words were low and whispered directly in Wynona's ear.

She nearly lost her tray as she spun. "Rascal!" she cried. Her heart did that funny flip-flop again and a wide smile spread across her face. "I didn't know you were coming."

He put a hand to his heart. "And not see how all this turned out?" He tsked his tongue and shook his head. "It's not often I meet a woman willing to take on a murderer in order to serve tea." He leaned in. "I figured I needed to come and see it for myself."

That stupid blush. One day Wynona really needed to get it under control. "I'm so glad you did," she said softly.

Rascal tugged on his collar. "You don't happen to serve iced tea, do you?"

"I don't normally," Wynona said. "But for you...I think I can make an exception." She finished passing out the food, then walked up the front stoop. "I'm sure if we look around in the kitchen, I can find exactly what we need. And Lusgu is so efficient with the dishes that I have no doubt we'll even be able to find a clean glass."

"As long as your tea doesn't lead to any more cases like we just finished," Rascal drawled. "I think I need a break before another big one hits."

"It better not," Wynona said, smiling at her patrons as she weaved her way to the kitchen. "I have no intention of ever getting involved in a murder investigation again."

The kitchen was a quiet relief from all the chattering going on in the dining room and Wynona allowed herself a moment to breathe.

"Never?" Rascal pushed. "You have a pretty good eye for detail," he complimented. "We could always use good informants for the team."

"Absolutely not," Wynona said decisively, though she tempered the words with a smile. "While I'm extremely grateful for those of you who make it your life's work to put criminals behind bars, if there's anything I have learned from this experience, it's that I absolutely, under no condition, ever want to deal with the seedier side of Hex Haven again." She finished fixing Rascal's tea and handed him the cold glass.

"I'll drink to that," he said with a grin. "To the success of Saffron's Tea House, to killers being behind bars, and to beginning again." He nodded toward her, his golden eyes glowing with warmth before taking a sip. He paused, then sniffed the glass. "Is there rosemary in this?"

Wynona grinned. "Yep."

"Huh." He tilted his head. "How did you know wolves like rosemary?"

Wynona shrugged and leaned her hip against the counter. "Figuring out people's tea preferences is a gift of mine."

Rascal frowned. "And you're really sure you don't have magic? Like none?"

Wynona shook her head. "None. I tried for years under Granny's tutelage. If anyone could find a way through this curse, it would have been her."

"Hmm..." Rascal said in an absent-minded tone.

"Wolves."

They both jerked toward the sound.

Lusgu stood glaring at Rascal.

"Lu!" Rascal said loudly. "How are you today!"

A couple of large metal spoons began to swirl around Lusgu's head as he glared at Rascal.

"And that's my cue," Rascal said with a wink. Taking one last gulp of the drink, he set it down and raced out of the room. "Thanks, Wy! I'll be in touch!"

The kitchen door closed just as one of the spoons clanged against it.

"Lusgu!" Wynona scolded. "Stop!"

The brownie shook his head, but the spoons went back to their regular places on the counter. "Messy, messy, messy," he grumbled, turning back to wherever it was he came from.

Wynona huffed. "What in the world is that all about?" No one answered her and she figured they never would. Her eyes went to the door as voices filtered through the cracks. A slow smile spread across her face. She was open. Everyone knew she wasn't a murderer. And her shop looked like it was going to be a success.

Toss a handsome werewolf into the mix, and Wynona had a feeling her future was about to become very, very fun.

She couldn't wait.

THANK YOU!

I hope you enjoyed Wynona's first venture into
Solving mysteries! If you enjoyed yourself, I would
Encourage you to leave a review on your favorite retailer.
Kind words are the best way to thank an author
and help other readers find books they enjoy!

Sugar, Cream or Murder

Not ready to be done with Wynona and the gang?
Catch her next in "Sugar Cream or Murder".
Wynona and her team are back...but she's not exactly happy about it.
Wynona's sister, Celia, is at the top of Wynona's list of least favorite people.
But when one of Celia's friends ends up dead...Wynona can't bring herself to let it
go.
Despite having a little sleuthing experience under her belt at this point, Wynona
is completely out of her comfort zone as she's surrounded by some of the most
powerful witches in Hex Haven, trying to pretend she's not upset about her lack
of magical ability.
Wynona's family might not see her worth, but with Primrose, Violet and a dash-
ing werewolf at her side...Wynona might just find where she belongs, and solve a
murder or two along the way.
Grab it HERE![1]

---

1. https://www.amazon.com/dp/B097NLX294

CPSIA information can be obtained
at www.ICGtesting.com
Printed in the USA
BVHW040852240222
630005BV00017B/506